I0618639

Grace Under Fire

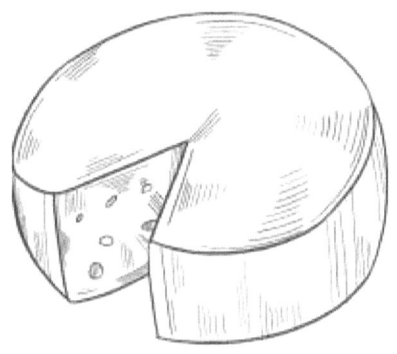

Jennifer Raines

Grace Under Fire
Copyright © 2022 Jennifer Raines
All rights reserved.

ISBN: (ebook) 978-1-958136-36-2
(print) 978-1-958136-37-9

Inkspell Publishing
207 Moonglow Circle #101
Murrells Inlet, SC 29576

Edited By Yezanira Venecia
Cover art By Fantasia Frog Designs

DEDICATION

**To Jonathan
For Your Love And Support**

JENNIFER RAINES

CHAPTER ONE

To hell with the naysayers and the doubters, she didn't give a tinker's cuss what they thought. Grace Anderson was slowly winning over the town. Next, she planned to charm the valley. It might have taken the northern New South Wales field day committee a few years to come to the party, but here she was, artisan cheesemaker with her own booth, her own banners and her own prize-winning products. Grace Anderson's farmhouse cheeses were smack bang in the middle of the Exhibition Hall, in the middle of the Northern Rivers Showground, reaping the benefits of the biggest crowds on record.

A single bite of her pale golden cheddar, with its hint of sharpness, and people were hooked. Her first experiment in unique cheese; it held prime place in her heart. It'd also won more blue ribbons than her soft cheeses, but a few more years and competitions would change that.

More than a decade of unrelenting work was starting to pay off.

An announcement cut through the buzz of the crowd: *The video presentation on the removal of woody weeds and revegetation with local native species will start in ten minutes.*

Grace's order book was bulging, and she'd made a few

solid business contacts today. She didn't mind the work, and the taste of success was sweet. Shoving her hands in the back pockets of her jeans, she rocked back on her heels and allowed herself a grin.

"You look pleased with yourself," her sister Ella said.

"I am." Grace leaned across the counter to hug her sister, placing a hand gently on the baby sling housing her four-month-old nephew, and held on.

"Hug *me*." The imperious demand from below the counter had Grace drawing back and backpedalling to come around the side of the booth. Ella had nursed their youngest sister, Chrissy, until her death two years ago and adopted her daughter.

Grace crouched to Tessa's height, and the little girl stepped into her arms. Her niece smelled of vanilla and Ella's soap. Tessa wrapped her sturdy four-year-old legs around Grace's waist, anchoring herself in place. Grace grinned at her sister. "When did you get here?"

"About half an hour ago."

"And Jake?"

"Seduced by a ride-on mower." Ella nodded in the direction of the pavilion showcasing farm machinery. "Shiny paint, huge wheels and gargantuan blades. The perfect toy for a hot-shot Sydney lawyer who lives in an apartment."

"How's the house hunting going?" Normal chitchat when her sister's visit this weekend was anything but normal.

"We've found a bungalow with wide verandas and a large garden." Ella's hand cupped her baby's bottom. "Perfect for the kids. Jake's put in an offer."

"Fingers crossed." Grace held crossed fingers in front of Tessa, who mimicked her action.

"A bit higher than the budget we planned," Ella confessed.

"Budgets rarely match dreams. I've fallen for a German curd vat." Grace winced. "Much more than the budget I planned."

"Are you hurting?" Tessa caught Grace's chin, turning Grace's face towards her.

"Kiss it better?" Grace pointed to her cheek, and the child planted a sloppy kiss.

"How much longer will you be here?" Ella gestured around the Hall.

"A few hours. Packing up will take another hour. I should be at the farm by about seven."

"Any clues why Mum and Dad called the meeting?" Ella's inquiry was laced with concern.

"You know what they're like." A united team. Grace had never known a time when her parents' love wasn't strong and real—an aura tangible enough to reach out and touch. "A family meeting only starts when all the family's present."

"But?"

"Mum's not getting any stronger." She'd borne witness to her mother's steady decline in recent months. Simple household tasks became harder by the day. Her mother thought Grace didn't notice the tricks her mother had adopted to disguise her frailty. Grace gave her the dignity of pretending not to see. "She's still struggling from her last bout of pneumonia."

"Tell me." With two words her sister shouldered some of Grace's burden.

"She couldn't make the bed by herself." Grace blinked back tears. Yesterday she'd found her mother sitting on the side of the bed, her fingers caught in the folds of the fitted bottom sheet trying to push it over the corner of the mattress. Grace had made up some story to explain her arrival, said she needed something only her mother could find. She'd coaxed her mother out of the room, then remade the bed. "I think they saw another specialist."

"Since our call last week?" Ella brushed the back of her hand across Grace's cheek.

"Are you trying to make me cry?" Grace sniffed, then winked at Tessa. "Another kiss to make it better." The child held Grace's face with both hands and placed a solemn kiss on each cheek. Grace spun in a circle, delighting in Tessa's squeals of joy. "I didn't say anything about the bed."

"Just like you haven't said anything about taking over shopping, the housework and the cooking?" Ella pumped Grace for details every time they talked.

"It's not hard to knock up extra casseroles and soups. They can eat them if they want them." The food disappeared almost as fast as Grace put it in the freezer.

"They're intelligent people. They must know it can't go on like this."

"They went to town Thursday morning. Dad asked me to do the afternoon milking even though they were home." She'd spent a sleepless night parsing out the implications of her father's absence from the shed. She could count on one hand the number of times he'd skipped milking over the years.

"We'll insist on an answer this time," Ella said firmly.

"For a family that talks about everything, they've been uncharacteristically closemouthed about this." Grace taking on more work didn't make a damn bit of difference to her mother's health. Grace nuzzled against Tessa's neck, the little girl's giggles a quiet comfort, smoothing over the tight clumps of anxiety holding Grace's body hostage.

"Hi, EJ, Grace."

The deep male voice—honey and smoke—brought Grace's head up, her antennae on alert. Tessa protested at her firmer grip. Grace hadn't seen him arrive, and with her sister as an audience, couldn't avoid the contact. Ryan Wilson was six foot two and topped her by a good four inches. His broad shoulders were encased in standard dairy-country uniform of blue chambray and sleeveless poly fibre jacket. The dark moleskins and battered R.M. Williams boots were another tell of Australian country boy. Ditto with the wide-brimmed Akubra perched on his head. Dark reflective sunglasses hid his eyes, but his mouth was set in a straight line above a square jaw. His skin was tanned to a burnished gold, chamois-soft for a man who lived his life outdoors. Word was Ryan Wilson had lived outdoors in the eight years he'd been absent from the valley.

"Ryan." Ella's ready smile curved in greeting. "Sorry I've missed you my last few visits home. We haven't left the farm."

Grace had been avoiding personal encounters with him in the two years since he'd been home. Quite a feat, given they were neighbours.

His mouth relaxed into a half smile. "You've been busy since I last saw you."

"Meet Tiger." Ella rested her hand on her son's head.

"Tiger?"

"He was on the move even in the womb." Ella laughed. "His birth certificate says Kit." She pointed at the child in Grace's arms. "Tessa's grown a bit."

"Did you want something?" Grace drew herself up to her full height. He had the edge, but she didn't back away. The prickle of awareness was new to her and oddly disorienting. *So, he'd turned into a hunk.*

"Just saying hello to all the new stallholders—as a member of the field day committee." Ryan dared Grace to object.

"Doggie," Tessa squealed.

Jake continued. "Asking if there's anything we can do to improve your experience?"

He could take himself off like he had ten years ago. Annoyance did battle with basic politeness. "I'm fine."

"On the committee?" Ella teased. "The Wilson boy made good!"

"A mover and a shaker," he replied ironically.

"Doggie." Tessa wriggled in Grace's arms, straining to get down.

Grace squatted to face the three-legged mixed breed leaning against Ryan, keeping Tessa within the secure circle of her arms. Ryan could have approached Grace at any time during the long day. Instead he'd used Ella to run interference. His tacit acknowledgement of Grace's confused hostility gave her pause. Her new-found edginess around him was as welcome as tick-borne disease in her cows and shredded the good manners her parents had taught her.

"Tessa would love a dog," Ella murmured.

The *Oh no!* in her sister's voice had Grace hiding her grin.

"Maybe not yet." Ella rubbed Kit's back. "Tess, say hello to Ryan, and he might introduce you."

Tessa lifted her head, tilted it further back and, giggling, toppled back against Grace. "Hello, big man."

He hunkered down and slid a hand over the dog's head, caressing one ear while encouraging the brown and white mutt to sit. His tongue lolled out the side of his mouth, and his liquid brown eyes adoringly followed Ryan's every move.

"Hi, Tessa. This is Satan," Ryan introduced his companion.

Figures! Grace wished she could see through those glasses, see if there was any hint of apology in Ryan's eyes. A melt-your-bones brown—not that she'd paid much attention to him years ago on the school bus. He'd been in Ella's class, whereas his younger brother, Danny, had been in Grace's. The brothers had shared the same dark brown hair and eyes, the same rangy build.

The stab of grief for Danny ambushed her. One of the reasons she'd kept her distance since Ryan's return.

"How'd he get his name?" Grace snatched at the conversational lifeline.

"Fought through hellfire to save a few lives. Or his namesake from World War I did. This one alerted us to a fire in a cabin. Didn't you, boy?" Ryan crooned. "We got the workers out safely, but his leg was badly burned. Had to amputate." He'd wrong-footed her again by showing a sensitive side.

"Poor baby." Grace stretched out a hand to the dog and waited until he accepted it before patting him. "Like this, Tess."

"He's very gentle. Likes kids." Ryan's hand covered Tessa's, bringing him closer to Grace. Close enough for her to smell man and shared history. Her breath caught in her throat as past and present collided.

"Good doggie. Ellie"—Tessa screwed up her eyes against the sun—"I want doggie."

"I know you do, darling," Ella murmured. "We can talk about it with Jake."

"She looks like Chrissy," Ryan lowered his voice so only Grace could hear. When she nodded, he continued. "I'm sorry Chrissy died. I haven't had the chance to tell you."

"I'm sorry about Dan." Old despair erupted in a messy accusation. "You *never* gave me a chance to tell you."

Ella winced at her sharp response, but Grace had looked to Ryan in the church ten years ago. For help to make sense of the madness? For reassurance? To see if he shared her sense of loss, of waste, of guilt in not being able to prevent Danny's death. Ryan had refused to talk to her after Danny's funeral, abandoning her to suffocating grief.

Ryan had been seventeen then to her fifteen, as tall as now but gangly. He hadn't grown into his build, but the promise of the man had been there. His shaggy hair had been longer. Not long enough to hide his tight, shuttered expression.

The pain of Ryan's rejection had smouldered inside her, only to flare up now. He'd left town straight after her best friend Danny's funeral. Hadn't stayed for the wake or to listen to community condolences. Ryan had spoken to no one. Not even her. Then disappeared. *When his mother needed him.* Grace had struggled to forgive him for that too. She'd taught herself not to need him, not to need anyone other than her family.

"I'm sorry I didn't speak to you." He rose abruptly to his feet, his hands held up in front of him.

She rose with him. Her heart hammered, her hands balled and her legs were planted wide in defiance.

"Are these handmade?" A short, wide woman in a rose-patterned dress had peeled off from the noisy pack surging through the Hall and stood at her stall.

Grace scurried to the counter, a plastic smile plastered in place. "Yes. Farmhouse cheeses from Blue Sky farm in the Ridgeway Valley."

"Can I try?" The woman gestured to the two breadboards, one spilling over with crackers and chunks of fruit bread with a large wedge of her crumbly cheddar in central position. The second hosted her soft cheeses, a less rustic display, more a sophisticated cheese platter presented as you might a share plate at an award-winning restaurant.

"What would you like first?" The potential customer held only half of Grace's attention, although her patter was too well-honed for the woman to detect her distraction. Ryan and his give-away-nothing reflective sunglasses occupied her peripheral vision. Ella had always defended him for leaving town. Hers was an easy friendship with him, something Grace couldn't imagine for herself.

"Nice to catch up with you, EJ." Ryan turned to walk away.

Ella caught his elbow and linked arms. "Why don't you escort Tessa and me back to Jake so I can introduce you?" She made a face at Grace, promising a reprimand later tonight for her churlish sniping. "See you later, Grace."

"The cheddar," Ms. Rose-Pattern said.

Grace lost her temper when her heart couldn't make sense of her world, which only compounded her sense of helplessness. She could have—should have—politely accepted Ryan's condolences for Chrissy. Instead Let Her Rip Gracie had ripped into him, reminding him of that dreadful day. Her gut clenched in contrition. From his reaction, she'd catapulted him back to the incomprehensible hell they'd inhabited after Danny's death.

"Can I try the cheddar?" Ms. Patient Rose-Pattern had to repeat her choice. The woman skewered the chunk Grace cut with a toothpick, wrinkled her nose as she savoured its earthy scent, then popped it in her mouth. "I like it." The woman reached for the second chunk Grace had cut. "What's your average cheddar weight?"

"About twelve kilos." Grace braced for the verdict, always personal when it was your own creation.

"I'll take one. I just love the branding. Pretty girls? Is that from the nursery rhyme?" Ms. Rose-Pattern leaned closer. "Are you one of those three girls in frilly blouses sitting on a bench in the photo on your label?"

Grace raised her voice to compete with the booming announcement of the winning ticket for the door prize. "I'm the middle sister. My Nana loved that photo—called it pretty girls all in a row." Except now Grace had only one sister.

"That's sweet." Ms. Rose-Pattern gave Grace a shrewd look. "And your blouse matches the one in the photo. Clever marketing. I'm guessing Blue Sky's your farm?"

"Family owned and run for four generations." When Grace took over, it would be five. The continuity was a rhythm beating in her blood, a source of pride as well as a passion. For now, she operated as a subtenant working and living out of the old house her grandparents had lived in until their deaths.

"Was that your sister and her husband?" Ms. Chatty Rose-Pattern stared at Ryan's retreating back, giving Grace permission to do the same.

"Ella's my sister. Ryan's . . ." *Not Ella's husband.* Relief pushed jumpy sparks of alarm along Grace's synapses. *I am not interested.* "A neighbour."

"He's reason enough to move to the country." The woman's low-voiced chuckle brought Grace's gaze back to her. "Easy on the eye," the woman commented. "Do your sisters work in the business?"

"They had other dreams." Unnecessary to explain her beautiful younger sister's early death from an aggressive cancer two years ago. Grace processed the payment, putting the cheese into one of the sturdy cloth bags she'd designed and made, and added one of her business cards. "I've given you my card"—she smiled—"in case you want more. Do you need help getting this to your car?"

"I'm fine, and I feel sure you'll be hearing from me." Ms. Rose-Pattern re-joined the river of people winding through the stalls.

* * *

Ryan was aware of Grace's gaze on him as he walked away. He'd planned to approach her today. They'd done enough pussyfooting around. She avoided him at those community functions where their paths crossed. But they were next-door neighbours as well as business people in a small community, and their standoff was starting to generate gossip. Enough to have his mother asking him questions.

"Are you here long?" Ryan asked. He'd intended to use his role as a committee member to approach the booth. EJ's arrival made it simple. He was sure of a welcome from her. Every time Grace saw him, she donned some invisible cloak of disdain to repel him, giving him the brush-off without saying a word. Her outburst gave him an answer. She blamed him for a silence at the funeral, which had taken every ounce of his self-control to maintain.

"A few days. There's Jake." Ella signalled, but Tessa had already taken off at a run to be caught and lifted high by a grinning pirate of a man with a ponytail and earring.

"Not quite what I expected," Ryan murmured.

"That was my reaction when I met him." Ella released his arm. "Jake, this is Ryan Wilson, a friend. Ryan, meet my husband."

"I've heard about you." Jake offered a hand. "No need to clam up. Just general stuff, about how you and your brother, Eleanor and Grace grew up together."

"Grace and Danny bonded as pre-schoolers." EJ leaned into her husband, each of them holding a child, the four of them a solid unit. Ties Ryan avoided.

"They were close," he agreed. And despite having

different dreams stayed close. He rubbed the back of his neck. Maybe their dreams hadn't been so different. It required creativity as well as determination to produce unique cheeses. Danny had wanted to do graphic design, although that was one secret they'd managed to keep from the small-minded, small-town busy-bodies who dismissed the creative arts as unmanly.

"Mum used to say they were joined at the hip." EJ faced the truth head-on. "Grace adored him."

Grace had shouted at Ryan at Danny's funeral, although he hadn't heard a word past the roaring in his ears. He'd seen her mouth moving, her arms waving, and hot tears pouring unchecked down her cheeks. If he'd tried to speak, he would have shouted too. Not at her. At the sanctimonious school principal who'd expelled Danny for sharing a kiss, and the bigots who'd taunted Danny. Shouting at the cowards who'd driven his brother to suicide would have turned to fighting. Ryan had wanted to beat the shit out of someone that day. But he'd clamped it down. For Danny, for his gentle brother, Danny. Then Ryan had got the hell out. Planned never to return.

"I know." His powerlessness was another regret. He hadn't been able to find any words for her. He'd let Grace down too.

More casual small talk, an easy goodbye. EJ, or Eleanor Jane—too big a mouthful for schooldays—made things easy for him. With Jake, and with Grace. A natural mediator, EJ had waded into the middle of a fight even when they'd shared a classroom. Not a close friend but a mate.

He rolled his shoulders, and Satan pushed his nose into Ryan's hand. Animals were more reliable than most people, but a trusty dog couldn't shift this kind of tension. Grace had run free at his place as a kid, even when she was a bit more than a kid. He'd liked her, liked her loyalty to Danny even more, but he'd never given her a second look. Today's kick to his libido had been unforeseen and irritated the hell out of him, given she treated him as if he had some contagious disease.

The contrast between the virginal white-lace blouse and her usual work shirts had his head spinning. It softened her hard edges, made his fingers itch to unwrap this unexpected delight. Turns out her normal plain packaging was camouflage. Useful for projecting a no-nonsense persona in the still largely masculine farming world. Up close Grace Anderson wasn't all cool businesswoman. Jeans and boots were standard. The flimsy white cotton with lace and frills caressing her breasts and gathered at the waist told a different tale. It matched the photo of the little girls on her label. *A sentimental streak?* Danny always swore she had a marshmallow centre beneath the quick temper, but that was a lifetime ago.

Her wide-brimmed hat had lain discarded on a box behind her, and her sunglasses had been tossed aside when Ryan had arrived. Her clear green gaze had bored unflinchingly into his shades when she'd slapped him down. Confident, right enough, mixed with a hint of vulnerability to twist his gut. Danny would have responded to her sensitivity, although even at fifteen, he'd been oblivious to the appeal of her soft scent, cluster of brown curls, not-quite-pretty face and firm body. And Danny, or rather his brother's death, stood between Grace and himself.

He smiled grimly. Grace would probably choke on her full-cream tasty cheddar if she knew she had him to thank for the inclusion of organics at this year's event. The old timers on the field day committee had taken some persuading. Logic had triumphed over prejudice, and wasn't that a surprise? He'd been a kid when he left town. Now a wealthy landowner, he was learning the benefits of playing with the local decision-makers. Not that he'd ever forget how they'd met his mother's pleas for more time to pay her bills with closed doors.

A landowner! Not in the sense of hereditary title. He bought, improved and sold land, refusing to be emotionally attached to any patch of dirt. He'd gone that route once. His current plan was to sell the family farm when he'd built it up a bit more. It no longer held special value for him. When it came to Grace—he looked back in the direction of her booth—they just had to be able to rub up against each other in public without setting tongues wagging.

* * *

The booths officially closed at five, with the first call at four-thirty. The doors running the length of the Exhibition Hall were flung open to allow easier access for stall holders packing up and for shoppers, who'd hung on for a last bargain, to leave. The field day ended with a celebration— fireworks, a dance—which Grace had planned to join until this unscheduled family meeting. She loaded her refrigerated van with her bags, flyers and banners and unsold cheeses— she'd sold more cheddars than she'd expected, fewer than she'd hoped.

Another van pulled up alongside. "Hey, Gracie. Did you see yesterday's cryptic crossword?"

"Yep." She nodded at Bluey. The grizzled old farmhand leaned out the window, his watery blue eyes squinting against the late afternoon sun. His muscled arm was a nutty brown in sharp contrast to the snowy white T-shirt he habitually wore. "Where are your sunglasses?"

"Somewhere. I'm stumped by one clue, 'two cheese omelette dead marched.' I've got as far as two words, four letters, then seven. I'm guessing omelette means it's scrambled. So, an anagram?" Bluey had started at the Wilson farm around the time Ryan left home and had become a fixture.

"I got that one," she admitted.

"Don't keep me in suspense, girl." Bluey scratched his chin and rolled his eyes. "What's the answer?"

"I'll tell you if you get yourself some sunglasses and start wearing them." She sauntered closer to his window. He'd also helped out at their farm in the past. He'd been a part of her life for forever.

"Deal."

"You say that all the time." She softened her rebuke with a smile. "But I live in hope. Are you sure you didn't get this?"

"Damn! I knew I should have got it." He slapped a hand on the steering wheel.

There'd been plenty of malicious gossip flying around Danny's suicide. Bluey's reliable presence had protected Mrs. Wilson from the worst of it. Ryan hadn't been around to help. Yet Bluey had stayed at the farm when Ryan took over, and she'd never heard Bluey whisper even the slightest criticism of his new boss.

"It's two words from 'dead marched.' 'Cheese' is another clue." She waited a heartbeat for his guess, then gave him the answer. "Edam cheddar."

"That's the answer? Edam cheddar?" He hooted with laughter. "You're a sweetheart, Gracie. Save a dance for me tonight?"

Her smile died. "Ella and Jake are up for the night."

"Say hello from me." Bluey's smile winked out. "Give my best to your mum and dad." A sensitive man for all his gruff exterior.

Grace didn't move as Bluey drove away. She was indifferent to the other workers packing up booths, the vans edging through the aisles of displays. Two years since Chrissy's death. Since Ryan's return. Memories surfaced. She'd shouted at him behind the church at his brother's funeral, and he'd stood silent, letting her treat him as her punching bag. She'd been oblivious at Chrissy's funeral, her gaze fixed on the wooden box housing her vibrant, irresponsible sister. Ryan's name had been in the condolences book she'd read a few months later. She hadn't known he'd been back in town when her sister died and wasn't sure what she thought about his attendance at Chrissy's funeral. He'd left town after one funeral and arrived in time for another.

"Let it go, Grace," she mumbled. Growing up had taught her to understand Ryan's need to grieve in his own way. Chrissy's death had helped her accept it. Grief didn't excuse his abandonment of his mother. Helen Wilson had lost two sons that day.

A vehicle tooted its horn, reminding Grace where she was. She returned to her packing. This part of the Hall would be cleared out shortly and converted into a dance hall. Getting the big machinery and larger displays disassembled both here and in the outside exhibition spaces would take a few more days.

A family meeting. They had them all the time. This one had an ominous ring to it. When she climbed into the cab, uneasiness settled in her stomach like curdled milk.

JENNIFER RAINES

CHAPTER TWO

The turnoff to Ridgeway Valley was a half hour from town. Grace's spirits lifted each time she made the corner. Coming home. It had been sanctuary, and more, since she'd taken her first steps as a toddler in the lush pastures surrounding the main house. Tonight, the pounding of her heart blocked out the familiar song of welcome.

For Pete's sake, Grace. It's a family meeting, not a court hearing! Fixing a smile in place, she pushed open the back door of the main house. Warmth, light, voices tumbling over each other and the fragrant smell of a beef casserole hit as successive blows. Her stomach cramped in rejection. A plate was thrust into her hand.

"We heard you arrive. We're eating in the dining room." Ella had taken charge of dinner, saying it reminded her of the old days.

She took over the conversation as well, talking about Kit's latest achievements and Tessa's discovery of dance, engaging their mother in one of her favourite topics—her grandchildren. Grace appreciated her sister's attempt at normality, but Grace's nerves stretched in anticipation of the discussion to come. None of them bought her excuse for not being hungry. They accepted it, though, passing bowls of potatoes and peas from hand to hand, while she fought the queasiness triggered by aromas she normally loved. Ella's breezy chat carried them through the meal. While Jake cleared the plates, Ella excused herself to do a final check of her babies.

"Another wine, Grace?"

"No, thanks, Dad." She was jumpy enough without the added stimulation of alcohol. "I think we should get started."

"At the kitchen table," her mother insisted, leading the way across the wide, polished wood hall. Her mother's breathing was laboured, and her steps were slower than at any time in Grace's memory. "The kitchen table makes it family." The kitchen had borne witness to generations of births, deaths, and every minor or major victory or disaster in between.

Grace swallowed a sob. "Yet we ate in the dining room." Catching her mother up, she rubbed her hand up her mother's back, the prominence of each vertebra in the slight frame highlighting Grace's helplessness.

"Ella, Jake, and the kids make it a celebration as well," her mother said. "Pleasure first, business second."

Family business signified the big stuff—farm succession, estate management, Chrissy's illness and now her mother's. They had regular meetings. This one came hard on the last one about the timing of her succession to the farm, feeding her sense of foreboding. Ella slipped into the room behind them.

"Are the babies good, Ella?"

"Yes, Mum, and I brought the baby monitor." Ella placed it on the table, flicked it on and smiled when Tessa's soft voice came through, "*Sleep time, Kit. Love you.*" "All good."

"Jake, you take the head of the table." Her father marshalled his troops. "Elaine and I'll sit here."

Grace glanced sideways at her sister, before settling on one of the paint-scarred wooden chairs her parents had bought twenty years ago at a land sale, intending to renovate. There'd never been time, and after a few years, no inclination.

"You're probably wondering why we wanted a family meeting now when it's only been a few months since we talked this all through."

"We're guessing something's changed, Dad." Anxiety was a lump at the back of Grace's throat. Under the table, Ella took her hand.

"A few things have changed." Her father's voice sounded too loud in the loaded silence. "All the decisions we've made, all the conversations we've had no longer apply."

"You're scaring me, Dad," Grace whispered, turning to face her mother. "Mum?"

"I'm taking too long to come back from this last bout of pneumonia." Elaine picked up the thread. "The specialist is recommending a different climate to rebuild my strength. It's too hot and dusty here."

"How long's a while?" Grace needed facts to build a solution.

"At least six months." Her mother glanced at Grace's father. She was holding back.

"The specialist says it must be done . . . and soon." Her father reached for his wife's hand. "Immediate and permanent would be better."

"Why didn't you tell us?" Grace tightened her hold on Ella's hand. This was worse than any of the scenarios they'd discussed.

"We wanted to get a second opinion." Elaine might be physically unwell; she was always indomitable.

"Will you be okay if you leave here?" Grace forced the words through dry lips. *Please say you'll be okay. I'm not ready to lose you.*

The hope in her father's smile eased the cold dread caused by his shocking announcement. "She won't be okay if she stays."

"Finally, something we can do." Grace smiled through tears. She and Ella had refused to talk about the possibility their mother might die, although the fear had stalked them both. Relief came through in the changed grip of her sister's fingers.

Elaine nodded. "Recovery will be slow, but away from the humidity and heat I'll do better." Elaine hesitated. "Brian?"

"There's more." Her father drew all eyes back to him. "There's been speculation for a while. The official offer from the milk processor came through last week." His sombre expression underlined the threat. "They're dropping the farm-gate price of milk by fifteen percent from the next contract period."

As Grace stared into the troubled faces of her family, she realised they were all looking at her, waiting for her to speak. "I'll increase my payments to the farm—for the milk, for the rent of the house and the cheese-making space to cover the shortfall."

"You already pay a fair rent and a fair price, Grace. It doesn't make sense for you to pay more," Brian said gently.

"Farm income will take a sizeable hit," Ella cut to the core of the problem. "You need money to move away, money to hire a replacement manager."

Grace held her breath, a new fear taking shape, too impossibly big for her to grasp.

"There won't be enough to pay for a manager and draw an income to support ourselves," her father confirmed.

"Let me give you more," she begged. The urge to cry out, *Stop now,* sped through her, as if stopping the words would stop what came next.

"That wouldn't be fair, Grace, and it's not an answer." Brian placed his and Elaine's joined hands on the table. "You all know the plan. I'd work another decade, then retire. We'd stay here, employ a full-time manager, and I'd do occasional farm work and draw a wage."

Grace nodded, unable to speak. Ella wrapped her arms

around Grace's waist, pulling Grace into her side. Grace's mind refused to work. She was looking at a jigsaw puzzle with lost pieces, missing some critical connection between her mother's health and the future of the farm.

"Pretty Girls would have had time to grow, with the idea that the estate would be split three ways. Grace would have everyone's backing to buy out the farm," her father restated the family succession plan crafted over years.

"Jake and I have talked about this." Ella glanced at Jake, and he nodded encouragement. "We know you want to make sure Chrissy is remembered in your will, but Tessa and Kit and any other children we may have will get equal shares in what we have. Tessa will also inherit a large amount from her father's side of the family. We've always planned to give Tessa's share of the farm to Grace."

"That's not fair." Grace struggled to focus on the implications of her father's words and her sister's offer. "I mean, it's not fair for Tessa to miss out."

"Eleanor and I planned to raise this at our next visit. Grace, you have an official contract as a subtenant, but you contribute in many other ways to the value and viability of the farm. Your share of the estate should be larger. But, to be blunt"—Jake met his father-in-law's gaze—"Brian's talking about whether current and future farm income can support him and Elaine to leave the farm. Have I got that right?" His quiet authority gave the madness a horrible reality.

"Unfortunately, yes." Brian's sigh of resignation shivered through her.

"What options have you considered?" Jake's calm, client-lawyer dissection of the problem terrified her.

"We've spoken to our financial adviser and the bank." Brian lifted his hands, then dropped them, the gesture summarising hours of futile negotiation. "Our best option is to sell the farm."

A roar of protest filled Grace's head, blocking out everything else. *This isn't real.* She rocked backwards and forwards. I'm going to wake up in a minute. This isn't happening. "Dad, you love this farm." That was real; a constant in her world.

"I do, but I love your mother more." He turned to his wife, brushing away the tears running down her cheeks. "Believe me, we've tried. There is no other choice."

Grace could barely breathe. Couldn't trust what might come out of her mouth. She understood they saw no other choice. She'd find a way. *There had to be a way.* This was her home, her dream. She straightened away from her sister's protective embrace.

"You love the farm too," her father said. "You're the one most impacted by this decision."

She stared at him, then slapped a hand over her mouth to stop herself from shouting. *Be quiet, and let me think!*

"Are there any buyers, or were you thinking of the open market?" Jake asked coolly.

"We've had offers in the last few years." Brian shifted his gaze to Jake.

"Ryan?" Focusing on Ryan gave Grace a legitimate target for the turmoil bubbling beneath her shock. "Offers? Has Ryan made a second offer?"

"About a year ago. Bigger farms have a better chance of survival these days. He likes what we've done, wants to diversify and introduce new practices," Brian said.

"He already bought out Donovan—the only other farm on this road! Why offer for us? He knows we're a family farm." Indignation gave her more control than the despair creeping through her. "We're converting to organic? The Wilsons don't give a rat's arse about sustainable practices."

"That's unfair and untrue, Grace. His mother didn't have the money to do much more. She started making changes at the same time as Donovan. Ryan's made more." Her father held up a hand. "And Ryan was joking. He knew I wasn't interested. Ridgeway Wellness Centre also made an offer."

"Like her bloody hide!" Ella beat Grace to outrage.

"After she scored big off our misfortune?"

"Rochelle Harkiss isn't responsible for how we lost the land." Elaine had always refused to blame the sophisticated entrepreneur at the end of the lane.

"You mean swindled out of the land by Smithhouse," Grace snapped out her objection, her voice rising on the memories. Her mother's tractor accident, the rising medical bills, Smithhouse's offer of a loan on a handshake, then his insistence on immediate repayment with a very specific piece of land six months later. "Rochelle Harkiss watched from the sidelines as he cheated us, snapped up the land before it went on the market, then magically got permission to rezone productive farmland for her Wellness Centre."

"And your point is?" Brian sighed. For him, the battle with Smithhouse was over.

Grace surrendered to the comfortable rage of an old resentment. "That stretch of the valley was prime Anderson land."

"Now it's not. Holding on to anger about what you can't change only hurts you, Grace."

"Are you selling to her?" She rose to her feet, stumbling back a few steps as the inconceivable became concrete, snapping tight bands around her chest. The farm belonged to her parents. This wasn't her decision to make.

"I'm talking to my family about our options." Brian reached out a hand, and Grace came back to the table. Ella leaned against her.

"I'm sorry." Grace raised a hand in apology. "It's not my decision."

"No, it's not. This hurts you more than anyone else, baby," Elaine said. "We've been going around in circles trying to work out the best way to handle it and decided we can solve it better together."

"If we put it on the open market we might attract more buyers; however, we have two viable options now," Brian explained, the weight of the decision heavy on his face. "That saves time. Ryan has demonstrated he's serious about continuing dairy production in the valley, and he's open to new ideas."

Grace snorted. Her father was right, but this was happening too fast, spinning out of her control.

Ella shared a look with her mother, then turned to Grace. "Honey, have you talked to Ryan about what he's doing?"

"Today's conversation is the longest I've had with him since he's come home." Grace had strayed too close to personal matters, scratching at the scab of Danny's death in their first conversation. He'd reacted. More than he had at his brother's funeral. She'd forced him back to that dark place and been helpless to handle the memories differently.

"You have a legal and binding year-on-year tenancy agreement." Her father reclaimed her attention. "We'd make that a primary consideration in any sale arrangement. Can we do that, Jake?"

"There are laws protecting tenants' rights," Jake agreed.

"Tenants can be evicted." Grace knew of cases and cursed her smart mouth when her father winced.

"You need reasonable notice for eviction," Jake said. "You'd get six months at least."

Six months! Her whole body ached as if she'd spent the day birthing a calf. Punch-drunk, her brain sluggish, Grace's desperation made her more determined. She'd find a different solution. She'd been outraged at Ryan's first offer for the farm, but it had spurred her to start putting money aside—a safety net. Before his first offer, she'd pumped every penny into growing her business.

A shiver ran down her spine. Years, she'd factored in years, if not decades, before her parents' farm succession plan came into force, and she'd need to approach a bank for the loan to buy out her sisters' shares.

"Rochelle said it'd enhance their image to have an organic cheese-making business as part of the Centre's activities." Her father was trying to make the unbearable sound workable.

"Would you like me to sound them out?" Jake asked. "Act as go-between, with you able to withdraw at any moment—?"

"That's what we hoped you'd say." Relief smoothed out the frown on Brian's forehead.

"My preference is for Ryan," Ella stated bluntly. "Rather than as an add-on for Rochelle's Wellness Centre. That sounds a bit cutesy-poo."

"As sound a reason as any for a business decision," Jake muttered.

"It's not. I've always liked him. Grace"—Ella pinched the soft skin at Grace's waist, a signal to haul it in—"Tessa liked him. Plus, he's got a three-legged mutt who adores him."

"Children and animals. Your failsafe way of assessing people." Jake smiled fondly at his wife.

"It works." Ella claimed she'd fallen for Jake because children and animals liked him. "And, without wanting to start any conspiracy theories, Rochelle still deals with Smithhouse and—"

"Smithhouse hasn't changed his business model," Grace finished, using the encouragement in Ella's eyes to steady herself. Her parents had carried this secret for weeks. Her dummy spit made a tough situation worse. "Satan's the best thing Ryan's got going for him."

Elaine's eyebrows shot up. "You think he's got the devil on his side?"

"Satan's the name of his dog, Mum." Grace had stopped paying attention. She rose to her feet, her heart pounding as if she'd run a race. Adrenalin poured through her. "I'll buy the farm."

"I know that's what you want," Brian began.

Her fingers curled over the back of the chair, gripping it with an intensity to match the determination flowing through her. "Then give me a chance. Market rates. Not charity."

She scanned each face in turn around the table. She had

Ella's support. That gave her Jake's as well. Her father was torn. He wanted her to have it, doubted she had the money and needed to act quickly.

"Let us sleep on it," Elaine said.

Grace needed to be outside before she blew it, before she wheedled and begged. Rounding the table, she slipped her arms around her mother's shoulders to bring her mouth level with her mother's ear. "Only if it works for you, Mum." Then she straightened. "I'll let Ella tell you the story of how Satan got his name."

"He kept the dog, Grace." Her sister used truth to skewer her. "I'm betting he rescued him."

"Tell someone who cares." Grace rolled her eyes. "Let me buy the farm. Not him. Do you mind if I skip cleaning up tonight?" Disappointment was eight hundred kilograms of prize bull slung across her shoulders.

"Jake and I are on kitchen duty." Ella waved her away. "You have the night off."

"Then I'll make a move. Another work day tomorrow." She kissed her father, blew kisses to Ella and Jake on the way out the back door. "Love you," Grace called, slumping against the wall when she got outside. Voices floated through the open window.

"Should I go after her?" Ella asked no one in particular.

"Let's talk some more," Brian answered.

"About how to help her make it work?" Jake asked.

"We have to be hard-headed about this." Brian sighed. "The bank will be. Elaine and I have crunched the numbers until we're cross-eyed and can't see any way Grace can do this. If you've got ideas, let's hear them."

At four the next morning, Grace trudged towards the milking shed in the dark. She yawned and blinked several times.

Had she managed any of the deep sleep experts said was essential to function properly if you were going to operate machinery?

Cows were waiting and started moving into position as she flicked the light switches in the milk shed, her soft whistles and nudges encouragement enough for their shared common purpose of emptying their udders. Yawning again, she closed the gate on the first sixteen. Then moved from cow to cow, attaching the teats to each in turn, murmuring endearments to them. The soft sounds of Allegri's *Miserere* coming over the loudspeakers announced her father's arrival. A pulse started beating at her temple, but she'd coached herself overnight to be patient. Two solid hours of milking before they could return to the house. Her parents would deliver their decision at breakfast with everyone present. She leaned forward to attach the next cow.

"Get any sleep?" Her father put his hand on her shoulder and bent to kiss the top of her head.

Grace's hand covered his work-hardened one. Tipping her head back, she leaned against him. "Some."

"Doesn't look like it." He searched her face with eyes people said she'd inherited from him. She'd inherited a lot more, but she'd yet to learn his calm acceptance when life slapped you in the face.

"Head couldn't seem to stop." She'd researched loan rates and financing options until her eyes had crossed and the figures no longer made sense. Then she'd cried. She'd muffled her bone-cracking sobs with her pillow, even though the main house was across the paddock. She'd cried for herself first, for the loss of her dream. Then she'd cried for her parents. They'd had this diagnosis for weeks and, despite the seriousness, had delayed acting because of her. Her final tears were because she'd behaved like a selfish monster. Shock was a feeble excuse.

"Has it stopped now?"

"Not really." She didn't know if it ever would. They were leaving and selling the farm. The knowledge pressed against her chest like a boulder—huge and immovable. Surreal to find it there.

He laughed. "You've always been able to multitask."

"I can milk cows in my sleep." She'd allowed herself to believe Blue Sky would be hers one day. Her love for this land was in her bones and sinews—her first waking breath in the morning and her last sigh at night. The air had a different quality. The trees she'd planted over the years whispered to her when she walked between them.

"Just as well." He walked beside her. "It's a hell of a situation. We'll give you three months."

"What?" She fumbled the milking teats, and he stretched out a hand to steady hers.

"You heard."

Her stomach lurched. "I thought you'd wait until we were together."

"Your mother guessed you hadn't slept." He grinned. "Said making you wait any longer constituted child abuse."

"I can be patient," she claimed. Hope was roman candles exploding in the pre-dawn sky, a soaring pyrotechnic display of colour and light.

"You are endlessly patient with cows, cheese, farming and any member of your family. You can be a little ragged with outsiders." He ruffled her hair. He, of all people, knew where she'd learned distrust. "You've got three months to line up a bank and finance, and the property is yours."

"You need to leave soon." She couldn't accept more sacrifices when her mother's health was at stake.

"We're going soon. We want to set up a few things first, tidy up a few loose ends." He was a man who never had loose ends.

"Are you sure?" She held her breath.

He raised an eyebrow. "You're the one who needs to be sure."

"I am," she breathed. "I am. Will three months work for you financially?"

"We wish we could sign it over to you, but we can't." He shook his head. "Contracts exchanged in three months or we sell to whoever makes the best offer."

She threw her arms around him, smothering him with

kisses.

He held her away from him. "If you can't make it work, we'll try and protect the subtenancy."

"It won't come to that." She moved along the row, attaching teats, while her father doubled back to start moving in the next group of cows. The music soared gloriously. A cow dumped a load of manure. A grin split her face. *Hers.* The rough texture of the slow-moving, big-bodied animals had always grounded her, the earthy smell when you leaned into them ambrosia. The sight of milk flowing through the lines a solid satisfaction. She'd make it hers.

Her smile was still in place when they'd finished, when they'd cleaned the lines and washed out the shed, when they'd fed the calves and checked the feed and water troughs.

Her father tugged on a curl. "I'm proud of you, Grace. I don't know if I've told you often enough. And I'm proud you want to make this work."

"You delayed because of me." There was fresh guilt in that.

"Your mother delayed for both of us." Tears welled in his eyes. "I can't let her do that anymore. I can't watch her grow weaker by the day when I have the power to change things."

Grace brushed her fingers across his cheek, caught a tear on her fingertip. "Knowing you love her so much makes me proud. If I could find another you, I'd marry him tomorrow."

"Look for a better financial manager," he said ruefully.

"You're the best father." Smithhouse's swindle cast a long shadow on their lives. Her father's legacy had been to doubt his financial judgement, while she'd vowed to own and operate the farm herself. Sharing control with a partner, an investor or someone offering a clever deal was a risk she wasn't prepared to take. "The farm's viable. When we complete organic certification, we'll be able to charge a premium for our milk and cheese."

"Your idea."

"You backed me all the way. And we've achieved more. My cheeses are in increasing demand." She did a little victory dance. "The cheese glitterati of Sydney can't get enough of me."

"That's because you're very good. That gold at the Royal Easter Show is just the first." He wrapped an arm around her shoulder, drawing her close. "I'd best tell your mother you're happy to be saddling yourself with a mountain of debt. No need to come back for the afternoon milking. Ella said she and Tessa will help today."

"I'll catch up later then. I've got some deliveries in town."

CHAPTER THREE

When Ryan caught sight of Grace's parked van, he accepted the coincidence as an omen. He'd been thinking of her, considering how she'd react to the agreement he'd reached with her father this morning. The opportunity to find out himself was irresistible. Pulling in behind her, he ordered Satan to stay in the vehicle. With his hat shielding his face, he took up a position against the side of her van and surveyed the businesses nearby. No banks, so she hadn't come to discuss money. A delivery? The café was possible, but he hadn't seen her products there. He'd checked. Her pitch to the field day committee said that she'd been growing the number of outlets that stocked or used her products. She'd need to grow faster to service a bank loan.

The quick kick to his gut when she emerged from the café pushing a trolley was the other reason he'd stopped. Locking horns with her at the field day had lit a spark he'd expected to fizzle out. He didn't have time to waste on a taste for a woman with a short fuse and a bad attitude. He let his eyes drift over her before she found him. No-nonsense jeans and shirt today, the lacy confection she'd worn yesterday might never have been. Except he pictured her in it in his mind's eye. He'd also gone from irritated to intrigued by the passion causing her to nurse a grudge against him for ten years.

"Morning, Grace." He pushed himself off the van.

She stumbled, halfway between a bounce and a jump, her barriers locking in place with the thud of a prison gate. "Morning, Ryan." She straightened her shoulders. Her smile was forced but lovely. It changed her face from not quite pretty to captivating. "Were you waiting for me?" She was wary, yet for some reason, willing. Brian probably hadn't had a chance to tell her about their deal if she'd been in town all morning. She must want something from him to rein in her reaction so quickly. *Curiouser and curiouser.*

"I'd like to talk to you," he said.

Her nod amused Ryan.

"We're not doing a good job of it so far," he pointed out.

Opening the back of her van, she lifted the trolley onto the tray, taking her time packing it away. Grace was one of the few farm kids who'd wanted to stay on the farm. Like him, she was the kid who'd done the mucking out, who had farming in their bones. His goals were different now. Although he had some sympathy for what she was trying to do, making it more important to establish boundaries in their relationship from the get-go. He wanted her off-balance, before she could unbalance him any more than she had.

Finally, she faced him. "I've got something to ask you too." She needed to work on her tone, however, her proposition was purely fascinating.

He wanted to touch her—*and wasn't that a surprise*—to slide his fingers through the short curly mop he bet she considered practical. It framed her pixie face, giving it a luminescent appeal. Her body was easy on the eye too. A bit on the lanky side, but she had curves. And dips. And the promise of lushness. He gestured over her shoulder. "Fancy a coffee in a public place?"

She jiggled the keys in her hand, assessing her options.

"Okay."

Ryan wasted no time, turning and heading across the street to the small café. He ushered her through the front door and into an old-fashioned booth. He dropped his hat on the bench seat beside him. She slid off her sunglasses, swinging them from side to side between her thumb and two fingers before looking pointedly at him. He flicked his sunglasses down his nose.

"Is there something you want, Grace?"

"Take off the glasses, Ryan. There's no sun in here." Her blue-green eyes twinkled. A family thing—all three Anderson girls had the same almond-shaped eyes and pretty lashes.

"I've got sensitive eyes." He folded his glasses and set them on the table between them, feeling more exposed than he'd expected by the simple act of meeting her gaze with no protection. Her small smile of victory irked him.

Resting her elbows on the table, she propped her chin on her hands. "What do you want to talk about?"

"Ladies first."

She opened her mouth, then spotted the hovering waitress and eased back in her chair.

"Changed your mind, Grace?" the waitress asked.

"Ryan changed it for me. Just a coffee please."

"I could do you a good cheese sandwich." The waitress giggled.

"Just coffee, please, Susie," Grace said.

"Same for me." Ryan turned back to Grace as the waitress moved away, enjoying the byplay. "I didn't know this café was one of your customers?"

"Not yet." She played with the salt cellar, her fidgeting confirming she was touting for more business. "I provided some samples to test their interest."

She needed a friendly bank manager.

Maybe she just needed friends?

Her father had sounded Ryan out a few weeks ago. Asked whether he was still interested in buying Blue Sky.

Brian's approach had been indirect, but Ryan hadn't doubted his purpose. He'd hidden his surprise, been as careful in his answers as Brian in his questions, but open to continuing the conversation. Once at his computer, Ryan had played with ways and means to make it happen. The older man had called back this morning to tell him it was no longer available. Because Brian knew Ryan could keep a secret, he'd said Grace was buying the farm.

"I'll go first then. Brian told me you're buying the farm." He waited for the explosion. Instead she crumpled, blinking back tears he couldn't not witness. *Damn.* "I've made offers in the past, and he was setting me straight."

"When?" she asked, her voice scratchy from swallowing her shock.

"This morning."

"I didn't know." She was clearly blindsided to discover her father had confided in him.

"And you object to Brian talking to me about the farm," he stated, frustrated by her wariness.

"It's not for me to object," she replied. The waitress set a coffee in front of her, the enticing aroma filling the space between them.

He nodded his thanks for his own coffee, waiting like Grace for the waitress to move away. Grace could keep a private conversation private. Good to know.

"Is that why you want to talk to me?" She had more prickles than an echidna.

Watching her expressions change as she battled with herself was instructive. Annoyance warred with curiosity warred with self-interest. She'd slap him down if he offered for the place. But whatever she wanted from him was keeping her at the table. *A guy could dream she wanted his body.*

She frowned at her cup, then gave him an up-and-under look. "To convince me to sell?"

"Faster to wait for hell to freeze over." He stirred sugar into his coffee. "Brian's one of the most decent men I know. There are things about our relationship you probably don't know."

Her wrinkled nose told him she didn't like him sharing secrets with her dad. She'd been her father's shadow for as long as Ryan could remember and resented interlopers. He respected Brian Anderson, the steady way he worked, the decency he showed anyone who worked for him or with him. And his composure.

"Spit it out, Ryan." She tapped her fingers on the table, the short nails making a rat-a-tat-tat on the bare wood. Grace's personality was more firecracker, although she and Brian had achieved a lot in the last two years. With time she'd grow into her father's legacy on so many levels.

"After Danny's funeral, your dad paid for a labourer for three months to help my mother." Ryan had her full attention. "I'd like to repay my debt now. Supply a labourer for three months so he and your mother can leave the farm immediately."

She opened her mouth, closed it, then opened it again.

"You look like a guppy."

"I don't." She frowned, then met his gaze. She was smart as well as sexy. "You've already made the offer to Dad."

"This morning," Ryan agreed.

"And he accepted?" She looked like she'd landed in a country where she didn't know the language.

Ryan nodded. She'd known nothing about the deal done a decade ago. Another debt he owed her father—Brian Anderson had safeguarded Wilson family dignity.

"Why now?"

He could see her working it out, sucking in her protest and appreciated the effort it cost her not to throw his offer back in his face. Maybe she had changed, tamed those high spirits so she didn't always attack first and apologise later.

"Because he needs it now, and I'm in a position to repay it." He gave her a part truth. Grace needed help now, and her father was giving her cover.

"Cocky bastard, aren't you?" Her fingers had restarted their drumming. "You've been back two years and could have paid him out at any time."

"He refused." Brian had told Ryan to forget it. Ryan had decided now was the perfect time to renew his offer. He prided himself on repaying his debts. Shifting the dynamics between him and Grace was a bonus. "Until now."

"I don't need your charity." Her words confirmed the rumours she wasn't good at accepting help.

"If Brian's selling to you, this is my last chance to pay him back," Ryan countered, confident his logic was irrefutable.

She studied him over the lip of her coffee cup, weighing the odds, weighing him, and more than lust for her stirred. Ryan admired what she'd made of herself, how she'd convinced her parents to go with her, the shift from the old to the new at a time when it was risky to do so. Buying the place now was a huge commitment and an even bigger challenge.

"What did you want to ask me, Grace?"

"I heard you're hiring." She stared over his shoulder.

"You were going to ask *me* for work?" His turn to be caught off-guard. She must love Blue Sky if she was prepared to set aside her animosity towards him and beg for work. Her determination to buy the farm or kill herself trying annoyed the hell out of him.

"I *am* asking you for work," she insisted.

"When the hell do you think you can work for me?" he demanded. Her resolve staggered him and reminded him of the boy he'd been when he'd have done anything to keep his family farm. "Between midnight and four in the morning?"

"I've got ideas." She peered down her nose at him, as haughty as any landed gentry he'd ever encountered, and damn if he didn't find that a turn-on as well. "You know that. Donovan would have told you I acted as an advisor on improving his property. Long conversations," she emphasised, "about restoring native grasses to reduce methane production and make him more self-sufficient in feed. That corridor of young trees in your back paddock was my idea."

"Advice at no charge." Ryan had already owned the Donovan place and had okayed every one of her suggestions. Talking to her about his own ideas had appeal—preferably in a big bed after a bout of hot, satisfying sex.

She shrugged. "Times change."

"I'll give it some thought." He swallowed the rest of his coffee, pissed off because he'd worry about her now. More pissed off because she'd reminded him of dreams he'd buried along with his brother. Her cup was long since empty. Still, she sat opposite. *What the hell was keeping her at the table?*

She started fiddling with the spoon. "I hear you're using some new-fangled 'inhumane' farming methods."

"Didn't know you listened to local gossip." Ryan was indifferent to the gossip but intrigued by her change of direction. "Not so new-fangled. I've heard the trash talk."

"Robots milking cows does sound cold-blooded." She was curious as hell and trying to be casual.

"Ever seen it done?" He threw out the lure. Like throwing Satan a bone.

"I've done some research." She was watching him intently.

"And haven't ruled it out?"

"The start-up costs are high, and an increasing number of people are in favour. Done right, it lets cows choose their time of day for milking and recognises individual animals. Overall, it increases yields and reduces labour costs." More conversation than she'd offered him in two years.

"I do it right." He was impressed by her concise summary, although he'd discovered since he'd been home, she was one of the most progressive farmers in the district.

"You aren't tied to being present for set milking times." *Was that a whisper of envy in her voice?*

He nodded. "That's one of the benefits. If you're a

family farm and relying on your own labour, reducing it sounds like a good idea."

"Are you keeping data on how it works?" She relied on data, not just hunches to improve her farm, another interest they shared.

"Sounds like you're not completely opposed to the idea. Want to see it in operation?"

She sat back in her chair, but he caught the flicker of excitement in her eyes. If robotics appealed to her, he'd let her play with them to her heart's content, and he'd use them to get to know her—not rely on his memories of his brother's best friend.

"Come to my place." Ryan waited a heartbeat, watched the flicker build to a fire. "Have a look around."

"Is that a bribe?" She shut down so fast his head was spinning, going from echidna to thorny dragon in seconds, her hostility a shield to deflect all comers.

"Why would I need to bribe you?"

"To gain respectability, acceptance in the valley." She tossed the hand grenade into the conversation. Accusing him of being an outcast when he'd exiled himself. Another grudge she held against him.

"As an organic producer, you've got your own problems with acceptance." He signalled for the bill. "You do have a low opinion of me, don't you?"

"I apologise for that. I was rude." She fell silent when the waitress arrived, then hovered as Ryan paid with his credit card. "Can I—"

"Replay the last twenty minutes, Grace. From my perspective. You were ungracious about having an extra worker and offensive when I invited you to my place. Yet you expect me to jump at employing you for your *superior* farming knowledge."

Ridiculous to be attracted to a woman who thought he'd crawled out from under a rock. Although he couldn't fault her for opinions forged in the hell of Danny's death. The man he was had grown from the boy who hadn't been able to save his brother. She couldn't blame him any more for his desertion of Danny than Ryan did himself.

"I've said I'm sorry." She got to her feet, raised her hands in surrender, then dropped them.

"You have to be sorry for an apology to mean anything. If you weren't so caught up in your own prejudices, you'd see I'm already accepted in this district." He let his cynicism creep through. "It's easy if you invest in land and throw a bit of cash around."

Ryan followed her out of the café, jamming his hat on his head and donning his glasses. She crossed the road, head down, making for her van. He matched his pace to hers, heading for his vehicle—separated by a gorge deeper than the Kali Gandaki.

"Grace, Ryan."

Hearing his mother's voice, Ryan removed his hat and took the few steps to bring him to Grace's side. Turning tail, as he'd intended, would bring a rebuke. Grace was one of his mother's favourite people.

"Hello, Mrs. Wilson. How are you?" Grace moved easily into his mother's hug.

"Hi, Mum." When Grace stepped back, he leaned forward to kiss his mother's cheek. Grace huffed out a breath, and he didn't care if she was pissy. She knew nothing about his relationship with his mother.

"Fine." The woman smiled, brushing her prematurely grey hair behind one ear. She was worn beyond her years, and the sense of powerlessness he'd known as an adolescent ripped through him. He'd never been able to earn enough, do enough to help her until he left the farm. Paying the bills, phone calls and letters hadn't filled all the gaps left by long separations.

"I nearly didn't recognise you through those aviator glasses, son." An old joke, but close enough to the message Grace had delivered in the coffee shop to make him squirm. "I heard your stall was a huge success at the Show, Grace."

"It went well." A wry smile replaced Grace's stiff

politeness. "Pity it took so long to convince the dinosaurs on the committee to allow organic producers to participate. Pure prejudice."

"A little bird told me you had a lot to do with the change, Ryan. Congratulations to you both," his mother beamed. Damn! He'd hoped to keep his involvement quiet.

"Ryan!" Grace squeaked, raising her glasses to peer at him. He'd never die not knowing what she thought.

"According to my source, a grumpy old bloke from the Chamber of Commerce, who shall remain nameless"—his mother chuckled—"didn't believe Ryan at the meetings, but my boy was right. Showcasing organic brought new customers."

"I've made representation to them for years." Disgust radiated off Grace. "Ryan swans in here and they accept his suggestions overnight."

"He *is* a man." With her tongue firmly in her cheek, his mother shredded all grumpy old men.

"It's ridiculously unfair," Grace wailed.

"Which bit?" Ryan said, however, Grace should know better than to get riled by the resident troglodytes. "That women don't seem to know their place is in the kitchen anymore? That I won them over where you didn't?"

"Damn you, Ryan." Clearly, she hated learning he'd been the one to sway the committee. *Did she hate him?*

"Does it matter, when you got to strut your stuff?" He let some of his frustration show.

"How's your mother, Grace?" His mother adroitly changed the subject.

"She's starting to kick the pneumonia." Grace hauled in her irritation. "Dad's taking her away for a holiday shortly."

Ryan pushed his hands into his pockets. For all her friendliness, Grace wasn't telling his mother the truth. Protective of her family? He would be too in her position.

"That sounds lovely." The woman observed him, then her eyes slid back to Grace. "And now I understand."

"Understand what?" Grace asked.

"Bluey said he'd be starting work at Blue Sky soon."

"I'd forgotten"—Grace sent Ryan an unreadable look over her shoulder—"I mean, I'd forgotten he boards with you."

His mother blushed, and Ryan raised a quizzical eyebrow. His suspicion about her relationship with the nuggetty farmhand was confirmed. Bluey more than rented a room from his mother.

He glanced at Grace. "He knows the work."

"Tell your mother I'll call by to see her," his mother said to Grace, then tugged Ryan down to cuff his ear. "You can get your mind out of the gutter."

"That's not where it was!" He laughed.

"Mum would like a visit." Grace waited until his mother turned the corner before confronting him. "How come I was the last person to know about the debt you're repaying?"

"You were a child at the time." Whereas his brother had been an innocent. They all grew up overnight when Danny died.

"I was fifteen. You're two bloody years older than me. How did that make you an adult and me a child?" She threw a hand in the air in exasperation.

"You're the one throwing the tantrum," he growled, although she'd taken a risk letting him know she was looking for more work. Sharing the information she'd do almost anything to keep the farm was a kind of trust, whether she knew it or not.

"Fine." She slapped a hand against her thigh. "Good."

He reached out and caught her arm as she swung away, pulling her back so she bumped against his chest. *She fit in his arms*, and he took a risk. "Your father understood how desperate Mum and I were. And is decent enough not to trample our pride. He's desperate now in a different way."

Her breath was warm against his cheek.

A second's truce, making him want more. "Are you going to stuff up our deal?"

"That's offensive." Tough words but she sounded chastened.

"As offensive as you suggesting I need to be anointed by you to be accepted in this district."

"I apologised for that." She bit her lip, her voice a whisper of regret.

"I guess we'll find out if I should apologise for telling you to engage your brain before your mouth." But he'd worked out her gripe against him. Not just his refusal to talk to her after Danny's service. But his absence. "The invitation to the farm's still open."

Her head lifted, her expression bewildered, and Ryan inhaled her fresh flowery scent, cursing himself for his instant weakness. Close enough to catch the faint whiff of coffee. *Would she taste of it?* If he laid his lips against hers, would he taste coffee or the woman? Insanity, given her prickliness.

"Not every family is cookie-cutter perfect like yours, Grace." He released her when she flinched, disgusted with himself.

"When would it suit you for me to drop by?" she asked quietly.

"I'll let you know." Now he needed space. Wanting to make her problems disappear confused the hell out of him. "Don't turn me into a barbarian in the meantime."

CHAPTER FOUR

Grace recognised the brisk knock, winced at the squeak as the door swung open. Fixing it had been on her list of chores for yesterday. Before the bombshell had wiped her brain clean. A family joke—squeaking doors always dropped to the bottom of the to-do list. The crumpet popped up. She transferred it to a plate and turned around. "*What a surprise.* And without the kids."

"You took off like a bat out of hell this morning." Ella gave her a hip bump. "Don't spoil your dinner." An old rebuke.

"I skipped lunch." Grace could have ordered a sandwich at the cafe, except her stomach had been as unsteady as a newborn calf getting to its feet. "If you want a crumpet, make it yourself." Then she added another crumpet to the toaster and passed her plate to her sister.

"Charming way to treat a guest." Circling the table, Ella took the chair where Grace had planned to sit.

"Why are you my guest?" Grace was half paying attention. Her first attempt to play neighbours with Ryan, and she'd blown it. The whisper in her heart was relentless. *He left.* Lots of local kids left for work.

Her sister ignored her question, dribbling honey on her

crumpet and studying the room. "I like what you've done in here. The blue changes the whole mood."

"I wanted to capture the sky on those perfect summer mornings," Grace said. *Where had Ryan woken up in the years he'd been away?*

"An artist as well as a prospective landowner." Ella bit into her crumpet. "How far have you got with your notes?"

Grace pointed to the spreadsheet on her open computer. "See for yourself."

"Sources of direct cash: raw milk to the processor, cheese, the farm-stay cottage rented on average thirty-six weeks a year for the past two years, weekly classes in cheese making at the community centre in Casino and savings," Ella read aloud. "You haven't tallied up yet?"

"I've only just started." Grace's morale took a pounding just hearing the short list of incoming funds she'd identified. She'd probably stuffed up any chance of selling her skills to Ryan.

"The next item is interesting. Additional sources of cash: direct sale of own organic milk, upping occupancy of farm-stay cottage, organic eggs, private lessons in cheese making here. When did we buy chickens?"

"Next week." Grace pulled a face. Would Ryan follow up on his invitation to tour his dairy? *Would he even speak to her again?* "I'm brainstorming at this stage."

"Are you planning to sleep?"

Grace swallowed a mouthful of tea too fast and started coughing. She'd factored in sixteen-hour days, seven days a week for the next few years, but the prize was worth the effort. "I'm young, strong and not afraid of hard work." Maybe if she apologised to Ryan again she might be able to convince him to pay for some of her farming ideas?

"You're not talking hard, you're talking punishing." Ella held up her hand for silence, reminding Grace of their father. "Have you got a price for the farm?"

"I'm estimating around a million from a check of Stock and Station Agent sites last night." She tried to sound casual, but the sum made her knees shake.

Ella's nod confirmed she'd reached the same estimate. "The biggest issue is the deposit on the loan. Can you get that?"

"I'll give it a bloody good try." Grace had three months—thirteen weeks—and the absolute will to make it. Although she'd failed at mending fences with Ryan this morning. She'd need allies or at least no new enemies. He supported organic farming. She cringed inwardly at the resurfacing of her fifteen-year-old self shouting out her confused ramblings. She'd missed him, and some of her angry resentment lingered.

"We'll help." Her sister switched to her calm-the-clients' contralto, her "have I got a solution for you" voice. "Jake will do the legals pro bono."

Grace forgot her fight with Ryan. "I can't—"

Her sister continued as if she hadn't spoken. "That's a gift from him to you and Mum and Dad. Next time you see him, you say, 'Thank you, kind sir.'"

"Do I curtsy as well?" Grace flopped back in her chair, overwhelmed by the gift. "That's incredibly generous."

"I'll bankroll you for the next three months."

"I can't let you do that," Grace protested. "What about your new house?"

Ella reached a hand across the table to take Grace's. "You might forget the money you transferred to me month after month when I was struggling on my own, but I don't. What counted more than the money was knowing you had my back. Jake and I are more than fine. Let us do this for you."

"I don't know what to say." Grace squeezed her sister's fingers.

"That'd be a first!" Ella returned to her crumpet. "I'll cover the money you normally pay Mum and Dad for rent, milk, utilities and cover all farm costs."

"The cost of doing Dad's labouring is already covered." Grace grimaced. Whoever said confession was good for the soul didn't have Ella as a sister. "I saw Ryan today."

"Did he use some kind of hold spell?" Ella's crumpet stopped halfway to her mouth.

"Not funny." Grace's surliness yesterday had invited the comment. Her plan to magnanimously offer her skills for a price had backfired stupendously.

"And?" Ella waved a "keep going" with her crumpet, and honey dripped onto the table.

"You're as bad as Kit," Grace muttered, reaching for a sponge. "Ryan said he owed Dad three months' farmhand work. He and Dad have agreed he'll repay the debt, starting when Dad and Mum leave the farm." Another man would have taken the opportunity to forget the debt. Crazy to have this burr under the skin because Ryan was behaving honourably.

"Didn't see that coming." Ella's ignorance allowed Grace to forgive herself a little bit. Her shock was reasonable, her ungraciousness unforgivable. Ella continued. "Did he say anything else? Did you know about it?"

"First I've heard. It's the sort of thing Dad would do, and quietly." Grace admired her father's capacity to be generous after all the knocks he'd had. "Dad paid for Bluey to work for Mrs. Wilson for three months after Ryan left town." She nursed her cup, still puzzling over Ryan's choice of farmhand. Whichever way she looked at it, she couldn't find an ulterior motive. "Ryan's asked Bluey to do the three months here."

"Ryan always was observant," Ella said admiringly.

"What?" Grace demanded.

"I doubt there's another labourer in the area you'd have allowed on the property. You'll be here alone. You need to trust whoever it is. You might have sucked it up for a week or two to reassure Mum and Dad and to pretend you'd let Ryan pay off the debt. Then you'd have asked whoever it was to leave—but you love Bluey."

"You know me too well." Grace frowned. Ryan had left

her with no way to say no. Her sister had never wavered in her support for Ryan. "Why are you so keen on Ryan?"

"Because he could be an ally. Give the guy a chance. Judge him by his actions. Stop rolling your eyes. His actions now. Are you the same person you were nearly a decade ago?"

"No." Grace pushed her plate away and stood, then crossed to stare out the window. Everything she'd ever wanted was within sight: the home paddocks and—on the other side of them—the milking shed and main farmhouse. But her dream wasn't just about working the land. This stretch of hills and river and sky were part of her. Turning to face her sister, she huffed out a breath and some of her jumbled emotions. "Danny's death changed me."

Ella cocked her head to one side, concern in her calm eyes. "How?"

"It taught me you need to be independent to be strong." The grief had been visceral—wanting to shout at the sky, run until she was so exhausted she fell down, pinch herself hard so she'd feel something physical rather than the frightening emptiness and heaviness that wouldn't let her breathe. "That you can only rely on yourself."

"I'm sorry you felt so alone," Ella said gently.

"It cemented when Smithhouse swindled Dad." Grace made her second confession.

"Smithhouse changed us all," Ella admitted. "I vowed never to let justice be bought. Smithhouse would never have stolen the land, except for an unscrupulous lawyer who misused the power he had to help Smithhouse."

"Smithhouse taught me to mistrust offers that look too good to be true." *And never to share the farm with anyone.* Her sister would worry about Grace's isolation. Ella shared everything with Jake.

"It's not a weakness to need people, Grace."

"Love suits you and Jake. I'm not looking for that." *Her dreams for the farm made it impossible.* "Independence, especially financial independence, is a strength."

"You don't have to prove to us you can make it alone." Ella wanted everyone to have what she and Jake shared.

"To myself then." People leave and people take, that's what Grace had learned, and Ella's happiness, like their parents' marriage, was a rare and precious thing, but not for her. Grace returned to the table. "You've just proved I'm not alone. You and Jake and Mum and Dad are all on my side."

"What have you got against Ryan?"

Grace searched for words to explain her complicated reaction to Ryan. "He left." She held up her hands and dropped them. Saying "he abandoned me" sounded ridiculously melodramatic. "He wouldn't talk to me."

"And we're a family of talkers." Ella sipped her tea. "That's the way we deal with disasters. We talk. Not talking doesn't mean he doesn't care."

"Mrs. Wilson never talks about him." Although she'd been pretty quick to credit him for getting organics included in the Northern Rivers Show today.

"I've often wondered why. Mum has too. She's also wondered where Mrs. Wilson got the money to pay a deposit on her house in town, when the farm's still in her name."

Grace took another bite of crumpet and chewed. "You think Ryan's bankrolling her?"

"Dad paid for Bluey's first three months. Mrs. Wilson couldn't have paid for Bluey all these years without help. Then she talked about wanting to retire. And hey presto! Ryan landed back in town, took over the workload at the farm, and she set up in town."

Grace didn't want to give him the benefit of the doubt and didn't like herself very much for her lack of generosity. "The damn man convinced the show committee to include organics." She couldn't find an ulterior motive for his support with the committee either, and she wasn't the only local to benefit. "One year he's on the committee. I've spent ages trying to convince them."

"Fancy doing you such a bad turn!" Ella marvelled. "I've just realised something else. Mrs. Wilson's a proud woman. She must have been desperate to accept Dad's help back then and to send Ryan away. I bet going was Ryan's only option to earn enough money to pay the mortgage." Ella's conclusion landed like a kick from a cow, hard and fast.

Ryan *was* proud, and he'd admitted to desperation, not a confession she'd share with anyone. Grace had been so caught up in her grief about Danny and her need to talk to Ryan about Danny, she'd only seen that he'd abandoned her. *Ryan had been the one truly alone.*

"This morning Dad said Mum delayed because of him. They delayed because of me," Grace confessed. Engineering their quick departure might go part way to addressing that imbalance.

"They delayed while they worked out what to do," Ella said bluntly. "Dad acted pretty fast today calling Ryan. He'd go in a heartbeat if he believed you were on friendly terms with Ryan."

"You think?" Grace's reasons for resenting Ryan were starting to look petulant.

"Dad's always liked him, and he respects what he's doing now." Her sister should have finished law. She built her case with evidentiary precision. "All you have to do is let Dad know you'll call Ryan if there's a problem. I thought you got on okay together when we were kids?"

"We did," Grace drew out the words. Her relationship with Ryan had been unusual. Allies probably summed it up best, linked by an unspoken allegiance to Danny. As a kid she hadn't bothered analysing her feelings for Ryan. Now she could admit liking and respect had been mixed with a bit of hero worship. Heroes weren't supposed to abandon you.

"Dig for that feeling," Ella hesitated. "In that hideous custody case when I was terrified we'd lose Tessa, my lawyer asked me three questions as part of the compulsory mediation before moving to court. What was my ideal outcome? What would I settle for? What could I live with to prevent the matter going to court?"

"My ideal outcome is working beside Dad for at least another decade." *Grace wasn't ready to lose him.* "And this won't go to court."

"Your question is different." Her sister was relentless. "What compromises are you prepared to make to keep the farm?"

"Me? Compromise? Wash your mouth out with soap." Her feelings for Ryan were more complicated than she'd admitted to her sister. His rejection of her after Danny's death was just the start. His aloofness, his easy possession of land and influence when she was dismissed as a flaky greenie irritated her. The unwanted tug of attraction irritated her more. Her reaction to the irritation was to avoid him or needle him. "Have you forgiven Drew for trying to take Tessa?"

"The situations aren't the same." When Grace remained silent, Ella sighed. "Moved on is a better description. He's Tessa's biological father, Jake's cousin, part of our lives. He ditched Chrissy knowing she was pregnant and reappeared when he thought he could profit from Tessa's existence. He didn't, doesn't, really love Tessa. I don't think he's capable of love. He's never apologised. That's the hard part. But if you're constantly looking for payback, you miss the moment." Ella held Grace's gaze. "Don't miss the moment because Ryan didn't do what you expected when Danny died."

"I'm working on it." Grace made a vow to work harder. "I'll tell Dad I had a coffee with Ryan today. Thanked him for Bluey."

"Did you?"

"Did I what?" Grace knew where her sister was heading. "Thank him for Bluey?"

"Not graciously enough," she confessed. Like Ella, their father had always chided Grace for her animosity to Ryan. Even before Ella had told Grace about his probable contact with his mother, she'd seen him on his land. Seen the changes he was making, how he'd merged the Wilson and Donovan properties. How the improvements Mr. Donovan had made in his last few years on his farm had laid the groundwork for Ryan's current activities. "You know which buttons to press."

"Make nice." Ella grinned. "I've seen you do it."

"I love you too."

"He was always kind, and you're usually fair. He's giving you Bluey."

Fair! Justice and fair play were biggies in her family, even before the Smithhouse affair. Her parents' integrity was reason to hold her head high. Ella's attack stung and brought a new insight. Grace had hung on to her anger at Ryan's departure as a way of coping with Danny's death. She'd thought she'd shatter without Ryan's support. Anger had provided a good substitute.

"They need to get away soon." Her sister changed direction, and Grace struggled to catch up.

"I agree." Her brain was turning slower than a hand-held butter churn. *She'd miss Ryan again if he locked her out, and she'd spent less than an hour with him.*

"Dad might stay a few more weeks if Mum is safe somewhere," Ella mused.

"He wants to be with her." Despite her reluctance to accept Ryan's offer, Grace could see its possibilities. "I have an idea."

"You're always having ideas." Ella grinned. "What's this one?"

"The Blue Mountains. Jake's aunt and uncle's place?" Grace had spent a blissful few days there last year. Her only holiday in close to a decade.

"We had the same idea." Ella snapped her fingers. "Jake's going to talk to them today."

"Dad said they planned to stay a few more weeks. They won't like us organising their diary." Grace hadn't thought of a way to sugarcoat the suggestion.

"Are we? Dad lined up Ryan. He's ready to go. It's Mum who needs a nudge. Jake and I discussed this. We'll ask his aunt to issue the invitation. And"—Ella smiled smugly—"we'll add a sweetener. Me and the kids. I'll go up for a few weeks with Tessa and Kit. The grandmas can bill and coo over them to their hearts' content."

"You don't want to go to the mountains for two weeks. Jake won't be able to stay with you." Grace added up the sacrifices her sister was making for her.

"Sadly, no. He took leave for Kit's birth. But it's the best I can think of to help—the best *we* can think of to help," Ella corrected herself. "Don't go all early Christian martyr on us. It's our turn to share the load, Grace." She carried her plate to the sink. "I'd best get back to my babies." She turned around when she reached the door. "I'd trust him with Tessa or Kit."

Entrusting Ryan with her children made him family for Ella. Grace wished her feelings were so simple. Her pulse had skittered when they'd crouched beside each other at the field day. Her gaze had followed his hand as he'd caressed Satan. Long, lean fingers—strong, she had no doubt of that, but with the ability to gentle—an animal, a child, a lover. She'd itched to tip those dark glasses down his nose, to see his eyes, to try and take her measure of the man. His mouth had curved in a half smile when he'd spoken to Ella. Again, when he'd introduced Tessa to his dog. He hadn't smiled at Grace.

Today she'd trotted out her prejudices over a coffee he'd paid for, and every one of them was flawed. She'd had the chance to study his eyes today, tawny brown with hints of green. His expression had given little away. Resenting him was easier than respecting him. Despising him was easier than having her pulse skitter and little balls of lust explode in her belly.

Grace slung the last bag into the boot of the hatchback

her parents used for off-farm travel. All done.

This is the way the world ends
Not with a bang but a whimper.

She couldn't remember the rest of the poem from high school, but those words by T. S. Eliot had stayed with her. She'd never imagined they'd apply to her life. She searched the mid-morning spring sky. Where was the storm and tempest to mark her parents' leave taking? A little meteorological melodrama seemed called for, for the end of an era. They'd visit, but a visit wasn't the same as sharing a life.

Her mother had had another episode overnight, and the urgent family confab in the early hours of the morning had voted for an immediate departure. Grace couldn't claim desertion when she was urging them to go. A breath hitched in her throat. She tipped her head back to stop the tears from falling.

Her father leaned against her and followed her gaze. "A mackerel sky."

"Change is coming." She gave him a wry smile. She'd giggled as a little girl when he'd first told her about mackerel skies. "A fish sky, that's silly, Dad." Yet she looked for those rare days, and the symbolism was another kind of magic.

"It's happened so quickly." He slipped an arm around her shoulders, drawing her to him. "I'm not sure I'm ready."

"Neither am I. I'll miss you."

"I'm at the end of the phone."

"Just as well, because I'll be ringing daily." She worked to keep the mood light for both of them. "Where did you hide that thingamajig?"

"Bluey will know the answer, and unlike most of the planet, he'll know what you're talking about." Her father was reassured by Ryan's choice of Bluey. "I'd hoped to go with you to the bank."

She'd hoped he'd be with her too. "I'll be fine." Five days closer to her deadline, but who was counting? Her gut went into freefall every time she let her mind stray to potential pitfalls.

"Make sure you push for ten percent deposit," he repeated his favourite mantra.

"Got that bulletin, Dad." Rural properties traditionally required higher deposits than houses in town. She was gambling on the family name to keep it lower than a newcomer to the area.

"You need a margin for error." He restated the warning learned from hard experience. "Farms always have unforeseen expenses—a sick animal, wild weather, broken machinery. It's risky not to leave yourself with a buffer."

"You think I should buy more chickens?" She elbowed him in the ribs. The chickens were waiting to be picked up. She'd reworked her figures, had approached the tourist office about greater promotion of the farm stay and had upped her promotional activities. The café had placed a paying order—small, but an order—and she hadn't finished her door-knocking. The chickens were another link in her very fragile buffer.

"You hated raising chickens as a child," he muttered.

"But these are organic chickens," she teased.

"Like that makes a blind bit of difference!" He turned as her mother came out of the house, hurrying back to take her arm.

"I'm glad Ryan's lending you Bluey." Her mother made her way slowly up the path. "He could have sent someone else. He remembered you love Bluey."

"He said that?" She stared at her mother.

"He had a few hands available." Her father settled her mother in the car. "I was surprised he suggested Bluey, didn't think he'd give him up. He said Bluey was family to you."

"I'm not some helpless female," she protested. Ella had tagged Ryan as observant *and* kind. Recognising Grace loved Bluey showed a perception she would have denied before the last few days.

"Hell no! You're an Amazon trained from birth to fight

dragons and defeat small nation-states." Her father laughed at her.

"I am *not* overreacting." For her parents' peace of mind, she needed to negotiate a truce with Ryan.

"Just asserting your independence," her father deadpanned.

Her independence was all she had. She was riding a pretty rocky see-saw between hope and fear. When she walked the gentle hills of the farm or milked the cows or zoned out in her cheese-making room, she couldn't imagine losing Blue Sky. Sometimes in the early hours of the morning, the memory of Smithhouse's swindle invaded her dreams, and she'd wake to the taste of failure.

"Call me when you get to the mountains." She bent to kiss her mother.

"We may be feeling far too independent to do that." Her father kissed both Grace's cheeks. "If we forget, you call us."

She stood, long after they'd driven away, before turning back to face the empty farmhouse. Taking responsibility for the farm wasn't an issue. She'd done it before.

She'd been alone before. She was used to working alone. Liked it.

Today loneliness crept like a dreary mist up from the river to descend on the house. Turning her back on it, she crossed to lean on the fence of the yard housing the poddies, as she and her father did every morning after milking. Today he wasn't at her shoulder. The sensation of being hollowed out was the surprise. She shivered. Then, impatient with herself and unable to settle, she drove into town to collect the chickens.

"You want some help, Grace?"

She turned with a smile. "That would be good, Bluey."

"Branching out?"

"Testing an idea. Organic eggs, although it'll be months before these chicks earn their keep," she said. They lifted the boxes of chicks into the van. "We've only got one more inspection to pass for organic farm status."

"Chickens aren't my thing." He sounded apologetic, but she recognised a declaration on the division of labour when she heard it. "Got another clue you can help me with," he said.

"Can't see you wearing any sunglasses."

He slipped a hand into his pocket and pulled out a pair, pushing them onto his nose with a grunt. "Can't get the hang of them."

She leaned across and planted a smacking kiss on one cheek. "For that I'd do anything. I love you, Bluey."

His gaze slid sideways, his face crumpling into a smile. "I love you too, Grace girl."

She nudged him. "I've heard you'll be working at Blue Sky for the next three months."

"Your dad called Ryan this morning. Sorry about Elaine. I'll be there tomorrow." He accepted his new role with a wave of the hand. "I've got another anagram for you. Two words, nine and four letters. I've worked out enough to know it's got something to do with cheese again."

"My speciality." She collapsed the trolley and loaded it into the van. Despite their disagreement, Ryan hadn't delayed even a day before sending her Bluey. No game playing, no delaying to make her have to remind him.

"I like cheese. I know cheddar, and now I know Edam is a name, but I'm a plain man, and this has got me stumped."

"Did you try cruising the dairy section at the supermarket?"

"Don't be daft, girl. 'Rooftop timber became two cheeses.' 'Rooftop' means top of roof, that's the first letter of roof, right?"

"Right."

"So, I've got R plus 'timber became.' That gives me the thirteen letters."

"Any guesses?" she asked.

"If I had any halfway decent guesses, I wouldn't be

standing here wearing a damned pair of sunglasses and hoisting chickens." He lifted his hat and slapped it against his thigh.

"Mrs. Wilson has some of my cheeses," Grace said slyly.

"What's that got to do with anything?" He put Grace firmly in her place.

"Camembert and brie."

"You're having me on." He snorted.

"Nope. French words. I produce those soft cheeses. Give me your phone, and I'll write them on your notes page."

"Who says my phone has notes?" He tucked his glasses back in his pocket.

"You only pretend to live in the last century, Bluey. Your brain's like a steel trap." She tapped out the words in the phone he passed. "Thanks for the help. And for swapping Wilson's for Blue Sky."

"I expect you to help me with clues." He hid a smile.

"A small price to pay." She had a new puzzle as she drove back to the farm.

Ryan had forced a chink in her defensive wall. His repayment of his debt to her father guaranteed she'd bank a ten percent deposit, although she doubted her bank balance featured high on his list of motives. Dismissing his choice of Bluey as a random act of kindness was a cop-out. The itch between her shoulder blades returned with a vengeance. No insensitive monster—just a kid who'd been too overwhelmed at seventeen to do more than retreat to lick his wounds. The child in her, who'd felt abandoned after Danny's death, had refused to forgive him for not being able to undo what was done.

CHAPTER FIVE

A month!

Ryan had let her stew for four weeks before inviting her to see his robotics. Not that Grace had been sitting on her backside in that time. Yard work, cheesemaking and deliveries each day, endless paperwork in the evenings, while her sleep had been fractured by a restless conscience insisting her half-hearted apology to Ryan in the coffee shop hadn't been good enough. He'd touched a nerve that day. Like an aching tooth, it wouldn't let her rest. Her family wasn't perfect, because she wasn't perfect. Her temper could be as foul as the smell of her chickens' poo.

She pulled into the side of the road. Crossing her arms on the steering wheel, she leaned forward to rest her head. She'd been up eleven hours and had work for the next eleven. She hadn't ticked off half her list any day this week. Bluey had taken to appearing wherever she was at regular intervals and standing over her while she ate. A ham sandwich, an apple, a chunk of cheese. Despite the butterflies rising en masse in her stomach, Ryan's invitation was a welcome break in her grinding routine.

Raising her head, she scanned the horizon. Her valley. Ryan's as well. She pulled back onto the road, slowing as she drove past the old Donovan place—now part of Ryan's holdings. It had always been known as the Donovan place, and people stuck with the known. Like the Wilson place. The farms had names. In the past, few locals had used them, instead talking about the Wilson place, the Donovan place. Theirs had always been Blue Sky, as if it held a magic for others, not just her. She'd hugged the enchantment to her chest growing up, a secret pride. Blue Sky and so often the skies were a pure bright blue to dazzle the eyes and make the world seem brighter, lighter somehow. No clouds today—not in the sky—but she was grappling with some weighty issues. Not all of them called Ryan Wilson.

Her plan was to offer regret, demonstrate respect and set the growing lust to one side to negotiate a friendly truce.

Ryan lounged against the veranda post when she pulled into his yard, Satan at his side. Some nights the insults she'd thrown at him were all that filled her head—her small-minded bitchiness for Ryan's perceived sins of the past. Man and dog came down the steps to meet her. Ryan's body was long and lean, and his face was shaded by the broad brim of his hat. His eyes were hidden, and she had the urge to whip his glasses off. Again. The hitch in her breathing was more than nervousness about the apology she owed him and had been practising for most of the journey here. Pushing open the door of the Ute, she stepped down.

"You came," he said.

"Thank you for the invitation." She put her hat on. Her glasses were as effective a shield as his own. "I need to clarify something from our last meeting."

"What's that?"

"I think Mum and Dad are pretty perfect. Ella's always fair, even when she suffers because of it." She tipped her glasses down her nose, her gaze steady. "I tend to speak before I think sometimes."

"Just sometimes?" He sounded as though he was enjoying himself.

She huffed out a breath and offered her worst dummy-spit for his judgement. "I didn't speak to Chrissy for more than a year. I only started again when she was diagnosed with cancer. Two years later, she died. I'm ashamed of that temper tantrum."

"What brought it on?" His immediate acceptance she'd had a reason settled the jingle-jangle in her head.

"Chrissy ran away to Sydney with Ella's boyfriend. Neither of them said a word." Grace's hands fisted. "Just disappeared, leaving Ella to deal with the gossip and snide remarks." Chrissy's disloyalty to Ella had enraged Grace. With time, the memory of her anger had muted, flaring occasionally like an old injury from a disgruntled cow who'd stepped on her foot.

"Mum's not big on sharing spiteful gossip," he said. His dislike of narrow-minded, malicious gossip probably began when Danny started high school. "I didn't know."

"It was years ago. After Mum's tractor accident. Ella was working her butt off to care for Mum and help run the farm. Chrissy was looking for a ticket out of town. I was furious." Grace took another deep breath and let it out with a whoosh. "Anyway." This confession was part apology, part thank you and all peace offering. "I like your mother. I visited a lot after you left. She wanted to talk about Danny. More, to hear me talk about Danny. The stories she didn't know." Grace wanted to explain herself to Ryan, and explaining herself to a man was new for her. "I need to talk, Ryan. It's how I process the big stuff."

"I don't talk about Danny or my family much," he said flatly.

"You loved him." She pushed because his answer mattered to her. In her darkest moments she'd questioned whether his silence at the funeral was because he'd been ashamed of Danny.

"Do you have to ask?"

Scanning Ryan's face, she noted the sculpted cheekbones, the determined chin and his strong nose. Danny's had been broken in a fall they'd had as kids.

Otherwise they might have been twins. They'd been best friends as well. Like her and Ella.

"No. No, I don't. Any more than I had to ask if he loved you." Their love for Danny had united Ryan and Grace as teenagers, although they'd never acknowledged their shared role as sentries. She touched his upper arm and inhaled his calm—a hard man, of necessity. "I've come to ask for a truce."

"I can do that." He made it easier than she deserved.

"Let's go see your robotic milking setup." She pushed her glasses back into position.

"It's this way." He gestured. "How's Bluey working out?"

Paying a debt to her father was none of her business. Lending her Bluey made it personal. The butterflies rose again, and she pressed a hand to her stomach. "He knows me, knows my rhythm, is there before I need to ask. You worked that out."

"You told him to skip the morning milking." Ryan must have been asking questions about her. Bluey wasn't the garrulous sort. "Mum told me."

"Do you object to them being a couple?"

"More reason to demonise me, Grace. I'm so narrow-minded I don't want my mother to have a lover."

"Wow!" She halted. "That picture's stuck in my head now."

"You brought it up," he chided her.

She scrunched up her face. "I'm not looking for another reason to have to apologise to you."

"I like it when you're chastened."

"Then you'll like what I have to say next." Grace sent him a sideways look as they continued across the paddock. The urge to snatch his glasses and fling them into the tall grass hugging the fence line made her fingers tingle. "Dad called this morning. He's been chatting with Mr. Donovan."

"I remember them being close." Ryan turned his head, and she wanted more than ever to see his eyes.

Serious eyes, maybe more chestnut than tawny. At the café they'd flashed when she'd accused him of needing her seal of approval. She'd guessed they were as hard as petrified wood when he'd accused her of a temper tantrum. "Aren't you curious about why I'm bringing it up?" she asked.

He ran his hand over his dog's head, a habitual gesture. "I'm curious about you." His husky growl momentarily silenced her, a quicksilver slide under her guard.

Her heart dropped to her toes. "You bought him out three years before you took over. You let him choose his own departure date."

"It suited me." His strides ate up the distance.

"It made a huge difference to him." She had to hurry to keep up. Her father said Donovan couldn't stop singing Ryan's praises.

"From a callous bastard to a Good Samaritan." He halted abruptly. "That's quite a leap, Grace." His tone scalded.

"I'm not granting you all the virtues." She was trying to navigate around ten years of silence. "Giving Donovan control was decent and shows you understood how hard it was for him to leave." Ryan's treatment of an old man demanded Grace's respect and provided a blueprint for how he might treat others.

He's already lent you Bluey.

Distrusting strangers was an early lesson for Grace— cause and effect had stamped their mark on the faces of people she loved. Her father still doubted himself because of Smithhouse's swindle. Scars remained from when Tessa's biological father had tried to steal custody of her. Not because he loved her. To punish Jake and Ella for falling in love. She knew it was wrong to watch people, always expecting to be tricked or lied to, but she couldn't help herself. Ryan's actions had given her pause; first Donovan, now he'd repaid a debt to her father. Bluey said little, although his occasional laconic asides added weight to the view Ryan paid attention to people.

He shrugged. "He was decent to me."

"I forgot." She trawled through her memory. Ryan had started doing odd jobs when he was twelve. She'd been pretty sure even then his pay went back into the farm. "You worked for him sometimes, didn't you?"

"His girls were much older than us. It was already clear they didn't want to take over the farm."

"He had secret hopes of grandchildren for a while, especially his oldest grandson." She'd trade information for a chance to prolong her first almost friendly conversation with Ryan.

"He didn't say. What happened?"

"The digital revolution held more appeal." She whistled as they entered the shed. "City folk tend to forget we've got our own digital revolution. Wow!"

"Take all the time you want. I'll be in the office"——he pointed—"over there."

"I just might." Grace waited for him to disappear before she did a happy dance. For a blissful hour, she poked her head into every corner, examined every piece of equipment, did a quick survey of the area immediately outside the shed and observed healthy cows lazily chewing cud. Ryan called out to her. She pushed her hands into her pockets as they headed toward the house.

"I visited a pilot farm at Camden, on the outskirts of Sydney a few years ago." She couldn't contain the questions bubbling inside her. "How'd you get interested?"

"An old bloke I worked for in New Zealand experimented a bit. A shortage of decent hired help, he said"—Ryan paused—"before me."

"No family?"

"He sent his kids away to school and uni. They lost interest in the farm. Like too many farmers these days, he'd told them it was tough for so long, they weren't prepared to try it." He slowed his pace, matching his strides to hers. Walking together was companionable.

"It's a common enough pattern, plus family farms don't

often support more than one child taking over." That's why Grace's parents had worked so hard on a succession plan.

He stopped, his hands in the air. "Don't tell me! EJ was busting a gut to be a farmer."

"About as much as Chrissy was. Mum and Dad had a succession plan—me. And an estate plan." Her parents had broken a country taboo and talked about land and distribution of inheritance with their children.

"Smart man, your dad."

"Reality has slapped our plans around a bit." She liked hearing Ryan praise her father.

"When my bloke died, his kids got the dividend. He was open-minded, flexible and had the curiosity of a child. I loved working for him." He gave her another piece of himself.

"Why did you leave?" She hadn't known he'd been in New Zealand. *Had he ever considered not coming back?* He hesitated, and she had her answer. There'd been a time when he planned never to return. If Danny's death had driven him so far away, what had induced him to come back?

"He encouraged me to move to bigger spreads, get a range of experience, especially in Australia. Because I'd come from here." He was answering her questions, actually talking to her, and Grace hungered for more. "I can offer you tea and cheese biscuits. Good cheese I've been told," he added cheekily. *He bought her cheese.*

"You'd get it cheaper if you bought it directly from me." Her stomach did a double flip. Another reason for her humble pie today. "The last two calls I've had for cheese said you referred them."

"Just being neighbourly."

A harmless word when he wasn't. Not to her. Accepting help required a level of trust. Hard for her when suspicion about backstabbing deals had become her starting point—a necessary protection. Her physical response to Ryan didn't fall under the heading of harmless. A steady hum of excitement when she got close. *Don't go there!* "Who made the biscuits?"

"Perhaps I did."

"I'm not that gullible." She smiled, pushing her hat back.

"So, are you prepared to risk tea and biscuits with the devil?" He halted at the veranda steps.

She pointed at the dog. "House-trained, is he?"

"As much as I am."

"Then I'll give you both a chance."

Pushing the unlocked screen door open, he waited for her to precede him. A few steps took her from the unseasonal heat haze of the day to the welcoming cool dimness of the dark wainscoted hallway. She removed her hat, letting her eyes adjust, and he bumped into her. A second. Long enough to know his body was work-hard, to feel the solid outline of him against her back. A pulse in her temple jumped. She inhaled his distinct woodsy scent and had to fight the urge to lean back into him for more. Her breath stalled in her throat.

"Straight down the hall, Grace," he growled.

She knew her way blindfolded. And *befuddled*! The layout was as familiar as her parents' home. Built around the same time but without the additions and renovations her parents had made. His kitchen was new. He must have gutted the original to make way for this spacious, open-plan space. Only the fuel stove stayed in position, although the ancient relic she remembered from her last visit to the property had been replaced by a new top-of-the-line Aga.

"I like what you've done here," Grace said. The back wall had been knocked out, replaced with insulated floor-to-ceiling glass, letting in light and a gorgeous view of the distant hills. Every piece of furniture had been replaced, from the sideboard holding crockery and glassware to the wooden table dominating the centre of the room. Second-hand furniture, so he hadn't opted for modern when his mother moved out, just different.

"Thanks." He passed her to move the kettle onto the hotplate. The dog curled up on a mat beside the fireplace with the ease of a regular routine.

"It was dark and depressing the last time I was here." She'd avoided the place since Ryan had taken up residence.

"It was always dark and depressing," he replied.

"Only after Danny died and you left. Before that it was filled with laughter. His laughter, your mother's, even yours." She remembered Ryan's smile from their childhood. Rare, slow in coming, a gleam appearing in his eyes while his face remained sombre, then his face would crack as if a belly laugh had burst inside. She'd liked seeing it as a kid, had taken it for granted as an adolescent. "I don't think I've seen you smile since you got back."

He tipped his glasses down his nose, crossed his arms and leaned back against the stove.

"Ella and the babies coaxed a half smile out of you. That mutt of yours manages more, but me, I haven't seen a real smile yet."

"Do you want me to smile at you?" He dropped his glasses on the table.

Her toes curled in her boots. The tremble in her loins when he'd offered only a fraction of it to her sister and child warned her his rare smile would have an entirely different effect on her now. She slid into one of the chairs drawn up to the table. "I'll accept a cup of tea."

Efficient and practised in the kitchen, he was a man used to looking after himself. As well as working regularly at Donovan's, he'd picked up a contract doing well-paying grunt work at a mine, where he'd been the day Danny died. Expected to be a breadwinner from childhood, Ryan had shouldered those burdens without complaint. Loaded with work and responsibilities, yet free of the cares troubling him now. Danny's death had shaped the present for both Grace and Ryan. Unless they talked about it, they'd never be friends. *Where had that thought come from?*

He warmed the pot, spooned in tea leaves from a vintage canister and took mugs from the cupboard then set them on the table. "Milk, sugar?"

"Milk, please." She raised an eyebrow when he placed a milk bottle on the table. "No milk jug?"

"It can be arranged." His voice would curl bark.

"No need." She'd liked the hesitation, the sense she'd thrown him off-balance, when she was the one off-balance. In a home she knew well but didn't know at all. Winning his smile might settle her.

"Help yourself." He placed the teapot and a plate of biscuits on the table. The dog's head lifted, and his tail thumped. Ryan threw him a biscuit. Took one himself.

"So, what do you think?"

She stirred milk into her tea. "Does it matter what I think?"

"You've got a good head for business."

Her gaze lifted to his, first her cheese, now her business sense. Another compliment, but she was unsure where he was heading.

"Yours was the best booth at the field day, the most eye-catching. And you were the brains behind the picnic hampers walking off a neighbouring stall all day." He added sugar to his cup.

"Who told you that?" She sipped her tea, studying him over the rim of her mug. Another compliment. His compliments were an intoxicating surprise.

"They did. They stock fruit and pickles. You suggested they team them up with bread, a wedge of your cheese and a good bottle of local wine." He confessed to cross-examining her friends.

"I was pleased with their success. I didn't know you convinced the field day committee to include me this year."

"Pissed you off though." His accurate reading of her initial reaction when he'd been generous with his compliments threw her back into the role of bad-tempered shrew.

"They should have included me and the other organic producers on sheer merit," she repeated an old grievance, although Ryan had given his support for the field day long before her parents made the decision to sell, and she wasn't the only beneficiary.

He held up his hands in the universal gesture of surrender. "I agree. For the record, the mayor, the woman from the tourist office and a few others came in behind me. They argued we'd attract a bigger crowd, make more money for the town and local guesthouses and cafés."

Grace had expected him to make her feel beholden to him. She'd read him wrong on this too. She moistened dry lips. "Thank you for your support."

"Sticks in your craw to have to thank me." He was teasing her—a common occurrence in the past—and enjoying watching her squirm.

"I am *not* a bad-tempered shrew." She scowled at him. "I'm trying to be reasonable here, Ryan."

"If you were being reasonable, you'd use that clever business brain to look at what I'm doing." He drummed his fingers on the table.

"What exactly are you doing?" Her curiosity trumped her annoyance.

"Getting the properties ready to sell."

She'd heard that rumour and hadn't believed it. Couldn't believe even now he'd choose cash over his heritage—*willingly leave the valley when he could afford to stay*. "You want someone else to benefit from your sweat and tears."

"Staying isn't in my plans." He drained his cup and rose to his feet.

Confusion had her staring up at him. "Then why the offers for Blue Sky?" Would he tell her the truth? Grace met his gaze. A different tension entered the room. A new negotiation. She'd never accept anything less than a meeting of equals in any area of her life. But her mouth dried—he incited a throb in her blood, a sense of anticipation, a sense he might make love to her with the same intensity he brought to his work, and she'd thank him for his time.

"Scale is everything in farming. When your father refused—"

73

"You must have expected he would?" she said. His misreading of her father seemed out of character.

He continued. "I went for robotics to achieve the same productivity gains."

"Productivity gains!" She exploded. His cool calculation of costs and benefits seesawed her back to irritability.

"A seductive promise in modern farming." His voice made a different promise, tipping the seesaw to something more primitive, and Grace shivered. "Then you've got what you want."

"Not quite."

His gaze lingered on her lips.

Her heart stuttered. *He was as interested in her as she was in him.* A heady sensation.

"I'd like some of your river frontage."

She gasped. "In your dreams." Images of his rare, crooked grin and work-hardened body had invaded her dreams. She stared at her empty cup.

"How's it going with the bank?" He was multitasking—simultaneously seducing her and talking business.

"Why is that relevant?" Waiting for the bank's decision on her loan was akin to water torture—the slow drip of each passing day without a decision like a steady drip of water on her forehead. The initial meeting had been tense. At least on her side of the table. Grace had never had to sit in front of someone detailing her finances, her expenditures, her forecast earnings, hoping they'd find her case convincing.

"I'm guessing your biggest worry is the deposit." He was relentless. "What percentage are they pushing for?"

"What percentage did they want for Donovan's?" she countered.

"Forty percent." Ryan didn't bat an eye at the mouth-watering amount.

She sucked in a breath. She didn't have a hope in hell of pulling that kind of money together.

"I'd been out of the district for five years, no credit history, and Mum's place was—to put it politely—

unimproved. I also chose to use the local bank to build a relationship."

"The local bank is my only option. The broker is supportive. He said he'd push my arguments with the higher-ups." She bit her bottom lip. Her father had the credit history. She'd tried to do all her transactions for the cheese business with cash. Waiting until she had money before she took each step to expand. "I'm negotiating ten to fifteen."

"If it doesn't work out, call me," he said casually, adding nothing more while waiting for her to precede him onto the veranda. He stayed close to her heels, catching her arm before she stepped off, trapping her between him and the post.

Her body went on alert. "You're crowding me, Ryan."

"You're tempting me. But you know that. Fancy a roll in the hay?" he deadpanned.

She choked on a reluctant laugh. "Only city slickers have fantasies about rolling in the hay." Memories of her own adolescent experience tumbled back to ambush her. Innocent and joyful. The wicked glint in Ryan's eyes promised one of the two. "Country people—like you and me—know how uncomfortable it is."

"Necessity can be a killer." His voice was a purr, his breath warm and his body close enough for her to be enticed by his spicy aftershave.

"True confessions?" She placed a hand on his chest, creating breathing space. The temptation was shocking. "You don't like me."

"I like your honesty." He traced a finger down the side of her face, the rough pad surprisingly gentle.

The directness of his play for her appealed. The disinterested older brother of a friend had changed in the time he'd been away. He'd developed an elusive charm the boys who'd stayed behind didn't have. More, he'd developed a fascinating contrariness, making her want to understand the contradictions between the man who revealed admirable qualities to relative strangers, and the man who kept a cool distance from most people. Danny's death explained part of the puzzle.

"The prickliness is a bit of a trial, but I can cope. And we're both old enough to know there's a buzz between us."

His touch had ignited a fire. Heat pooled low in her belly. "A buzz!" Grace fanned a hand in front of her face. She wasn't ready for this. She especially wasn't ready for it with a man with such different goals and dreams. "To return to your very romantic offer. Not right now. But I'll bear it in mind. Now, I must go."

"The offer's separate to any business we might do." He stepped back, instantly giving her space.

The late afternoon sun crept under the veranda. Ludicrous to be mesmerised by eyes she knew as well as her own. Except lush lashes shadowed the brown depths, making the fanciful part of her imagine his eyes were the colour of liquid chocolate. But they hid secrets. Secrets she was intrigued enough to dig for.

"I took it that way." She smiled. The man was full of surprises today, and each one had slipped past her guard. "Thanks for making it explicit."

She'd never been so attracted and so cautious with a man before. Mating, birth and death were as natural as breathing to her. She'd had her fair share of tumbles in the hay, friendships that went a step further, but nothing to distract her from her goal of becoming the best cheese maker in the area, the state. Hey—international competitions were her next step. Ryan had slipped under her skin in a different way. She wanted to be the one who brought a smile to his face. Her way of equaling the odds because he made her feel as giddy as a schoolgirl.

Aware of him at her shoulder, Grace slid her glasses on, imagined him doing the same as they crossed to her vehicle. "Were you serious about the bank?"

If he was surprised, he didn't show it. His fingers stilled on the head of the dog who rarely left his side. "I have some ideas on alternate financing options."

Another surprise. He'd been buying and selling property for years—successfully. She could afford to listen to his ideas, if it came to it. Listening didn't commit her to anything, and her pitch to the broker had been strong.

When she glanced in the rearview mirror, he hadn't moved—a man and his dog. The flutter in her tummy when she was near him was a new sensation. Disconcerting to be physically attracted when she was unsure of the man. Today he'd revealed more of himself. His contribution to their truce. He'd had next to no choices when Danny died, and her rush to judgement then had been unfair.

She was more confident about what he was doing as a farmer. He'd invested in more than robotic milking equipment. There were improvements to pasture and plans for more collaboration with universities and others of like mind in other countries. They were pragmatic decisions. Another contradiction. He worked the land, nourished and nurtured it, but refused to be attached. He'd repair and improve this land and then move on. Leaving her land would be like tearing her heart in two.

CHAPTER SIX

For two weeks Grace mulled over her visit to Ryan's. He'd made offers—financial advice and a quick tumble. Both were tempting. Examining her slow-growing bank balance gave the idea of adding his financial genius to her arsenal appeal. Simple human warmth had a different appeal. She missed her father's hugs, the brush of her mother's hand across her hair when Grace was bent over a task. Ryan could make Grace laugh, and she could talk to him about farming and know he'd take her seriously. Lately, when she'd soaped herself in the shower, she imagined Ryan's hands slipping over her, of him massaging her shoulders, sliding a hand down her spine to—

Stop! She sucked in a breath to steady herself. "Focus."

She pulled into the reserved parking place at the community hall with Ryan still filling her head. Indirectly, he'd prompted today's outing. Rumour had it that Bess Riley did some housekeeping and baking for him. Bess was also the president of the local country women's association.

Although Grace had a website, self-promotion wasn't in her lexicon. She'd relied on the taste of her cheeses, word of mouth and recent competition success to build her brand. Offering to speak to the association was an expansion of that approach.

With her trolley laden with pre-prepared tasting plates, Grace entered the hall to find herself in the middle of a chattering crowd. A lot of old biddies who came to gossip about other people's business. *Influential biddies*, she reminded herself. With six weeks left to secure her bank loan, she needed the community on her side.

Bess waved to her from the opposite side of the hall, and Grace started to navigate her way through the crowd.

"I haven't seen your mother at one of these meetings in a while." An imperious septuagenarian stepped into Grace's path. The old lady had ruled the town library for thirty-five years and remembered every child who'd had or lost an overdue book.

"She and Dad are away at the moment, Mrs. Hornblower."

The woman inspected Grace's trolley. "Are these yours?" she asked.

"Some samples for after my talk." Grace had never fully believed there was a Mr. Hornblower. Danny's theory was that the librarian had co-opted the name of the fictional Napoleonic Wars-era Royal Naval Officer as her own after a torrid affair with a sailor.

"I'm looking forward to trying them." The woman suddenly chuckled. "All those books you had me order were put to good use I see."

Grace edged forward another few feet. Bess was signalling wildly in the background and pointing to the clock above the stage.

"How's your mother, Grace?" The receptionist from the doctor's surgery laid a hand on her shoulder.

Grace turned around and found another three women waiting for her answer. *Hell!* Until the last few years, her mother had been a regular fixture at these meetings. "She's good. She and Dad are staying with friends in the Blue Mountains."

"Was that Chrissy's daughter I saw at the field day?"

asked the publican's wife.

"Ella and the babies were up that weekend. Excuse me." Grace extricated herself from their kind clutches. When she'd told Ella last night she'd be pitching to the country women's association, her sister had said, *"Go, girl!"*

The girl had come! Kicking and screaming, but she was here. Unless Grace engineered a bigger, steadier boost to her cash flow, she'd never make the mortgage repayments. Farm income also needed to cover wages for Bluey's permanent replacement.

"Let's get this show on the road," Bess said crisply, helping Grace unload the trolley and set up her display. The woman, about as wide as she was high, sported a smile that had worn deep tracks in her face. Housekeeper to big interstate landholders, she'd retired to the area with her husband about five years earlier. An irresistible force in the district, Bess would tan her hide for lumping her in with old biddies or gossips.

Grace scanned the crowd while Bess made her introductions. A few strangers, a few business people as well as farmers and farmers' wives. She'd expected Rochelle Harkiss, the petite owner and manager of the Wellness Centre, to come. Her makeup and carefully layered long hair were Instagram perfect. Her flowing pants and loose blouse left the impression she floated across the floor—an elegant bohemian who always made Grace feel like a pregnant cow beside her.

"Ladies. Today's guest speaker is Grace Anderson, our local cheesemaker."

The audience fell silent.

Rubbing her sweaty palms on her jeans, Grace rose to her feet. She sucked at public speaking, but, hey, another compromise. If she wanted support, she had to ask for it, but asking for any kind of help went against every promise she'd made to herself after Smithhouse.

What compromises are you prepared to make? She recalled Ella's question.

Grace covered the cheese-making process, the different types of cheese available to sample at the back of the hall after her talk, showed some slides and made a few jokes. Then she took her biggest risk—a plea to the women of her community for their moral and practical support.

"Mum and Dad are retiring." She waited for the shocked gasps and ripples of "That's terrible," "I'm so sorry," "Elaine" and "I wondered" to die down. "Blue Sky has always been a family farm. That will continue. I'm taking over from my father." She didn't need to be explicit.

These women were shrewd enough to connect the dots, to realise her mother's health had driven the decision, and Grace was buying the farm. The dairy farmers amongst them would be painfully aware of the hit from the reduced milk price on incomes. It was a short step to understanding her cheese business needed to grow exponentially for her to finance the buyout. A few of these women had worked off-farm over the years to keep their properties afloat. In a very real way, she was appealing to her tribe.

"Congratulations on buying the farm." Rochelle approached Grace as she descended the stairs from the stage.

"Dad told me you were interested in buying," Grace said bluntly. Best to get it out in the open.

"Given the way you lost the land I'm on, I never had much real hope of success." The older woman laughed lightly. Mutterings had commenced when Rochelle bought Grace's parents' land from Smithhouse on the same day they'd lost it. There'd been more talk at the lightning-fast council building approval for the Centre, but no proof of corruption. Grace's father still insisted Rochelle wasn't part of the swindle. "I did get an idea while you were talking."

"What's that?" *Keep an open mind*, Grace lectured herself while her neck and back muscles clenched. *Open mind. Open mind.*

Rochelle's choice of landscape gardener had put more noses out of joint. Not local, the burly man in workman's clothes, early thirties, blonde, bronzed and built was often at the side of the Centre's owner. His edge of rough was at odds with Rochelle's smooth and languid style. More toy boy than gardener but over time the locals had accepted him, when he used local landscape suppliers and made a few friends in the district.

"An opportunity to expand." Rochelle bared her orthodontically-curated perfect teeth in a triumphant smile. "You could offer tours, demonstrations, sampling and sales, which I'd promote through the Centre."

"You'd take a cut." Grace halted.

"We'd both benefit." Rochelle glided over Grace's abrupt response. "I admire what you've achieved. I know how hard it is to fall over the line with the deposit."

"I've got the deposit covered," Grace stated firmly. That was a big fat lie until she knew what percentage the bank wanted.

"I can help you to grow." Rochelle's smile turned to pity and carried cold calculation as well, as if Grace was the village idiot. "Include you in my regular promotional flyers, introduce you to potential buyers."

"I haven't thought of tours while I work." Grace forced a friendly smile and resumed her push towards Bess with the dedication of one of Ryan's cows heading for his robotic milking machine. "I'm not sure it's the best use of my time."

"Depends on the price. We both sell products that aren't off the shelf." Rochelle's honeyed tones, close to her ear, were as hypnotic as any top-of-her-game magician. "You rely on people paying a premium to buy your cheese, just as I rely on people paying a premium for what I offer."

"Food's a different product. I'll give it some thought." *Not in this lifetime.*

"I feed different appetites." Rochelle fed *multiple* appetites. "We have a lot in common. I think we'd work well together."

Who the older woman shared her bed with had nothing to do with business. Grace hadn't listened to the gossip about Rochelle using sex for favours before and wouldn't start now. Ryan? Her gut cramped in instant rejection. She'd seen them together. *It wasn't her business*. Pity the green-eyed monster standing like a devil at her shoulder prodding her with its barbed trident didn't get the message!

Bess bustled towards them. "You'll have to share, Rochelle. I have some other ladies with questions." Bess steered Grace back towards the tables spread with cheeses, biscuits, dried fruit and a few bottles of wine alongside the usual tea and scones.

Grace sweated through another hour, handing out flyers with details of her website and social media sites, her smile fixed in place. She'd come to sell, yet she'd screeched like a wild cat at the first offer—the only offer—she'd received. Discomfort prickled her skin beneath her increasingly limp shirt, and she searched for the source. Rochelle bought local, including Grace's cheese, and hired local.

I'm not the jealous type. Grace did battle with herself all the way to her next stop, a new delicatessen. Another referral from Ryan, and the contradiction between following up on Ryan's suggestion and dismissing Rochelle's with a "when hell freezes over" curse made Grace squirm even more uncomfortably in her seat. Rochelle's motive was pure greed, whereas Grace suspected Ryan's actions, like this referral, were more a clever chess move in their dance of desire than an attempt to take a share of her profits. She hadn't had a chance to thank him. Thanking him involved seeing him.

Seeing him would aggravate her itch, his buzz.

Did it matter if they sampled each other if he wasn't staying? A no-strings-attached torrid affair. Whoa! He'd planted the seed—she groaned at the pun—and she couldn't stop thinking about what it would be like to get him naked.

The delicatessen was an unexpected innovation in a town that had gone from old family-run shops to supermarkets, convenience stores, assorted chains and boarded-up shopfronts. The locals were ready for something beyond the bland. Housed in a pretty old pharmacy, with bow windows and blue-and-white-leadlight glass, the business might just survive. A different concept. A new approach. Their add-on, if successful, could be an income booster for her as well. A café to serve good quality, fair trade coffee and cakes, sandwiches, quiches and pies made on the premises.

"How did you meet Ryan?" She shook hands with the owner, Bob, on the finished deal. The image of Ryan trawling shops on her behalf looking for sales was both foolish and heart-warming.

"I bumped into him at the tourist office. He encouraged me. Said the area was ready for something different."

She'd had the same idea, and that made her twitchy— that she and Ryan might see eye to eye on more than farming methods.

"Hi, Ryan." Bob waved.

A public place and her nerves were jittering. Grace hadn't felt this awkward since her first official date— holding hands with a boy and walking down the street for every gossip in town to see, feeling eyes crawling over her and dissecting each tiny gesture she made. She swung around. Ryan's hat was settled low on his forehead, and his glasses were firmly on his nose. Strong and silent and she was tempted by the idea of shattering his steely control.

"How's it going?" Ryan shook Bob's hand.

"Improving by degrees." The man nodded in her direction. "A great tip of yours, stocking *Pretty Girl* cheeses."

"I appreciate the opportunity." She pushed her hands into her pockets. That way they couldn't embarrass her by whipping off Ryan's sunglasses.

Bob turned back to his shop, then pivoted. "I'll let you know how sales go, Grace. But I'd say have another shipment ready."

"When's the opening?" she asked.

"Saturday," he replied.

"I'm planning on being here," said Ryan. "You could always have a cheese tasting in conjunction with the opening."

"That's a great idea. Are you free for an hour on Saturday afternoon, Grace?" Bob asked.

"I can do that." She waited until the man had disappeared into his shop. "You're spending a bit of time promoting my product, Ryan."

He rubbed his chin. "Should I stop?"

"Yes! No! Why?" she muttered. He reduced her to speaking gobbledygook, and that was plain mortifying.

"You have a good product I'm familiar with. If I'm asked if I know anyone who produces cheese, I give your name."

"Is that the only reason?" She studied him, her head cocked to one side, unsure of her ground. He asked for nothing in return for these small acts of kindness. Rather, he gave her no choice but to accept his generosity.

"Small businesses need to help each other to survive. The more a community prospers, the more everyone prospers. What other reason could there be?" He almost crooned, the deep gravel of his voice a caress.

The shimmering sexual buzz was a beat in her blood. The combination of heat and affection threatened her independence in a more disturbing way than Rochelle's offer for a slice of her profits.

"Okay!" He shrugged. "I confess. You suck at marketing. You're best when you let the cheese speak for itself."

He got that. Another reason his offer was different to Rochelle's.

"Last night I picked up an order from a contact I made at the show. Six cheddar wheels a week for twelve months."

"Congratulations."

"You should take some of the credit for that order too, since you supported organic being included in the show."

"I said you suck at marketing, Grace. Your products speak for themselves."

"I've started tossing around ideas for doubling production," she defended herself. "Fast-tracking some new product ideas."

"Any word from the bank?"

"Not yet." Waiting for the decision ate at Grace's self-confidence. It made her question if the small steps forward, the single sales, the garnering of support would be enough to convince the bank. She was riding a rollercoaster where she didn't know if success or disaster waited at the bottom of the next run. Like a kid with her eyes squeezed shut and her hands clamped on the safety rail praying for the madness to end. Terrified she'd be found in the wreckage. The lack of control was the killer.

"The waiting does your head in."

"Ain't that the truth," she muttered. The broker had promised an answer in the next few days. Still, it wouldn't hurt to drop by, see if he had any news while she was in town. "I was spruiking to the country women's association earlier." She started pushing her trolley towards the van.

"I didn't think you had time for such frivolous activities." He fell in beside her.

"Am I that obvious?" She wrinkled her nose in distaste. "Don't answer. I represented Mum a few times when she was sick. I asked to be the speaker today. To promote my cheese. To promote myself—new owner of Blue Sky."

"How'd that go?"

"Positively for the most part. Rochelle offered to advertise tours of my place for her customers." Grace hadn't intended to blurt out Rochelle's offer first. "In return for a cut of any revenue." *Or to confide in him*. Grace couldn't afford to alienate anyone, much less Rochelle, who'd woven her business into the fabric of the town so tightly no one dared cross her.

"That's how a successful businesswoman operates."

Grace halted, stung. "If that's a dig at me, I'll never be successful. I don't have the stomach for taking a cut of other people's profits. *And* I don't have the ethereal looks, floaty wardrobe and follow-me-home stilettos."

"I liked the lace and frills concoction you wore to the field day." With his glasses firmly in place, the rumble of his voice was her guide. Like the rich symphonic music she played to the cows the sound soothed and inflamed. He leaned forward to run a finger down her cheek. "Like I told you, a buzz." Before she could object to his intimacy, he continued. "Who else was there?"

"Bess. She said she knew you."

"Asking questions about me, Grace?" He ensnared her with his intimate whisper. "It's good to know you care and don't just lust after my body."

"Another woman was pumping her." She denied responsibility for starting the conversation, but a pulse jumped in her throat, anticipating how he'd translate the words lust and care to action. "I came in at the tail end." She waved a hand dismissively.

His mouth curved in disbelief. "Did she tell you my old boss put me in touch with the station owner where she worked, gave me a good reference, and they took me on? Bess was the backbone of the domestic staff. She has a soft spot for me."

A lot of people around the Northern Rivers had Bess pegged as one of the toughest old birds around. *Soft spot? What was it in Ryan that brought out Bess' softer side?*

When he tugged on a curl resting against Grace's neck, the gentle pull had her swaying towards him. "She does a few days for me."

She placed a hand on his chest to keep him at bay. "Do you pay her in diamonds?" Bess hadn't wanted to retire, so she worked occasionally for a few select customers.

The corner of his mouth lifted. "She says I need all the help I can get."

"Bess made the cheese biscuits."

"She did." He inched closer. "Want to come over for some more?"

She closed her eyes on dangerous temptation. "Time to

step away, Ryan."

"Why?" He released the curl, the back of his hand brushing the bare skin between her shirt collar and neck, then trailing over her shoulder in seductive retreat.

Putting some distance between them, she divulged her dilemma. "I haven't found a single person who has a bad word to say about you. Mr. Donovan, Bess, Dad. You're stacking up the referees."

"Do you need referees?" His question was loaded enough to start a flashfire in her blood.

"I make up my own mind." Apart from her family, Grace gave her trust sparingly. Relying on herself in her business and in life had risen from the ashes of Danny's death and Smithhouse's swindle. Ryan was shaking up the certainties she'd depended on.

"Have you made up your mind about me?" He dared her to answer.

You tempt me as a man. You confuse me in the way you do business. "Almost."

"Have dinner with me tonight?" The intimacy in his husky invitation shivered through her.

"Why?" She, who never played games, was flirting. *Yes, please.*

"Consider it a job audition. You said you wanted me to hire you." He switched to business. "Here's your chance to prove you're more than just talk."

"It would be better to have the conversation out at the farm." She'd flunked flirting as badly as she'd flunked self-promotion.

"I'm doing the hiring." His mouth tipped up in a grin. "I get to nominate the location for the interview. Antonio's, I think."

The best restaurant in the area. "I'll meet you there."

CHAPTER SEVEN

Ryan rose when she appeared at the restaurant entrance. She'd dressed for business—country business, jeans and her boots. But the jeans were black, not her usual blue. The shirt brushing the tops of her thighs was a deep bougainvillea pink. She wore her hair short, and he'd bet she'd cite practical reasons for it, but it suited her, following the shape of her head. He liked the way the curls clustered when she was hot and sweaty after her deliveries. He'd like to get her hot and sweaty. She smiled at the guy allocating tables. Ryan knew the moment she spotted him. Her smile became uncertain, and she stood a little straighter. The blood drained to his groin. Yeah. He'd known the moment he'd got close to her at the field day he had a problem.

"Hi, Grace." Ryan moved behind her to pull out her chair. Her light, fresh scent teased his nostrils—flowery, and he remembered—Sweet Peas. His mother's favourite flowers. They'd filled the house when he was a child, and he'd never had a single lustful thought. "Would you like a drink while we look at the menu?" He gestured to the leather-covered folder in front of her plate.

"A glass of wine, please. Red, dry."

"They have a good merlot by the glass." He watched her

eyebrow shoot up. "I checked before you arrived."

"Sounds good."

Ryan signalled the waiter and ordered the drinks. "Eat here often?"

"We came for Mum's birthday last year. They do some clever things with vegetables." She opened the menu. "I've copied a few recipes."

"Do you like to cook?" he asked.

Her head lifted. She had a strong face. The light makeup couldn't hide the impact of unrelenting work days and worry about the bank's verdict on her future. He ached to trace the dark circles under her eyes, to make them disappear, but touch wouldn't pay her bills, and touching her would make him want more.

"If I've got time." She turned the conversation back to him. "What about you?"

"Grills, simple dishes on a regular basis. Got tired of eating takeaway, plus I was on a budget."

"Saving to take over the world?" She relaxed a fraction.

"You could say that." Although all his income in the first two years had gone back into helping his mother, paying for Bluey, paying down debt. He'd kept enough to survive.

The waiter returned with wine, poured them each a glass. "Can I take your order, now?"

"Give us a few more minutes, please." Ryan opened his menu. Something had happened to distress her since he'd seen her this afternoon. He wasn't sure how he knew, but he did. "Any suggestions?"

Her head was bent in deliberate study. "I remember the duck being wonderful."

"Duck it is."

The waiter magically reappeared, took their orders, then returned with fresh bread rolls.

"Is your cheese on the menu here?" Ryan started with an easy question.

"Not yet."

"I like your optimism and your ambition." He'd had it

once. Dreamed of turning their farm into a district showcase with him building a life in the valley.

"Are you teasing me?" She flopped back in her chair.

"Guilty as charged. You demand it. You're so single-minded." He'd teased her when she'd run free in his home, when she and Danny were like puppies rolling over each other. Now, Ryan wanted to help her. For once he didn't know where he was heading with a woman. They had no future, yet her eyes, her hair, the smell of her, and the feel of her skin—silk—the few times he'd had a hand on her were a constant distraction.

"I thought you wanted my ideas on your farm?" She took a cautious sip of her wine.

"And heaven help us if we deviate, by so much as a hair's breadth. Any room in your life for nuance, Grace?"

"I can do shades of grey," she muttered mutinously. "But some things are right and some are wrong."

"Indeed, they are. But I'm talking about casual conversation. You say something, I say something, you reply."

She stared at him blankly.

"Do you think you can handle that?" He waited for her to take the bait.

"Ask me a question," she snapped.

Ryan tore a bread roll in two. A small victory, leaving him wanting more. "Why did your father sell some of his best acreage to a charlatan like Smithhouse?"

She swirled her drink, then set it down. "Surely there are people all over town rushing to answer that."

"I'd rather hear your version." His mother had told him about Elaine's tractor accident and about mounting medical bills. She hadn't talked about Grace.

She shook her head as if baffled. "A few years after you left, Mum had a serious tractor accident. We needed cash. Smithhouse advanced some on a handshake and verbal deal with Dad."

"Any witnesses?"

"You *do* remember Smithhouse." She sounded grim.

"I've had the odd run-in with him," he replied. Smithhouse had wanted Donovan's farm for a housing development and had been mightily pissed when he'd discovered it was sold before it went on the open market. Not a good enemy to have.

"Ella was the witness. Didn't stand up in court, because she was nineteen, related, and likely to lie."

"Did the person making those claims recover from the beating?" Ryan soaked up Grace's helpless rage.

"We lost, had to sell to pay the debt." She winced. "Smithhouse claimed the deal included the top of the valley." Then, as if the words were forced from her, she added, "Dad took a long time to come to terms with the loss."

She'd been her father's shadow for as long as Ryan could remember. She adored him. An attack on him was an attack on her. It explained her reluctance to accept help with the farm—her sometimes aggressive independence. *Memo to self: any deal he did with her would have to be watertight legally for her to feel safe.*

"It made Ella more passionate than ever about justice. She's manager of a community justice centre." Pride brought a brief smile to Grace's lips.

"Is that how she met the big-shot lawyer?" He'd done his own research on Jake Taylor, Taylor Law, one of the top Sydney firms.

"Two years ago, his cousin, Tessa's biological father, who'd never shown any interest, tried to take Tessa away from us." Grace would have seen that as theft as well. "Needless to say, he didn't succeed."

"The Andersons stick through thick and thin." Ryan admired her family's loyalty, her loyalty to those she loved, even when she ranked him as an outsider.

"With the minor exception of my ostracising Chrissy." Grace rolled her eyes.

"Surely it's time to forgive yourself for that." He also

admired her capacity for self-reflection and contrition—after she'd blown a gasket. "I wouldn't have made Brian an offer if I'd known what you were dealing with back then."

She lifted a shoulder. "We didn't spread it around."

"How did the luscious Rochelle get to own the land?" He liked Grace's furrowed brow, her quick scan of his face, her slight irritation, and hoped she'd reacted to the term "luscious." Testing her interest in him was half tonight's purpose.

"I've never fully known." She frowned. "She must have been waiting in the wings, because while we were still reeling from the loss of the land, she'd moved in and started building."

"Interesting," he murmured. Closer to fascinating if Rochelle had been on hand to take advantage of Smithhouse's duplicity and get all the building approvals up so fast. She appeared to have the ear of the council heavyweights.

"To be brutally honest, she's created jobs and buys local." Grace made the reluctant admission.

"A paragon of virtue." He raised his glass, watching her over the top.

Her brows drew together. "Better than some of the alternatives."

"So, Ella focused on justice for the underdog. What did you channel your rage into?"

Grace was silent a long time, and he'd given up on an answer. "Making the farm viable. Trying to make it future-proof."

"Life's a bitch!" Ryan observed. But her honesty gave him an opening. "What happened between this afternoon and now?"

She fiddled with a fork. "Why do you ask?"

"The shadows under your eyes, the worry in them. Any news from the bank?"

"I dropped in to see the broker." Her huff of breath lifted her fringe. "The valuation's in, and he says the bank's getting antsy."

"I'm guessing over a million." He kept his voice easy, afraid of spooking her because Grace Anderson sharing her worries with him shifted something inside him. "Define antsy."

"I expected the valuation." She traced the outline of a dollar sign with the fork. "The deposit will be higher than I hoped, although the broker's positive he can keep it to twenty percent."

"That's steep. Did the bank have other suggestions?"

"They said if I had a partner it might make my proposal more appealing." She bristled like a chook who'd had an egg pinched from under her.

Ryan was getting used to her instant default to fight not flight. Now he'd learned more about how they'd lost their land, he understood her defensiveness. Understood it bumped between them, complicating their relationship. Initially Danny's death stood between them, but she didn't want a partner in her land or life any more than he did.

"It's a big responsibility for a young woman," she repeated someone else's words.

Ryan shared her disgust. He could picture the fat-cat banker mouthing them.

The waiter returned with their meals. "Would you like another glass of wine with your meal, madam, sir?"

"I'll sit on this one," she said. "I'm driving."

Ryan shook his head. "That's a kick in the teeth when you had a succession plan in place. Doesn't our banker know that?"

Slicing into her duck, she sampled a mouthful. "It's delicious."

Ryan picked up his knife and fork. "Changing the subject?"

"Eating a good meal while it's hot."

"Then we'll enjoy this and the rest of the wine before we talk business." He forked up a bite. "It is delicious. If you want to try and imitate this recipe, I'd be happy to be your guinea pig."

"In your dreams."

"You're very interested in my dreams, Grace. Tell me about yours?" he purred.

She flicked him a suspicious look, and he winked.

"If they're anything like mine, they're probably X-rated."

She lifted a hand to disguise the giveaway heat rising up her throat.

"Indeed. Best stick to talking about cheese making," he murmured. "At least over dinner."

She did, interspersing her descriptions with hand gestures and her own questions about the use of robotics on organic farms as well as non-organic farms.

"They work, despite the scuttlebutt around town." He'd worked hard to be impervious to mean-spirited gossip.

"I try not to listen to gossip. Mostly because it often slips into mud-slinging." She wrinkled her nose. "I like to make my judgements based on evidence and facts."

The waiter moved in to remove the empty plates. "Coffee or dessert."

"Perhaps a coffee in ten minutes," she said.

Ryan nodded in agreement, and they were alone. Unwilling to disturb the harmony they'd established over dinner, he was tempted to lean closer, to touch her with more than his gaze. The urge to keep talking about her dreams was harder to explain, an intellectual intimacy that made him yearn for a different kind of life. But he'd invited her here for a purpose, other than the one he'd admitted to. "There's another option for you to own the farm."

"I have to make a lot more cheese to reach a twenty percent deposit in six weeks."

"Sell me some of your land."

She withdrew as he'd anticipated into her protective shell. "I don't want a partner."

"I'm not offering to be a partner," he insisted. If she accepted that basic principle, he might have a chance of helping her. "I'm offering to buy some of the land, so you have the deposit to buy the bulk of it. Free and clear in your name."

She picked up her glass of wine, then replaced it, untasted. "Why?"

"I've told you. Scale is everything in farming." He gave her the plausible excuse.

"What about my scale?" she asked crossly.

Ryan leaned back in his chair. "You ultimately want to convert your entire herd to organic milk production or cheese making. You'll have the premium that comes with organic and the control of your own farm. It'll take years before you want or need to grow your herd." Logical arguments were the only pathway to a win-win outcome.

"Is this what you've wanted all along? Why you've pretended to be helpful?" She lifted her chin combatively.

"I'm not Smithhouse, Grace." He took a swig of his wine to wipe out the bad taste left by her suspicion.

"I owe you another apology." She pleated the linen serviette and drew an audible breath. "You paid above market rates for the Donovan place."

He didn't need her trust. It was a business deal, pure and simple. And if they went to bed, that was a different transaction, consenting adults acting on an attraction. He didn't need her trust there either, so why was he sweating on it? "Do you object to me leaving town or earning enough money in my absence to join Donovan's farm to Mum's?"

She cocked her head to one side. "You don't see it as yours."

"Is this some word game?" he snapped. "Mine. Mum's? Who cares?" His mother had given most of her adult life to the farm. His contribution had been cash and a failure to be there at the most important moment in his brother's life.

"I do cryptic crosswords, and I like word games, but I was making an observation." Grace's voice dropped. "To be honest, my animosity is because you weren't here when you were needed."

"I can't change that." Ryan absorbed the sting her words

brought.

"I needed you." Her expression told him she'd surprised herself with those words. "I mean—"

"I know what you mean." Ryan lifted a hand and let it drop onto the table. His fingers curled into a fist. "I couldn't talk to anyone that day. I couldn't bear to bury him." Some of the bastards in town had taunted Danny as if it were a blood sport. Brutish, mob-rule baiting had contributed to his brother's death. They'd made it easy to cut emotional ties to this place. "If I'd opened my mouth, I would have abused every bastard who came to gawp." He pressed his fingers flat. "Or have beaten the shit out of them."

She reached across the table and covered his hand with hers. The warmth offered comfort to the boy he'd been. "I'm sorry I shouted at you."

He turned his hand over and linked his fingers with hers. "You cared, and you were angry. That meant a lot."

Her courage in refusing to ignore Danny's death when everyone else in town pussyfooted around it acted as a balm to his bruised spirit. She was prickly, argumentative and he couldn't for the life of him explain why that added to her attraction. Her eyes opened wide, and for a moment he imagined drowning in those sea-green pools. He knew he wouldn't feel a thing. Just go slowly under, mesmerised by the lure of those depths.

A tanned, telegenic early forties woman was veering in their direction. Ryan released Grace's hand, easing back in his chair. Soon after his return to the valley, he'd made it his business to find out about the woman regularly heading down the valley road in the direction of the Ridgeway Wellness Centre. She'd made it her business to introduce herself at business forums, to be omnipresent at community ones. She'd weighed him sexually and professionally and found him wanting. That amused him. His taste didn't run to women who'd swallow you whole. In the last fortnight Rochelle had unexpectedly dropped in, claiming she was just passing and wanted to catch up on local news. His mother didn't raise an idiot.

"Why, Grace, it's unusual to see you here."

"Hello, Rochelle."

"And with Ryan?" She pushed a thick wave of auburn hair behind one ear, a deliberately provocative gesture, and leaned closer. "How fascinating."

"We're talking about robotics," Ryan offered.

"Not a partnership?" Rochelle wore another of her flowing caftans. This one in muted colours, designed to accentuate her femininity, yet despite her gruff exterior, Grace struck him as the softer woman.

"I'm not interested in a partnership." Grace made the blanket statement.

"You made that clear today." Rochelle gave a tinkling laugh. "But you want to grow your business. I'd like to help."

"Not on my time." Ryan got the pissed-off vibes loud and clear. Dollar signs flashed before Rochelle's eyes whenever two people had their heads together. Ka-ching!

Grace buying out her parents was now public information, and she was unlikely to have sworn her broker to silence. He recalled seeing Rochelle with the man, sharing an intimate meal here, shortly after he'd returned home. Rochelle wanted a piece of any action, and her new-found interest in Ryan was explained.

"I'm sorry your mother's health has precipitated this." Rochelle continued to smile. "I'll let you finish your meal."

"Good night," Grace said.

Rochelle waved a farewell. Ryan waited until she was out of earshot. "Smooth."

"That's the gossamer fabrics and regular visits to the beauty salon," Grace muttered.

The waiter brought coffees.

"Thank you."

"Another example of your open mind?" Ryan drained his wineglass and set it down with a snap. "She could increase your business."

"Only if I'm prepared to be a wind-up doll on call when she wants me to perform," she said tartly, tapping her neat unvarnished fingernails on the table for a few moments.

"She's very competitive. Probably ruffled her feathers to see you talking to me. She likes to keep a finger in every pie going." From his observation, she cooked up at least half the deals.

"We could be on a date."

Ryan couldn't contain his grin. "It's an open secret that you're barely on nodding acquaintance with me."

"People should have better things to talk about." Grace looked adorably haughty.

"People should." He nodded in sober agreement.

"Don't patronise me, Ryan."

"I wouldn't dream of it." He studied her over his coffee. "What are you going to do about her?"

"I've said I'm not interested, so nothing at this stage."

"She's a barracuda," he said. Rochelle didn't take rejection well.

"Is that a warning?" Grace met his gaze, a question in her eyes.

"Call it friendly advice. My offer's genuine." Ryan enjoyed having her sit across the table from him, sharing her thoughts and fears. Wanting her to confide in him was a dangerous and unexpected development. He didn't do binding ties. "I'll meet top-market price, I'll continue the move to organic status, and I'll make sure the land I buy remains an operating dairy farm."

She searched his face, as if it held the answer to some puzzle she needed to unravel. He had no answers, not to the sort of questions a woman like Grace asked. He'd let Danny down, hadn't been able to answer his cry for help.

Ryan signalled for the bill and waved away her offer to pay half. "I'm wooing you, Grace. And you blush delightfully. But I was referring to our business deal."

"No deal."

"Then we'll focus on the buzz." His mouth curved.

"We haven't discussed my business proposition for you," she protested.

"Next time. I'll walk you to your car."

"I'm unlikely to get lost." She collected her coat from the coat rack at the entrance.

"Let me." He took it from her, holding it while she shrugged herself into it. It carried her scent. Acting on the urge to turn her into his arms probably wasn't a good idea at this stage. He rested his hands on her shoulders a fraction longer than politeness needed before reaching around her to open the door. Another tickle from her teasing fragrance, and he gripped the handle more firmly.

"Really, there's no need." She turned up her coat collar and pushed her hands into her pockets.

"Humour me." He fell into step beside her when she headed down the block.

She took a left turn and then another halfway down that block, leading into a short, poorly lit laneway.

"You're kidding, aren't you—?" He didn't get a chance to finish. Headlights flashed to high beam, and a car roared out of the darkness. Ryan dragged Grace against him and swivelled to push her against the wall, covering her body with his. The wind from the speeding car slammed into him, and he pressed her head into his chest. The car took a sharp right, wheels squealing as it made the turn. "Are you okay?" He eased back, one hand on the wall near her head.

"Stupid kids," she muttered.

"Would kids do something like that?" He stared after the car. "They could have hit us."

"Playing chicken."

He scanned the buildings around them. "Any CCTV here?"

"These aren't the mean streets of New York," she mocked.

"Still." Her perfume filled Ryan's senses. It was dark, she was close, and with the adrenalin easing out of his body, he needed to step away while he still could, but his feet refused to move.

"Thanks for shifting me out of the way." She stroked his jaw with fingers shaped by years of hard work, yet her touch was tender.

"No trouble." Ryan's fingers encircled her wrist.

She leaned in to brush her lips across his. "I now know what it's like to lose a younger sibling. They leave a hole that can't be filled. At Danny's funeral I was mostly consumed by my loss. I'm sorry for yours."

Ryan stared into her eyes. Her few simple words broke through barriers that had stood solid for years. She offered understanding and comfort, and the isolation balloon he'd sealed himself in burst. He wrapped her close with one arm, exulting in the snug fit of her against his body. Tipping up her chin, he covered her mouth with his and lost himself in her. Arousal was instant and powerful. In his arms her dips and curves became womanly handholds to keep her close. She tasted of heaven, with a dash of the coffee she'd ordered to finish the meal. Before he was ready, her free hand pushed against his chest. He eased back, aware of where they were.

"I need to go."

"Of course." Ryan checked the laneway in both directions. "Where's your van?"

"I'm using the farm Ute tonight." She walked a farther ten metres into the dark.

Ryan followed her, then stood behind her while she unlocked the vehicle and slid in. With his arm on the top of the driver's door, he leaned forward. "Don't park here next time."

She raised an eyebrow. "Close the door, Ryan."

He did as she said and stepped back, waiting until she drove off before he wandered back up the lane. Maybe he shouldn't have made the move, but she'd wanted the kiss. His gut told him she'd called a halt to going deeper in a public place. And because she was as stunned as him at what had happened. He couldn't blame her. Zero to liftoff from a brush of the lips was a new experience for him. He itched to test whether that would happen a second time.

CHAPTER EIGHT

When her alarm sounded for the morning milking, Grace groaned and rolled over. The second alarm she'd set up penetrated pillows, doona and was just out of reach of her outstretched hand. A private joke, Avicii's *Wake Me Up*, didn't seem so funny this morning. She downed coffee and stumbled outside, her mind tugging at her problem as her fingers might pull on a loose thread in a scarf. Her plans were unravelling as fast as she made them.

Mist hung in the air as she crossed the yard, dewing her sweater and limiting visibility to the home paddocks. She shivered as the isolation she normally welcomed enveloped her. The urge to pump heavy rock through the milk-shed loudspeakers to blast away dismal reality had her fingers poised above the player. The lead cow turned her head as if to say, "Don't even think it," and Grace settled for Mozart.

Seven weeks of prevarication from the broker and the bank had ended with their offer right on close of business yesterday. The positive vibes she'd sent into the universe had produced another slap down. She'd reworked her budget in her dreams, each calculation taking her further from the twenty-five percent deposit the bank stipulated. She hosed out the shed, took the time to check the calves had food and fresh water. The rhythm of work and music helped with her decision.

"Compromise isn't defeat," she murmured to a tardy cow. "A conversation isn't a commitment."

She opened the kitchen door, and Bluey passed her a coffee.

"The scones are still warm." He gestured to a plate covered with a tea towel as he headed for the door. She wanted to weep at the kindness of a man who'd known her all her life, at the kindness of Ryan's mother who'd started to bake for her because she was looking peaky.

She sank onto a chair. Her mind jumped from her list of chores for the day to the bank's decision to Ryan's offer, a never-ending loop draining her dwindling confidence. Swallowing half the coffee in a single mouthful, she lifted the edge of the tea towel and inhaled the warm, doughy smell. Then dropped it back in place as her stomach protested.

"Compromise isn't defeat. A conversation isn't a commitment," she repeated, massaging her stomach in slow circles to ease the nausea.

Weeks ago, Ryan had said business and pleasure were separate. But that was before he'd kissed her in the alley, before he'd blown her expectations of what kissing him might be like into the stratosphere. Heaven didn't begin to describe the toe-curling sensation of being in his arms. For seconds, she'd forgotten everything, caught in the rush of sensations his kiss created. Desire more than lust, a giving and sharing rather than a taking.

She'd draw courage from that and take a gamble she'd vowed never to take. She'd talk to Ryan about his offer. She'd be careful, promising nothing, asking questions, taking nothing at face value.

"Ryan, it's Grace," she began. His perky response was a reminder the lucky sod had robotic milking for his cows and hadn't had to keep a four-a.m. appointment in the damp, Tolkien-like mist.

At dinner last week, she'd said no deal. Although that hadn't stopped her from turning his offer over in her head, checking it from every angle to find the trap. She didn't want to deal now. The bank's email had narrowed her options to zero. Ella was right. Grace couldn't afford not to explore Ryan's offer. She'd interrogate every fair proposal to keep the farm.

"What land are you interested in?" she asked, then answered his avalanche of questions.

"I received it last night." Grace had seen the email when she'd stopped work around eight. Unable to sleep after reading it, she'd refused to lie helpless in bed staring at the ceiling. Instead, she'd worked on her website, added to her list of shops that might stock her cheeses, and sent out exploratory emails. She'd woken stiff-necked, her head resting on her arms on the kitchen table and crawled into bed for the two hours remaining of her night.

"The bank settled on twenty-five percent upfront to approve the loan," Grace admitted. The number still hurt, still had her breath catching and her heart hammering.

"Of course, I feel like bloody shit!" Sucking in some steadying breaths, she listened for the low of contented cows as they made their way back into the fields and ordered herself to focus on her goal. The plate of scones caught her eye. She couldn't work if she didn't eat. *So, she'd eat.* After she finished this call.

"Where?" She'd missed his instructions to the piece of land he was interested in.

She didn't want to be beholden to him. Wouldn't be beholden to him, but if he was throwing her a lifeline, she'd be insane to turn her back on it.

"Midday. Got it." Grace walked to the window, her eyes straining through the mist as she repeated his directions. "The road in from the school bus drop-off."

* * *

Ryan pulled up on the dirt track behind her. She'd been leaning against the side of the Ute as he'd approached. With the valley as backdrop, and her womanly figure lounging negligently against the horsepower of the white work vehicle, she could have been posing for a motoring advertisement. Her short hair was tucked under her hat, her sunglasses hid her eyes, although at this distance, he couldn't read her expression anyway. Couldn't smell her either, but he knew her scent. Each time he got a sniff, he was aware of a new complexity.

Just being here marked a new step in their relationship. Did she know that, and was she prepared for the consequences?

She pushed herself off the vehicle as he pulled up and turned to face him. Her mouth curved in a welcoming smile. It cost her but slammed into him, making him want things he had no business wanting.

Walking towards her, Ryan saw the smile wobble, then right itself. He had a flashback to the first property he'd bought. A tiny, derelict house on a small square of land at the edge of a country town. A renovator's delight according to the selling agent. He'd renovated it himself, using specialist trades when he needed to quote licence numbers for building clearance—electrician, plumber. He'd turned a nice profit. Not before a lot of sleepless nights and backbreaking days of looking over his shoulder to see if the bank had changed its mind and would foreclose, of skipping meals to make the next payment. His only investments had been time, sweat and money, and he'd been scared spitless. Grace was gambling all that and more. He bet she hadn't slept much last night. She'd see having to sell any of her land as a failure. *Her failure*. Her courage grabbed him by the balls every bit as much as her work-toned body did.

She nodded when he reached her. "This place has lots of memories."

"Waiting for the school bus." He understood the desperation prompting her call. If small talk about their shared history was her way past gut-churning worry, he'd oblige. "Summer heat hazes drugging you into a semi-stupor, or icy winter winds sneaking under your collar and making your teeth chatter." He coaxed a genuine smile from her.

"You're forgetting the rain and the dust."

"I ate my share of dust." He fell into step beside her when she turned towards the river. "Good times."

"Some. Every square inch of this paddock has memories for me," she spoke carefully.

"Guess the bus doesn't come down this road anymore?"

"The Wellness Centre is a child-free zone," she mimicked Rochelle's polished tones.

"Hard to guarantee tranquility with kids running around," he observed. They continued for a few minutes in silence.

She stopped, opened her mouth, closed it again, then spoke as if the words were dragged out of her. "Did you know this was Danny's and my special place?"

Ryan raised a hand in denial as the words catapulted him back a decade.

"I figured that was why you picked it." She searched his face.

He saw himself reflected in her glasses. Neither of them giving anything away. A powerful sense of loss swept through him. For his brother, for their lost innocence, for Grace having to give up land she loved. "I didn't know." He whipped his hands behind his back to stop himself from reaching for her—not to make a move on her, but to share simple comfort.

"We had a few spots," she continued, some of the constraint leaving her voice. "His, mine. This was one we shared. We used to park our bikes in the old shed at the bus set-down. Some afternoons we'd skip chores, play hooky and come down here."

"I remember when he didn't get home in time to do his share of the chores."

"You covered for him, just as Ella covered for me."

Ryan scanned the surrounding area. "In my head, it was good land, clear access to water. It's also a place to dream in."

"He was a dreamer."

"I don't remember the poppies." He stared across the field in the direction they'd been walking.

"There'll be hundreds in coming weeks. I planted them for him. Not hardy natives, because he wasn't." Her voice softened. "The delicate red and white poppies of France. Red, the emblem of the war to end all wars and white to represent peace."

"You understood him." The grief had never left Ryan, nor the anger. Her tribute ambushed him.

"Your mother wanted to bury him in a traditional church graveyard as a statement that he had a right to a place in this community, but I can't go there," she replied quietly.

"This is right." Ryan hadn't understood his deep need to talk to someone who'd unconditionally loved Danny. Until she'd started speaking about Danny most times they met. Without demand, as if sharing memories was natural, a way of building a future by accepting the past. He hunkered down to touch a fragile bloom.

"Danny battled his demons," she whispered. "In those last months, he was at war more often with himself than he was at peace."

"Mum thought you were a good influence on him." Ryan started to walk again, movement making the words flow more easily. "Did you know that?"

She grimaced. "She thought I was his girlfriend. I was his—'girl'—friend. He loved me. He never fancied me."

Her openness cracked the lock on his grief. "Did he talk to you about being gay?"

"Sometimes. We joked about me being his cover." Stopping again, she turned her head to look at him. "If I think about it now, we didn't have the maturity to articulate what was going on, but we both knew he shouldn't need a cover, that he was normal." She pulled off her hat. "More than normal. A funny, smart, generous individual."

"I agree." A picture of Danny's cocky grin as Ryan waved him goodbye flashed into his mind.

"You accepted who he was," she stated, as if she had no doubt.

"Yeah." It felt good to find common ground with her, to finally heal the rift his behaviour at Danny's funeral had created. "I knew it would be hard in the valley. The town has pockets of narrow-mindedness. We talked about him leaving when he finished high school." Ryan had been watching, had begun to guess bullying at school was the biggest threat to Danny's self-esteem. "Sooner if needed."

Satan barked and started to lope ahead of them.

"What's that smell?" She started to run.

Picking up speed, Ryan caught her at the edge of the river. Satan stood barking, rushing backwards and forwards towards two metal drums. They'd been deliberately punctured—huge, gaping holes. A thick liquid seeped into the ground. The odour caught the back of his throat and stung his eyes. They'd been dumped a few metres from his gates on Grace's land.

"Hold on." He grabbed her arm. "Stay back. You don't know what it is."

"I can guess. It's reddish yellow and smells like rotten-egg gas." She shook off his hold and edged closer. "There's sulphur in it, and it shouldn't be here."

"Then stay the fuck back!" he yelled. *His gate.* He had drums like this. Enough to make him prime suspect. Although his had been empty the last time he'd seen them.

She eyed him balefully but stepped back.

"Satan, here." Ryan snapped his fingers. The dog came to his side. "Who comes down here?" His brain was calculating possibilities while he spoke. *Rochelle?* She'd been on his land recently—supervised. His crew knew to report any unauthorised arrivals or movements, plus he was known to use CCTV.

"Dad and I do from time to time. It's part of our buffer with your property to meet the organic certification requirements. It's where the properties meet, our closest point. That's why we chose it." Her eyes focused on the source of the spill.

"How wide's the buffer?"

"Twenty-five metres at this point."

"Then you should be safe."

Grace glared at him. "We'll need to notify the certification body, get a fresh inspection."

"What's the worst-case scenario?" Dumping chemicals didn't feel like Rochelle's kind of crime. Ryan didn't doubt she bent the law, but there'd be one helluva scandal if Grace lost the farm to sabotage. Rochelle had spent years encouraging collective amnesia about how Ridgeway Wellness Centre had miraculously sprung from prime Anderson farmland.

"It could set organic certification back months"—Grace hugged herself, her voice bleak—"and it'll cost to clean it up."

Ryan read the subtext. The delay in certification would reduce her week-by-week takings. The cleanup would be a massive hit. A one-off, but it'd cost hundreds if not thousands of dollars. Fury fisted his hands as he scanned the surroundings. The narrow track they'd walked down was the one Grace and Danny had ridden as teens. On his side of the river, the track was wider. Overgrown but still wider. They'd driven down it years ago to go swimming. He couldn't remember the last time he'd used it—the last time any of his crew should have been down this way.

"Have you got your phone?"

"There's no reception here," she snapped.

"I left mine in the truck. Use the camera. Get some shots." If not Rochelle, the field of candidates widened considerably. "How do you want to handle it?"

"I want to make it vanish, but the police need to see it. If I find out who did it, I'll press charges." She didn't have the headspace or resources for a legal challenge, and whoever had sabotaged her back paddock knew it.

"Any ideas?"

She stared blankly at him, surveyed the devastation, and her mouth set in a firm line.

He checked his watch. "Can you get reception from the Ute?"

She nodded.

"Take the shots. Go back and call the cops. It's bleeding into the river and going downstream. I'll check further down to see if there are any other dump spots nearby and meet you back at the vehicles." He didn't add, "You can fight me then."

He smelled a fight coming.

* * *

"How long?" Grace snatched off her sunglasses and watched Ryan walk towards her. Her land and water deliberately poisoned. Suspicion was a rampaging bull firing her blood, making her heart race and her hands clammy. "Twenty to thirty minutes," she repeated the cop's answer for Ryan's benefit and turned off her phone.

"It's meant to look like I did it," he stated.

"Are you saying you didn't?" Grace's muscles stretched tight enough to make her bones hurt. She'd confided in him, about the bank's position, about how desperate she was for the deposit. *Only him.*

"I've got some old drums, not all of them empty, and the makings for this cocktail," he said flatly.

"Something you could knock up." Sunglasses hid his eyes from Grace, but his body braced, not for the first time in their encounters. The poison on the land contaminating the air around them.

"If it's lime sulphur, the recipe's on the internet. So, yeah, I could knock it up," he agreed. "The ingredients are legal."

"Legal doesn't mean they're not deadly!" Grace flung up a hand. The timing favoured his involvement. Dinner a few nights ago could have given him the idea; this morning she'd admitted she needed help.

"Are you accusing me?" His voice was icepick cold.

"The circumstantial evidence is pretty persuasive," she muttered. It was too hands on for the "luscious" Rochelle, and Grace's parents had always insisted Rochelle was opportunistic rather than criminal. Besides, Rochelle might guess Grace was financially vulnerable, but she'd handed Ryan the information for free. She'd broken her cardinal rule, and hey presto—instant disaster.

"Why?" His frustration was tangible.

"Poisoning the land makes it worth less money. The cleanup could push me to the wire, so I'm forced to sell whatever the price." Even as she catalogued her reasons aloud, none of them fitted Ryan. "You get these few paddocks for a song. Maybe a chance at the lot."

"That's crap, and you know it." He gripped her hands, forcing her to face him. "Has anyone objected to your shift to organic?"

"Yes!" Grace wanted to roar at the senseless waste. "Years ago, when we started." Her father and she had nurtured the land with painstaking care. Impossible to tell the extent of the damage until she got an organic chemist to test the soil and water. Insurance wouldn't cover it all.

"When do you think it happened?" He was pushing her to analyse, not react.

Grace pulled herself free, crossing her arms to hold the rage and fear inside. "Last night, maybe the night before. The overnight rain helped spread it."

"You only told me about the bank's decision this morning. Unless you think I have an informant at the bank!" He took a few jerky steps away from her.

His back was rigid, clenched muscles straining against the worn work shirt, tucked into equally well-worn jeans. As unmoving as a mountain. She'd lashed out at him because her first instinct had been to ask for his help. A few weeks ago, she wasn't even speaking to him—she couldn't afford to lean on anyone. *Stupid! Stupid!* It made sense to consider the possibility he was the perpetrator.

He whirled to face her. "Why would I suggest meeting you here today if I'd dumped poison in the river?"

"You tell me." Grace tried to stare through his glasses, a shiver trembling through her. "We don't have random acts of vandalism this far out of town."

"You're making me your prime suspect? That shows a remarkable lack of imagination, Grace."

Bees buzzed, a light breeze rifled the trees, high clouds swirled, tiny dots on a broad blue sky. Quiet enough to hear branches bumping each other. A perfect day, except for the malicious destruction beside the river and the chasm she'd opened between them. They stood silent, readying for a shootout at the O.K. Corral.

Ryan moved first, opening the toolbox on the bed of his truck.

"What are you doing?" Grace moved closer.

Leaning into the box, he extracted gloves, a trowel and two glass bottles before turning back towards the river.

"Shouldn't we wait for the cops?" She trailed behind him.

"It's a crime scene. They'll probably call for forensics, and we won't be able to cross the tape." He stopped short of the site.

"You're crossing 'the tape' now," she pointed out. Police forensics could take days to report on the contaminants. She didn't have days.

"We've had rain. I can't see any clear tracks from either direction." He donned the gloves, pulled the handkerchief over his face and walked a large circle around the site. "Stay back. No point in both of us inhaling this," he ordered when she made to follow. He approached from the river, his boots in water, then moved fast to scoop some of the contaminated dirt and some of the seeping liquid into the cylinders.

Screwing the tops closed, he retraced his steps. "Move." He drew her further away, dragged his handkerchief down and sucked in fresher air.

"Are you okay?"

"Thanks for asking." He gave a half smile, which was more than she deserved, given her knee-jerk accusation. "The police will send out a team and get it tested. We can do it faster. Take whatever remedial steps need to be taken." He handed her the precious vials and turned back to the vehicles. "They'll cut that siren when they turn onto the track." He returned the equipment to his toolbox.

Grace moved ahead as the police stepped from their flashing vehicle. "Hi, Bill, she addressed the senior cop. "I'm guessing you know Ryan."

"From way back." The officer grimaced as if he'd rather forget whatever happened "way back." "Morning, Ryan. This is Pete." He gestured to his off-sider. "What's happened, Grace?"

Donning her glasses, she led the police towards the river, the smell threatening to gag her with each step. Ryan followed more slowly. Her feet dragged as doubts about the justice of her accusation grew. They'd been talking about Danny. She'd stomped on the fragile friendship she'd been forging with Ryan with all the finesse of a herd of wildebeest. Ryan wouldn't do this. Insight cut through the noxious stench. Emotional closeness scared her, so she'd rather strike first than be hit from behind by the return swing of the gate.

"Looks like it was dumped from the other side." Bill raised an arm and pointed to the tracks they could see. "That's your place, isn't it, Ryan?"

Bill's readiness to cast blame made Grace wince. Her crossed arms and scowl when the cop had arrived hadn't helped. Blue Sky had been attacked for a reason, and the who as well as the why were critically important.

"You know damn well it's my place, Bill." Ryan sounded

annoyed rather than guilty. "I have drums like this in an unused shed. I haven't cleared all of them off the property yet."

"I imagine every farmer in a hundred-kilometre radius has some," Pete said neutrally.

"Is it yours?" Bill asked.

"You mean, did I dump it here? No." Ryan's voice stayed level, but tension radiated from him. "Is it part of my store? I did inventory before I locked the shed. It won't be that straightforward. My drums were empty when I locked them away."

"Anyone got access to the keys?"

"You know the drill, Bill. We keep a key board in the common area so whoever needs to collect something from a shed doesn't have to waste time." He shot a glance towards Grace. "I operate on trust with my team."

The words flicked Grace like a lash.

"Everyone has access," Bill noted. "Pete, can you tape the area?"

"It's not such a big stash anymore. I've been working my way through the backlog when I have time, getting the EPA to assess and recommend disposal. You're welcome to check before you start a larger search." Ryan's offer confirmed his innocence to Grace, and damn—maybe she should cut out her tongue. Ryan added, "It could help in identifying whatever it is, its age, maybe its toxicity."

"That's mighty cooperative of you." Bill's tone became more conciliatory.

"Drums labelled like some on my property. Dumped at the bottom of a lane leading from my place to the river. This was designed to implicate me in a malicious damage charge. Or at the least cause me major embarrassment," Ryan recited her assumptions.

"Designed to damage your relationship with the Andersons." Bill looked from one to the other, his interest roused. "Why would anyone do that?"

"I'm buying the farm," Grace said.

"I heard rumours." The cop studied her intently. "How widely is it known?"

"Hell!" Grace rolled her shoulders, remembering her little bit of self-promotion. The bush grapevine travelled at lightning speed. Add social media, and no secret was safe. "I gave a talk to the country women's association the other day. Anyone could put two and two together and get four."

She'd broadcast the news she needed money. She glanced at Ryan. His stance seemed to scream "about time."

"Could be the whole state knows." Bill grimaced. "I told my wife there'd be fallout from the new milk contracts."

A reasonable assumption, but not the truth, and in his folksy, low-key way, he was pushing for the truth. "They're selling because of Mum's health," she admitted.

"So, it must be sold, whatever the price?" Bill rubbed his chin, as if giving the idea serious consideration, his gaze straying to Ryan with a curiosity he didn't bother to mask.

Ryan stood hipshot beside her, seemingly calm, quiet. Rage was a fellow traveller to both of them, a constant companion since Danny's death. Ryan concealed his, while she exploded in messy rants. She could feel how tightly wound Ryan was, as if he'd whispered his frustration in her ear. Being so attuned to him was disconcerting in its intimacy. She'd hurt him with her instant suspicion.

"If I can't get the finance the farm goes on the open market." Not news she wanted to share, but Bill was studying cause and effect.

Bill let his gaze travel across the open space, the spiked drums, the nearby river, the buffer of trees. "Someone wants it on the open market."

"If you're looking for motive, I've made two offers for the property," Ryan interrupted. "I could have dumped this shit to cost Grace and her parents money they don't have to drive the price down. A nice addition to my spread—at the right price."

Grace's temper tantrum had fizzled out, leaving her miserably ashamed of herself. Whipping off her glasses, she faced Ryan, trying to communicate an apology without words.

"That would be out of character." Bill was laconic. "I know your mum. I know your history. I check the people who move into the district. Just enough to know if I need to keep an eye out. You don't even have a parking ticket." The last was said almost in disgust.

"Sorry to disappoint you." Some of the rigidity left Ryan.

"Any special reason why you're down here today?"

"Sheer luck," Grace blurted, struggling to make amends. "I invited Ryan to have a look at the poppies."

Bill looked from one to the other with new interest. "*Of course* you did."

"Rochelle Harkiss has also made offers." *And while an unlikely candidate herself, Rochelle did consort with unconvicted criminals like Smithhouse.* Grace edged closer to Ryan, branding him an ally.

"We'll keep this quiet. Make a few discreet inquiries." Bill nodded to the junior officer circling the dump site with police tape, a handkerchief over his mouth and nose. "I'll speak to Pete. You're close enough to town for others to have an eye on the property, developers, light industry. Anyone expressed interest in mining?"

"Over my dead body," Grace muttered.

"Are there more sites?" Bill asked.

"I checked a few hundred metres in both directions. Didn't find anything. This one's enough," Ryan answered.

"It's serious enough to threaten my organic certification." Grace shoved her hands inside her pockets. Rising fear was a cold shroud settling on her shoulders.

"Whoever did this took a risk." Bill scratched behind one ear, surveying the damage. "Has your property been unattended in the last few weeks, Ryan?"

"All my crew were at the field day."

"Mum and Dad only talked of selling on the Saturday night of that weekend." Grace baulked at the idea of premeditation.

"It's common knowledge your mum's been sick. Ella was up that weekend as well. She's been up more than usual lately. Could be people think it's because she wants to show off her baby? Could be people have been watching and adding up a number of coincidences?" Each new scenario Bill painted opened a Pandora's box of unknown evils.

"You're convinced they're linked?" Grace bit her lip. Her impulse reaction to blame Ryan had released the immediate rage. In a bizarre way accusing him made the problem manageable. "You think someone wants to force me out?"

"I've got a lot of thoughts. Most of which I'd rather keep to myself until we get a few facts to support them." Bill dragged out his investigator's notebook. "Got any CCTV at your place, Ryan?"

"Cameras to protect the new equipment I've bought." Light bounced off Ryan's glasses, and Grace desperately wanted to know what he was thinking, what he wasn't saying. "Nothing to pick up movements to the old shed."

"Checked the CCTV recently to see if they've been any unusual comings and goings?"

"Not for a few days. Satan lets me know if anyone's around at night. We haven't been disturbed." Ryan rubbed his chin. "To be honest, that's when I'd expect trouble if it was coming."

"Satan one of your crew?" Bill looked up from his notebook.

"You could say that." Ryan pointed to the dog beside him. "Meet Satan."

Bill surveyed the three-legged dog, and his eyebrows rose. "Check it out, and if you find anything, let me know. Somebody driving onto your place with an excuse ready if they're caught works. If they held on to the stuff for a rainy day, pardon the pun, then they didn't need to go back via your place but could have come in from this side. I'll need to ring your dad, Grace, to check a few things. The property's still in his name."

"Give me a few hours to tell him myself." Grace grabbed this new chance to make amends. "And let him know Ryan was here."

"I'll get forensics in as soon as I can. You'll want to know what it is." Bill signalled to Pete. "Let's head back."

"We took samples," Ryan volunteered, when they reached the police car. "We'd like to do some risk management today. Prevent it spreading further."

"I'll see what I can do." Bill climbed into his car. Pete slid into the driver's seat and they were gone.

"Bill didn't seem to be especially pleased to see you on arrival." Grace followed the police car with her gaze until the dust settled.

Ryan adjusted his hat. "As he said, there's a history."

She couldn't remember any stories of Ryan being picked up by the police as a teenager. He'd been too busy at his own farm or Donovan's to mix with a wild crowd. "And it's none of my business."

"That's right."

"You know more about my finances than anyone else!" *A pathetic excuse, Grace.*

"If that's an apology, it needs a lot of work!" he grunted. "More sleep might help you think straight." He started walking towards his vehicle.

"What's my sleep got to do with this?" She ran beside him.

"Lack of sleep is the kindest way to describe your muddled thinking. Nothing's private in this community. Before you got home from the country women's association they'd probably figured out your mum's health is driving the sale, calculated the value of the land and farm income and your worth. Their husbands are probably running a book on whether you'll get the loan. It's pub gossip every time I've entered a bar."

She grabbed his arm. "You're saying this is deliberate sabotage to force me out!"

"That's Bill's theory." He shook off her hand. "Don't

get pissy with me, Grace. Because if I'm not guilty, the field is wide open."

She scampered to catch up, her mouth dry and her heart pounding. "I know you didn't do it."

"You a clairvoyant now?"

"It makes no sense." She'd known in her bones before the cops arrived, but her growing reliance on him terrified her. "I've seen what you've done with your land. Poisoning the water hurts both of us. And poisoning land you want to buy is even stupider."

"But, gee, it would drive the price down," he said snidely. "Old Let Her Rip Gracie. Do you always make the nearest bystander your punching bag?"

"Nobody calls me that anymore." She'd largely outgrown her rash outbursts. Ryan stirred her in ways she couldn't explain. "Bystanders aren't usually caught in the crosshairs. Your strong-silent-type act throws me off my stride." Her sarcasm fell flat. "I was wrong."

"And then some."

"You seem to have a problem accepting apologies." She shuffled from foot to foot. *Did his milder tone mean he'd forgiven her?*

"You're suspicious of everything I do. But"—Satan stuck to Ryan's side, his loyalty clear—"I might suspect me if I was in your position right now."

"I'd have a right to suspect you if everything you said wasn't true. You did bring me here today. Otherwise I might not have come for weeks, and the damage could have been irreversible."

"Took you long enough to work that out."

"Do you want me to grovel?" She eyed his back mutinously.

"The idea has possibilities." He halted at his Ute and swung around to face her. "I want this land healthy as much as you do, Grace." Strength and purpose radiated off him.

Grace remembered. He'd looked poleaxed when she'd told him about Danny's memorial. He'd traced a finger over the fragile petals of a poppy. She'd held her breath imaging those rough, sensitive fingers on her, and the deep drag of that yearning had wiped her mind clear. Sensing she'd be powerless to resist his touch had primed her to attack.

"I know someone at the University who'll do the tests fast."

"Thank you." She accepted this one offer, a necessary part of her apology. Being unfair to anyone was a criminal offence in her family. "Blaming you was a distraction from thinking about who did this." Self-preservation demanded she keep her protective barriers in place. *He was leaving. She was staying.* Still, she made the admission. "An unknown enemy is scarier."

"You could ask Bill to organise drive-bys?" His voice gentled. "We can hire someone to stay at the house?" He understood she was afraid.

"I'll up the security around the buildings." Grace huffed out the breath caught in her throat by his concern. Folding at the first challenge to her ownership would permanently weaken her. "I'll do more spot checks across the property, but I appreciate the offer. Bill knows his job." Although he hadn't been able to charge Smithhouse with a crime.

"Your call." Ryan accepted her decision with a nod. "We need to contain it. A mix of sand and sawdust as a temporary cover, with a trench dug around it."

"I'll organise it," Grace stated.

"*We'll* organise it. Bluey can help me." The damn man was back to organising her.

"My land, my responsibility." She straightened her spine.

"You should get that tattooed on your butt."

"How do you know it isn't?" Grace whipped back, sparring with Ryan beat trembling with fear.

"I can't wait to see."

"When hell freezes over." *Had she really said that?*

The corner of his mouth tipped up. "We both know that's a lie." He surveyed the site critically. "Sand and sawdust will work as a neutralising agent to start. I'll bring a truckload through my place."

"Thank you . . ." She couldn't refuse this act of kindness without looking churlish. "Again."

"Later, we'll need specialist removal. They can come and go through my place. Reduce the chance of more damage to your land."

"How do you manage to turn things around so I look like a bad-tempered shrew and you look like a friendly neighbour?" He was new territory for Grace. Her blood quickened when she was near him. Her instinct was to lean on him, lean into him, absorb the scent of him through her pores, surround herself with the heat of him, because that's all she'd have when he sold up and moved away.

"You've had a shock. A bit of shrewishness is forgivable." He shrugged.

"That's very reasonable of you."

"It is, isn't it?" His chin wobbled—he'd almost chuckled. "If there's any connection between this stuff and my place, it's fair I deal with it." Anthony Callea's cover version of *Wake Me Up Before You Go-Go* interrupted him. "Interesting ringtone, Grace. Better get your phone."

"Bill." She listened, then ended the call.

"Forensics are on their way. We should be able to do basic clean-up in a few hours."

"'You put the boom-boom into my heart?' Really?" he patted his heart in time with the lyrics.

"If you must know"—she tipped down her glasses—"it was a joke with Dad. Payback for long mornings of classical music in the milking barn."

"My offer stands. This slice of land gives me access to extra water from both sides, and another exit directly to the main road. You've invested in its health. That makes it very attractive to me. My land has years before it reaches the same level, and some of it may never get there because of past land practices."

Ryan was matter-of-fact, quick to act, turning a catastrophe into an inconvenience they'd handle together.

The easy mingling of their interests became terrifyingly natural with repetition.

"I'll call the organic certifying body while I collect my protective gear." She pushed her glasses back up her nose. *Accepting help is not dependence.*

He caught her hand, turned it over and pressed a kiss into her palm. "Thank you for telling me about Danny."

The tremble travelled to her toes. "Will *you* tell me about Danny?"

"Maybe." Ryan tugged her closer.

"I have to go." She needed some space to work out what was happening to her. Madness, to want him to hold her. To allow herself to believe she'd find comfort as well as heat in his embrace.

"What about my offer?"

Her mind shot back to that other time when they'd been standing close together, when his offer of a quick tumble had amused and tempted her. To the alley, when his kisses had sapped any sense of self-preservation. With an effort, she returned to the present. "I need time to think about it."

He lifted his free hand and rubbed her brow. "You're frowning." Then he dropped his hand, as if he knew his touch addled her thinking. "How much time do you need?"

Never. Forever. There'd never be a time when she would be comfortable or ready to sell part of her heritage. Twenty-five percent deposit meant she no longer had that luxury. Sometimes you had to cut off a limb to save the animal, as he had for Satan. Only a coward delayed that decision. She stood straighter. She wouldn't let a cowardly attack cheat her out of her birthright. "Come to my place for dinner tonight."

"I'm happy to take you out."

"If we eat at my place, I don't have to travel and can kick you out early," she said. His mouth twitched at her awkward invitation. Having to make another apology annoyed her. "I could have phrased that better."

The bastard grinned. "I understand. You need your

beauty sleep."

She needed sleep to survive. Leaning against the cows in the dark milking shed, she dreamed of sleep. Some nights she considered skipping meals to get extra shut-eye. She had sense enough to know that was lunacy. "We're not dating."

"Of course not." He said so smoothly she wanted to slap him.

She jerked open the door to her Ute.

"Although the buzz is getting louder." His murmur was velvety dark and deliciously wicked.

"Six-thirty," she called over her shoulder. Her heart rate steadied as the short distance between them grew. Despite these last few weeks, Ryan remained an enigma. A brainteaser of a problem in very human form.

Buying her cheese was supporting local businesses and building community. Every landowner, producer and retail operator benefitted from a stronger community.

Engineering business referrals, even lobbying for her inclusion at the field day fit in the same category. Paying his debt to her father was honourable.

Giving her Bluey was personal.

Letting him pay for the clean-up would be crossing a line she'd drawn in the sand of her personal independence. Ryan's latest offers were personal in a whole different way; she was seriously considering accepting help from him. Like dancing on a tightrope without a net, the sensation was simultaneously exhilarating and terrifying. The prize was living her dream. The risk was losing the entire property. She had a piece of land Ryan wanted, and that's how she'd approach negotiations. She wasn't a supplicant or a freeloader and wouldn't be treated that way. She wasn't a taker either. She paid her own way.

Who was she kidding? She was only considering doing business with someone outside the family because the outsider was Ryan. She needed him more than he needed her.

Accepting help is not dependence. Maybe she should get that tattooed on her butt.

She buckled herself into the driver's seat before checking the side mirror. He stood beside his vehicle, watching her, as if he sensed her watching him. He exuded a sense of leashed power. Yet his movements were loose, unhurried. Snapping on the ignition, she pulled back onto the laneway, taking a last look in the rearview mirror. He hadn't moved and now dipped his hat, an old-fashioned gesture reminding her she was a woman. His mouth fascinated her, and his eyes. He'd have to ditch his glasses for dinner.

CHAPTER NINE

Headlights hitting the main farmhouse then turning off to the left, a dying engine, a car door slamming—Ryan announced his arrival for dinner even before her mother's old dog, Bailey, a permanent fixture on the back veranda, barked in welcome. Wanting to keep the heat inside, Grace opened the laundry door. Ryan held a bottle of wine in one hand and a box in the other. Satan and Bailey had finished sniffing each other, circling and remembering they'd met before. Satan pushed forward to nuzzle Grace's hand.

"Hello, darling," she crooned before eyeing the bottle suspiciously.

"You don't have to drink it"—Ryan handed her the bottle—"*darling*."

"We're eating in the kitchen." She turned and led him through the laundry, his husky endearment sending her nerves into a jig.

"That's put me in my place."

"I was living at Grandma and Grandpa's old house but moved across here this afternoon. I thought the family kitchen was the best place for a business transaction between maybe-friends, one of whom has brought a dog to dinner." She opened the kitchen door, and the temperature climbed several degrees, enveloping them in its warm, fragrant air. Pointing to a blanket in front of the fuel stove, she smiled when Satan obediently walked in a circle then curled up.

"Smells good." He sniffed appreciatively while his eyes travelled around the room. "I remember the chairs." He sounded delighted. "Your parents talked endlessly about their plans to renovate them."

"Work and a growing fondness for their battered state kyboshed those." She placed the bottle of pinot on the table. "Would you like a beer to start?"

"That'd be great. This room hasn't changed much at all." He crossed to the large sideboard backing onto the hall's wall and ran a respectful hand over its red timber. "Always loved this piece."

"The cedar came from the valley," she said, topping a beer and handing him the bottle and a cold glass. "You must have heard Grandpa's stories about the old timber cutters."

"I loved them. Rare to find a piece like this today. It's a good history to have, Grace. Are you going to join me in a drink?" he asked curiously.

"With dinner. If I have a drink now, I might pass out."

"That would be a pity." His deep growl told her whatever happened between them, he wanted her to be fully awake and aware.

Her body jangled with anticipation. He wasn't wearing glasses. That didn't give her the advantage she'd hoped for. His eyes, a dark chestnut in this light, studied her with a slow patience, making her body ache for his touch. She'd already been primed. Standing naked in the shower earlier, goose bumps had spread across her body imagining his broad shoulders and solid chest a short metre across from her at her kitchen table. She'd shivered, not from the cold. Now she swallowed a groan. "What's in the box?"

He set his beer on the table and lifted the lid. "A rhubarb and strawberry pie."

She peered into the box, then lifted her gaze to his. "A

Bess Riley award-winning pie?"

He nodded.

"Do I have to kiss your feet in gratitude?"

He pointed to his cheek, and she inched towards him, caught by the twinkle in his eye, the "I dare you" cockiness of his stance. She leaned in, planted a kiss on his cheek and quickly withdrew.

"You need practice." He settled his hands on her hips and eased her forward, pressing his cheek to hers. "I like your perfume. It reminds me of Sweet Peas. Mostly Mum grew vegetables, but she had a fondness for Sweet Peas."

"I remember them." She turned her head, and his lips met hers. A different texture to the smooth skin of his cheek, to the working man's thumb pad drawing circles under her ear, to the woven cotton covering his forearms where her hands gripped him. His lips were firm, knowing and seduced as they touched, coaxing her mouth to open. When his tongue teased across her bottom lip, she was afraid the sobbing moan echoing in the kitchen was her own. Then she surrendered to mindless pleasure and a dragging need at the apex of her thighs. Straining to get closer, she locked her hands behind his neck, feasting on his kisses with a craving only his taste could satisfy.

The timer on the oven shrilly demanded attention. He released her, and she struggled to focus. He was breathing as heavily as she was. She backed away, her hand against her mouth, while her pulse skittered. "That's d-d-dinner. S-s-sit," she stammered.

She'd set the table earlier and only needed to transfer the casserole from the oven to a heat mat on the table. *Hell's bells, Grace. It was only a kiss.*

"You'll need potholders." He stepped to her side, his hands already encased in the insulated gloves. "Let me."

More potent than their first kiss, and she hadn't considered a second kiss could taste better. "I'll get the bread." She slid the hot, crusty bread into a basket and set it beside the casserole.

"If it's any help, you pack a powerful punch, Grace."

She sank into the chair opposite him, tucking her legs under it, conscious that the slightest movement could tangle her legs with his. "You're"—she searched for a word—"unexpected."

His rare smile appeared. "But worth the effort."

She didn't know if he was talking about himself or her. Wriggling in her chair, desire was a ticking time bomb, and she hadn't been prepared for its speed or power. She hesitated to start anything until she'd resolved their business relationship. For a woman who didn't do partnerships, she was caught between physical attraction and an offer to trade, both of which had the potential to blow up in her face.

"I cheated," she confessed. "I made the casserole and bread weeks ago. Tonight, I defrosted."

"Smells great." He opened the bottle and poured two glasses. "I appreciate the effort."

For a while they ate companionably, the country music playing low in the background enough to keep the conversation ticking over as they talked about performers they liked.

"Troy Cassar-Daley did a gig in Lismore about three years ago. At the pub. Ella and Jake came home for the weekend. Brilliant to see him live."

The player flipped to a new track. "Garth Brooks keeps hinting he'll come to Australia," Ryan commented.

"Hinting isn't doing." She sighed. "Dessert?"

"The pie's a present. You can eat it instead of breakfast to get your energy levels up."

"Don't joke. I just might." She yawned. "Coffee or another drink?"

"I should be leaving." He poured himself a thimbleful more wine. "Any decision on my offer?"

"Why did Bill treat you as if you were something stuck to the bottom of his shoe when he first arrived?" She was procrastinating, delaying Ryan's departure when she should have been saying, "See you later."

"You noticed." He leaned back in the chair.

"Hard to miss." She allowed herself another small sip of her half-glass of his very fine wine.

"I asked my question first."

"What exactly is your offer?"

"This is your decision, Grace." He held his hands up in surrender. "You have control." A generous assessment when he knew the contours of her dilemma.

"Control within an increasingly smaller square, where every day my options are more limited." She voiced her frustration because any deal would only work if there was truth between them. "It's like severing a limb, to think of the farm being subdivided. It's not just land for me."

"I can walk away." He swirled the remaining wine in his glass, his gaze on her. "Or you can nominate a different piece of land."

Terrifying to discover she didn't want him to walk away, that she'd miss the friendship they were starting to establish as well as the buzz. Yet leaving was his long-term plan. "That's the most logical acreage for you to buy."

"Is that a no?" he asked quietly.

Their voices had dropped, the dark crowded the windows, although stars would light the sky, and the moon would rise later in the evening. A confidential conversation with the potential to change her world.

"I won't lose this farm, Ryan, even if I need to sell part of it to keep it." She took the biggest risk of her life. "I'd rather do business with you than anyone else in the offing."

"Are you sure your nose didn't grow when you said that?"

She kicked him under the table.

"Ah, a genuine compliment, Ms. Anderson." He pressed both hands to his chest. "Be still, my beating heart."

"Put your offer in writing, and I'll consider it." She was ninety percent sure she'd accept his offer. He was teasing rather than triumphant, but she'd read every word.

"Back to the hard-headed businesswoman." There was

no sting in his comment.

"Once bitten, twice shy. Now, spill it," she said.

He didn't pretend not to understand. "I'll make it short and take no questions. Bill found me and his very luscious daughter in a compromising position in his Ute in their backyard one night."

His unexpected confession made her giggle. "Define compromising."

* * *

Ryan let the carefree sound trickle down his spine. "I'll leave it to your imagination. Unless you'd prefer a demonstration."

Her gaze softened, and a blush heated her cheeks—tell-tale signs she was recalling their kisses—the brutal intimacy of them, the tingling awareness sparking between them whenever he touched her.

"The buzzing's getting awfully loud." Ryan reached for her hand.

"That means it's time to go."

"Spoilsport." When he wanted to sink into her, let himself be seduced by her scent so there was only her. "I want more of you." And knew she was as curious as he was. That behind the curiosity was affection and respect, which sharpened the edge of his need.

"Definitely time to go." She pushed back from the table.

"Let me help you clean up."

"You've already stacked the dishwasher." She held up a hand as Ryan came around to her side of the table.

"I didn't get to interview you the other night. I'll pay you for advice on land management. Wasn't that your offer?" And for Ryan, an excuse to see more of her. To help her, to check she wasn't working herself to the bone. Updates from Bluey weren't enough. Repaying her father wasn't enough. It wasn't personal. Well, only a bit personal in that it saved her work and money. And his interest in Grace was becoming very personal.

"You were right. I gave the information to Mr. Donovan for free."

"But you *liked* Mr. Donovan." Provoking her now that they were on kissing terms was more fun than he'd imagined.

"If you're angling for me to say I like you …"

"I'll settle for the buzz at this stage." He enjoyed the flush turning her throat a soft pink. "Although we could celebrate reaching a deal." He drew her to her feet and nibbled her fingers.

* * *

"Not there yet." Grace led the way back through the house, stopping at the back door, her hand on the doorknob.

His eyes gleamed with a question Grace recognised, an invitation to mate. She'd enjoyed his banter at dinner, the sensation of him dancing around her without touching, of touching with a look, a caress as real as if his blunt fingers had traced her cheek. He made anticipation exciting, but she wanted more of his kisses before he left tonight. Wanted to test if she could control her runaway attraction to him.

"I like what happens when we get close." He stepped closer until their clothes brushed against each other, and the knowledge there was flesh and blood beneath the fabric incited a riot of sensations. She wanted to grab and hold.

Her heart pounded. "The alley was adrenalin, a whiff of danger."

The memory remained vivid, and Grace couldn't blame it all on the wave of hot air buffeting her as the car sped past, the roar of engine and screech of brakes as the car spun, releasing the acrid smoke of burning rubber. Her face had been buried in his chest. Solid, unmoving, a shield between her and danger. His scent had surrounded her then, woven into the memory along with the pounding of his heart, then the smooth skin of his cheek.

What had made him escalate that kiss?

Then the taste of him. Not a man who fumbled with anything. His kiss had been as confident and as elusive as the man himself.

"And the kitchen?" he growled.

"Pent-up lust," she confessed. If the stove timer hadn't shrieked incessantly, they might be in her bed now. Her cautious soul was a few steps behind.

"Works for me." He placed his hands on either side of her, caging her against the door. "You're a dangerous woman."

She cocked her head to one side. "Been talking to Billy Brown?" When he stared at her mouth as if he'd like a bite, her knees buckled. "Kneed him in the groin when he tried to help himself without invitation."

"Invite me." He angled his head and leaned closer until his mouth was a whisper from hers. "Invite me."

"What the hell!" She reached a hand behind his head and closed the gap, making her answer clear. Better again this time. A different whip of danger. The taste of him was sharp and mysterious, like the man. A hum started low in her belly. She'd like hours to unravel the mystery and the man. Maybe days. She lifted her other arm to cup his face. "Yes."

Settling her more firmly against his body, he deepened the kiss, his hands holding her face, his fingertips pressed lightly against her cheeks. A gentle touch she hadn't anticipated from him, and more compelling than if he'd pounced. She liked his taste. A complex man, and she'd always liked riddles. He drew back first. She stayed at the back door until he drove away.

Grace sipped her second cup of coffee the following morning. A personal indulgence—fifteen minutes and a long black after milking, cleaning and breakfast to order her thoughts and mentally review her list of the day's activities.

The first hit of caffeine was necessary to get her brain and her body moving when she rolled out of bed at four; a chemical prod to keep her eyes open and her wits about her around large, unpredictable bovines.

Now, she closed them, letting the aromatic scent and roasty-sweet flavour of her preferred blend roll through her system, concentrating her energy. Mrs. Wilson had baked raisin bread this morning. Grace and Danny had stuffed themselves on it from the time Grace had been old enough to sit at a table. They'd picked out the raisins and eaten them first, reaching for the next slice.

She could picture Ryan's reaction even now. When Danny had reached for Ryan's slice, Ryan had bent over the table, elbows wide, protecting his property. *"Picking at your food is gross."* His grin had been evil, splitting his face from ear to ear. A laugh bubbled in her throat. She'd coaxed a few half grins from him recently. She'd developed a taste for more.

With the ping of incoming mail, her focus shifted from being a farmer to cheese-maker and businesswoman. The address was unfamiliar, *leinadfarms*. It tugged on some half-remembered story. Ryan opened with a brief greeting. The attachment contained the detail of his offer along with his lawyer's contact details and the insistence she pass it to Jake for closer analysis. On a first read, Ryan's offer was clear, simple and the answer to her prayers. *Could buying the farm really be this simple?* Stunned, she slumped back in her chair.

The landline trilled loudly enough to be heard two paddocks away. "Dad, I was planning to call you."

"When?" His purring-engine voice, scepticism wrapped in care, had always been able to get her to confess.

"When I had better news." She glanced at the open screen, where the numbers danced with possibilities. Ryan's offer made it hard to deny her family's collective judgement he was a straight shooter. She liked his directness. In business. *When he had his hands on her.* Her tongue traced her lower lip, searching to see if Ryan's taste lingered. "Sorry, I missed that."

"I called Officer Bill earlier. He's got some ideas, but he's not sharing. What does Ryan think?"

That I need more sleep.

That the buzz between us is getting louder.

That I'm a dangerous woman. He made her feel like a sexy, powerful and dangerous woman. She sighed.

"Did you say something, Grace?" Her father's hearing was acute, his perception even sharper.

She dragged her attention back to her problem. "Ryan agrees someone is trying to price me out of the market." Outside the kitchen window, the farm buildings gave way to open fields. Gentle hills flanked her western side, rolling down to the river and shrouded in trees. Contamination was another kind of swindle. Never again! "We won't sell this farm to a cheat or a thief."

Her father let her outburst crackle across the distance between them, then settle. "Anything else?" Her father's support hummed through the line. Brian Anderson could almost be in the room with her, savouring his second cup of coffee, letting long silences bleed into plans. "Spit it out."

"You're drinking coffee." A lump rose in her throat.

"Aren't you?" His mug thumped on a table hundreds of kilometres away.

"Ryan's offering to buy a stretch of land, bounded by the river at the north end and the town road at the south—"

"Where the spill is?" her father interrupted. He'd worked it out. "That's why he was with you yesterday."

"Yes." She waited for his verdict.

"Has he put a dollar price on the offer?"

She named the generous price. "His offer will cover the deposit without exhausting all my savings." A lifeline given no amount of creative accounting could lift her savings from ten to twenty-five percent of the farm's value.

He whistled. "What do you think?"

"It's your land, Dad." Tears stung her eyes. She missed working alongside him, ached to turn back time.

"We're selling to you." Relief was woven through his gruff response. "What you do is your decision. Jake can look at the legals for you if you're concerned."

"Ryan's already told me to send the offer to Jake and given me his lawyer's name." She'd asked for his offer in writing. His response was an invitation for her to have it sliced and diced by her highly competent lawyer brother-in-law to check for flaws.

"Don't keep me in suspense," her father nudged. "What are you thinking?"

"That my options are limited." Her options were vanishingly small. "The extra cash will guarantee the bank approves the loan."

"Ryan knows you're considering it?"

She nodded, then remembered her father couldn't see her. "He knows."

"Your mother will be thrilled. Keep in touch." Her father's voice was lighter than it had been at the start of the call. She owed Ryan for easing her father's anxieties.

She stared out the window. Ryan was an unlikely fairy godmother, but her body felt looser this morning than yesterday. Muscles, tight as steel ropes since her parents' announcement, slackened. A lightness of being. She'd heard the same edge of hope in her father's voice. She pressed her hands to her mouth to hold back the shout of relief. She could dream again. Not over, but possible. A shiver of excitement rippled from head to toe, and she laughed in growing delight.

On the point of closing and forwarding the document to Jake, her eyes were drawn back to the heading at the top of the page. The email address leinadfarms@ appeared under the business name Leinad Enterprises. The words danced on the page. Danny had shared her love of word games, and they'd played with their own names.

They made race, ace, ear, crag from the letters in Grace.

Nail, dean and lead from Daniel.

Leinad was Daniel spelled backwards. "I'll be damned!"

Leinad Enterprises wasn't a coincidence. Ryan had named his business after his brother, and no one had told her. Or more probably, no one had twigged to the trick Ryan had played. He'd channelled his ferocious grief for his brother into a business bearing his brother's name.

"He won't thank you for bringing it up," she said to herself.

A private man. A private grief. He'd always hated the stares and whispers so common to small country towns. He'd especially hated the viciousness reserved for anyone who was different—like his brother. He'd cut all ties. She understood better now the different shades of grief, the different ways people dealt with it. None better, none worse, just different. Ryan had had to lock his down to survive.

The last time she'd seen the brothers together, they'd been walking away from her. Ryan had reached out and wrapped an arm around his brother's neck and hauled him close. Danny was dancing around, swinging his fists and trying to break away. Ryan was stronger. Then Ryan had leaned across and kissed his brother on the top of the head.

She'd forgotten that. More likely buried it in the turbulent sea of emotions and memories she'd been drowning in. It wasn't the first time she'd seen Ryan kiss his younger brother. In the roughhouse, adolescent world they'd shared it was unusual. Most parents stopped kissing their sons when they graduated primary school, and kissing teenage brothers was unheard of.

No, he wouldn't thank her for bringing it up. His loyalty shifted something in her. She had no future with Ryan, but they could have now. A buzz, he called the spark between them. She'd claimed it was an itch. Describing this sensation as a physical compulsion diminished it. For her, it was a brightness, a shine to the day. She'd catch herself grinning at the cows for no reason, giggling when she unloaded the van and laughing like a loon when she chased those dammed chickens into their roost. Thinking of Ryan made her pulse quicken and her breathing come in short bursts.

When she was in his arms, her mind overflowed with him.

Like the slow reveal in a striptease, Ryan had given her pieces of the story about why he'd left after Danny died. This puzzle piece told her more about who Ryan was. Forced to be a loner. He'd opened the door a crack for her. She was giddy knowing he was within reach. Knowing she could make the first move.

A secret smile made her mouth curve. *He wouldn't say no.*

His masculinity was too ingrained, his confidence in the man he'd become too unshakeable to be threatened by her making the first move—touching him before he touched her—because she'd only be a split second ahead of him. She liked the smell of him, the feel of his big body against hers, the hum of his presence. She'd raise his buzz to a roar and to hell with the consequences. Skin to skin, flesh sliding over flesh, they didn't need words to communicate.

The day dragged. Grace went through the motions of checking on orders, preparing the makings for her soft cheeses and checking and dispatching stock. The sun bled into the clouds, the orangey-pink light streaking across the sky promised another sparkling spring day on the morrow. Waving to Bluey from the doorway, she'd turned for the bathroom before the farmhand was out of sight, kicking off her boots, shucking clothes as she made her way down the hall to the shower.

Time to stop lying to herself. She climbed into her Ute, her nerves a mass of popping corn, a cascade of tiny joyful explosions. His proposition was a no-holds-barred, all-out affair. He rejected the ties that bound you—to people and places. She'd found her centre in this land.

He was leaving town. She was staying. No strings attached. No crying foul when he walked away. Knowing the rules, she'd handle his leaving better this time—she was sure of it. Besides, she had the power to walk away first.

CHAPTER TEN

Liquid pooled in Grace's pelvis when he opened the door. She'd had to wait a few minutes, and his arrival explained why. Faded jeans—hastily pulled on—were slung low on his hips with the top button undone. Drops of water beaded his chest, drawing her eyes to his impressive pecs. His feet were bare. He was rubbing a towel over his head. Wet—his hair was darker than usual and clustered with curls. A rough-towelled Satan shadowed him.

She pointed at the dog. "Does he shower with you?"

"He needs a bath every so often." He shrugged, and she stifled a groan seeing his shoulder muscles ripple. "The kitchen's warm. I'll get a shirt." He turned to walk away.

Reaching out a hand, she touched his shoulder. He stilled on an indrawn breath. Damp, but warm, firm, but supple under her fingers. "You don't need a shirt," she whispered, tracing an S-shape down his spine, the pads of her fingers skimming his skin, flipping her from tormentor to tormented.

He spun around, caging her between him and the wall, his hands hauling her closer while his mouth devoured her. No hesitation. A demand and a response. Excitement streaked through her and a burst of power at the speed with which she'd flicked the switch to passion. Her hands moved into his hair, dragging him closer, her body moving into his because any space between them was sheer hell. Letting her head fall back, she opened her mouth to his. Their tongues danced in a game as old as time and as new as their mating.

"Lemon. I can smell lemon." She needed air.

"Soap. Mum left it." He swallowed her moan. This kiss was slower, more intimate. His hands caressed her breasts through her cheesecloth shirt, then skated down her flanks to coax her closer. Her blood heated where he touched, and her heart soared at his welcome. He reached for the button on her jeans. A practised flick of his thumb and forefinger and his hand was inching its way down the front of her jeans. Flat, warm, seeking—it splayed out across her belly. "You're wearing more clothes than me." His hand pressed and retreated, advanced and withdrew.

She cried out, meeting the blaze in his eyes. "I want you naked," she panted, holding on to his forearms to remain upright.

"Deal," he growled. His finger had reached her centre, and the on-again, off-again pressure was pounding through her. Her body contracted involuntarily against his hand.

"We can skip the foreplay," she faltered.

"I want to play." His chest was heaving, but his fingers retreated.

"More," she begged.

"Not that fast, Grace." He freed his hand and scooped her up. "Not that easy. I've been imagining this for weeks."

"I'm more impatient than you." She looped a hand around his neck, needing the contact.

"Generally, yeah." He grinned, and his hands cupped her bottom before he hoisted her over his shoulder. "In this. I'd say we're evenly matched."

She anchored her hands on his hips, glorying in this moment of feminine weakness. "Where are we going?"

He kicked the door to his bedroom open. Bending forward, he let her feet find the ground, trailing his hands up her sides as she stood upright. "Somewhere where you can have your wicked way with me."

"You make me feel wicked." *And happy*. Grace lifted her leg to rub her thigh against the outside of his leg, while she leaned against him. Satan circled them. "You really are inseparable."

"Satan. Kitchen." The dog reluctantly left the room. Ryan nuzzled her throat, and her leg dropped bonelessly to the ground.

"Sweet Peas, a hint of soap, and the scent of woman." He unhooked the top button on her shirt, his gaze holding hers, then slipped each button in turn, his knuckles skimming her torso. "What took you so long?"

"I had to separate business and pleasure in my mind."

They both knew that was shorthand. Business was accepting that his offer for the poppy fields wasn't entrapment. Pleasure was admitting she was here now because she fancied him like hell and trusted him as a lover.

"All sorted?" His white-knuckled grip on her lapels eased.

She nodded.

Holding her shirt wide, he stared at her full breasts, presented in white cotton edged with lace.

"What you see is what you get." She twisted her hands together, suddenly nervous under his intense study. His avid eyes made her wish she had sexier lingerie and the kind of lithe body gracing catwalks across the world.

"What I see is pure woman." He stroked the back of his hand down her cheek, across one breast, where the nipple tightened in response to his touch. "Never apologise for who you are, Grace. You're beautiful."

An impossibly romantic declaration from a man of few words. A caress to her confidence. It was why she'd kissed him in the dark alley. A kiss spinning into this unexpected adventure. His lips had been devastatingly sure when they'd covered hers. His kisses in her kitchen had been purely addictive. Each time she'd wanted more, which was why she'd drawn back. *Why she was here.*

Tonight wasn't supposed to be about romance, and so she buried the fancy, blaming the chemicals flooding her system for tripping her heart. Slipping her hands inside his jeans and over his backside, she rocked against him to shift her mood. "I like your welcome."

He let her lead, matching her urgency. With her mouth fused to his, she caught hold of his zipper, dragging it down, squirming in her rush to get him out of his jeans. In response, he freed her breasts, filling his hands with her. The glide of his palms over her nipples was an exquisite distraction. She moaned, her hands fisting in the denim. He backed her onto the bed, levered her boots off and tossed them over his shoulder, where they landed with a satisfying clunk in the corner.

"Your skin's smooth," he whispered between her breasts. "Wonderfully soft." He licked the underside of one breast. "You taste like candied honey. I want to touch you all the time," he murmured encouragement. Her skin tingled, and her body ached with need.

"No," she protested when he rolled off the bed, any separation a shocking loss.

Hooking his hands into the waist of his boxers, he pushed them and his jeans off. Naked, he was as self-confident as her prize bull, and desire washed through her.

"Me too." She reached for her jeans.

"Let me," he purred. She scooted backward on the mattress, and he stretched out beside her, warming her with his gaze. Still, he didn't touch her, and his delay changed the tempo from hip-hop to waltz—a step, slide, embrace. She read admiration and desire in his look, appreciation more than greed, and she trembled. He unbuckled her belt, dragging it through the loops inch by slow inch. With it discarded, he tugged her jeans down, the friction of the old denim a soft torment. Her shirt followed. Still, he dallied, tenderness joining romance in his touch, and her body ached for his possession.

She hadn't expected a slow love-making and was confused by his actions.

"I'm ready." Her mouth was dry, but she was wet where she wanted him.

His finger brushed across an erect nipple, and she shivered. "Cold?" he asked.

She pressed his hand between her legs. "What do you think?"

Skimming a thumb across the damp gusset, he released a shaky breath. "Better get these off." He stripped them away and reached into the bedside table for protection.

Who knew Ryan Wilson could make the practical donning of a condom sensual? Watching his strong working man's hands roll the sheath over his erection held her spellbound. Any man who took precautions into his own hands was a man who understood respect. Ryan lifted her hand and rubbed it over his cock.

"What do you think of the fit?" His voice was sinful.

"Perfect." She squeezed gently, and he jerked under her hand, his face a rictus of control.

For her.

Her sexy, practical lover rolled until she straddled him, gazing at her through a daze of desire and—joy. Wriggling into a more comfortable position, she waited for his groan when she brushed herself against him. She leaned forward, her breasts brushing his chest, borrowing some of his patience to tantalise. He was letting her make the moves, and the power made her giddy. With her face pressed to his chest, she absorbed the sensations of firmness and strength, inhaled the tart scent of lemon, and listened for his heartbeat. Racing, but steady and true. She turned her head to sink into another delicious kiss.

His hands were everywhere, exploring her curves, lingering at her waist, fondling her hips, sliding around to squeeze her backside. The tempo shifted again, becoming as urgent as the blood pounding in her temples.

"My turn." He flipped her onto her back and crouched

over her. He was panting but took the time to string butterfly kisses down her body. When he suckled her breasts, the pull reverberated in her core, making her yearn.

"Now," she cried out.

His fingers threaded through her pubic hair, to stroke and pull gently, arousing her further. Jerking upright, she fisted her hands in his damp locks. "No Sweet Peas here. Just pure woman," he whispered. He loved her with his mouth, a rhythm building to a crescendo, demanding she be the first to surrender to pleasure—a lover's gift.

While Grace shuddered through her release, he slid up her body and entered her, holding her gaze as he built the pace. Her body, matching his speed, meeting his need, was slick with sweat. Her cry erupted a split second before his. His head dropped to the pillow beside her, his weight on her solid and reassuringly close. Awash with I-think-I'm-in-heaven chemicals, her body melted like ice cream around him. She was relaxed, floating on a cloud of intimacy that couldn't be undone. Her brain exploded—a ball set loose in a pinball machine bouncing off every target. She hadn't fathomed the risk she was taking. Uh-oh!

"This doesn't mean anything." She rushed to deny the tenderness swamping her. She hadn't bargained on this dazed sense of oneness with Ryan.

"That's a crazy thing to say." He rolled off her and lounged on his elbow to study her.

"Okay." She sucked in air and let it out slowly, bringing her gaze from the ceiling to his face. His smile was secret—and satisfied—and simply happy. A warm glow of triumph enveloped her, but he'd stated the rules for this encounter. *He was leaving.*

This wasn't supposed to be about love. Lust, with care as a bonus.

"It means we're attracted," she decoded. "We wanted to find out what it was like to be together."

"What was it like?" He leaned there, relaxed with his nakedness in a way she found ridiculously appealing, his smile curving his mouth and proclaiming he was at peace with his world.

She couldn't resist smiling back, tracing his lips with a finger. "Good."

"Good!" He ran his palm across her nipple, and it stood to attention. "I can't have been trying."

She let out a half laugh. Crazy to get so lost in the heat of the moment. He was saving her from herself.

"*Very* good," she amended. He pulled himself into a sitting position to collect the doona, and the uneven ridge she'd traced during their lovemaking was revealed as a scar. She outlined it, not ready to break contact. "How did this happen?"

"Carelessness with a bull." He glanced down. "I forget it's there."

"Was New Zealand your first stop?" Absently, she kissed the scar.

He sucked in a breath and audibly let it go. "Initially the Northern Territory. Seemed about the furthest I could go." He stacked pillows behind them and tucked the doona around them while keeping her within the circle of his arm.

His ready answer told Grace she'd crossed another line in his defences. "My guess was the bad lands of Kalgoorlie."

"I wasn't on the run from the law." He referred jokingly to the gold town's reputation as a hideout for people in trouble.

"Just yourself." *Having him share his past peeled back another layer of intimacy.*

He silenced her with a mind-numbing kiss. "As I was saying, I drove cattle trains for a few months until I turned eighteen, got a passport, went to New Zealand—was never coming back."

"How long did you stay there?" Grace accepted the shift in direction, further confirmation for her that Danny's death had set his path as a drifter.

"About four and a half years. Probably saved my sanity." He linked his fingers with hers, lifted them to his mouth to nibble.

"In what way?"

"That job I told you about. Angus McHugh. Just the two of us. Barely spoke for the first month or two, then he started to prod." Ryan's understated pain burned like a branding iron.

"A patient man."

When he gave her another special smile—not in the aftermath of sublime sex—she fell off the end of the world.

"You could say that. Like pulling teeth, he used to say. The old way—strapping me down and using pliers. He talked me through my silence, talked me into believing I could make something of myself." He freed her hand to give her breast a friendly squeeze.

"Do you keep in touch?"

"He died a few years ago. Left me some money."

Grace connected the dots. With no father, Ryan had had to find his own role models. Her father, Donovan, but this man had done the hardest work. He'd been more of a father to Ryan than his own father ever had. A father in the way she understood the role—unconditional love, unconditional support and uncrossable boundaries to teach you right from wrong.

"Did he suggest you come home?" She was sorry she'd never meet Angus McHugh.

"Not home. It was never home after Danny died." He restated the boundaries of their relationship without realising it. He didn't intend to hurt her. "Angus pushed. Even on his deathbed."

"You were with him?" She'd stirred sad memories and made fresh ones.

"Yeah."

A complex man who pretended to be straightforward. She'd found him out in acts of kindness to others as well as herself. He was thoughtful. Maybe that's what had slipped past her guard—made her want to believe the things Ella told her. That people existed who were motivated by more than personal greed. Kind, thoughtful and he'd hate those terms. He hid his strengths behind a brusque exterior, a kind of touch-me-at-your-own-peril bravado, and she was beginning to see through it.

"I probably should be going." She eased herself up.

"Will you come back?" His roving hand was arousing the most amazing sensations, cupping a breast, smoothing a flank, coming back to turn her face to his. The driving need that had heated her blood and made her abandon inhibitions thrummed with fresh demand.

"No. Yes. I don't know." She sighed.

"Then we'd better work on excellent now." His mouth covered hers, teasing, inviting, promising heaven, and she was lost.

Grace wasn't sure how much later they surfaced, but she was warm, her body bathed in well-being, and she needed to leave Ryan's bed before she reached for him again. She understood passion, and they had plenty of that between them—heat and sparkle and an edgy need. Finding he wanted her pleasure as much as his own was a revelation. Finding he had soft words and phrases and used them as well as his magnificent body to encourage her as they rocked and rolled their way to sweet oblivion risked a dangerous addiction. The clinical term—sex—didn't begin to describe the magic they'd made tonight. They'd made love.

"I can only find one boot," she muttered, hobbling around the room.

"I'll check the kitchen. Satan might have pinched it."

She wrinkled her nose. "You work as a tag team?"

He laughed, returning immediately with the boot. He sat beside her on the end of the bed while she pulled it on. "You've missed dinner. Let me give you something to eat."

She turned her head to stare at him. "We both know what's going to happen if I stay."

"I know what I want to happen." His shoulder nudge was affectionate, not demanding.

"That's why I need to go." She got to her feet, leaned

into him and kissed his cheek. "Thank you for a lovely evening."

"My pleasure." He lifted her off her feet and swung her in a circle. "Want to drop past my place tomorrow and try an advance on excellent?"

"I'll give it some thought." She let him walk her to her vehicle, then press her against the driver's door to nibble on her mouth until her knees were weak, and every blood cell yearned.

"Send me a text to let me know you got home okay. And don't look at me as if you didn't have some sort of code with your parents." He closed the door on her.

"I'm a big girl now," she drawled.

"Thank God!" he said with a reverence that kept a smile on her face all the way home.

Before she'd reached the back door, she sent the text. "Home safe." His thumbs-up emoji brought another smile. She nuked some soup while she showered and drank it in bed. Not enough hours before she needed to be up again. She was too on edge to sleep.

She was also in serious trouble.

Despite knowing the rules, she was falling for Ryan Wilson. He'd be horrified if he guessed. Vowing to stay away from him was the safest way to protect her heart. She rested her hand over that unreliable organ. It beat as strongly now as it had when she'd been wrapped in his arms. Turning off the light, she accepted she'd take whatever risks she needed to with her body, mind and heart to keep him in her bed while he was in the valley. She was strong and independent—loving him couldn't change that—she'd cope fine without him.

* * *

Ryan found Grace by the river, standing hipshot, her faded jeans and worn shirt clinging faithfully to her figure. Her hat was perched on her head, and her glasses settled on her nose. Strong and resilient—he didn't doubt that. But this had to sting—a personal kick in the teeth. Yeah. He hadn't forgotten the taste of being powerless.

At least she kept a safe distance today. On the afternoon they'd discovered the spill, she'd insisted on taking part in the temporary containment, despite his objections. Both in full-body suits, with protective face coverings they'd covered the land and the holes punched in the drums with a sand and sawdust mixture before dumping more as a barrier between the drums and the river. They'd worked at a fast and furious pace, aware of the potential for harm. Bluey had set up a pump and run an input hose from the river. He'd sprayed them down when they finished before helping them strip off their suits.

Her insistent independence was a tripwire encircling her. She might trip over the bloody thing one day! In his bed she was a constant surprise. Never submissive, always an equal who somehow made him feel like a king.

"How long have they been here?" Ryan moved to stand beside her. He shouldn't be surprised she'd changed her mind and come to supervise the final removal and decontamination. Not a matter of trusting him or the Environment Protection Agency personnel. A matter of land husbandry and making sure the job was done.

"A few hours."

Ryan slid a glance her way. "Been here all the time?" While they didn't yet know the physical legacy left by those caustic white crystals mixed with water and sulphur and heated to boiling point, the emotional legacy was already writ large on her face. Pale and set as she witnessed the scouring of ground she'd painstakingly nurtured.

At twenty, Ryan had cracked the code. Found a way to control his life. The buying and selling of land gave him power. Earning the money to buy and sell property on a whim, to have choices and no attachments filled the void in him. He'd renounced his boyish dreams of tending his family farm. Loving land he managed was a luxury, not a driving force. Better to have money in the bank and none of your emotions invested in it. Unlike Grace, whose face revealed every joy and every kick in the teeth.

"Yeah." She shrugged.

The Environment Protection Agency staff finished loading their truck and moved to one side to start their decontamination routine.

"You look like someone's been using you as their punching bag," Ryan muttered.

"Silly me!" She bristled. "Forgot the makeup this morning! Whatever was I thinking?"

"I was trying to tease." He'd never been much of a comic.

He'd put in sixteen-hour work days at the beginning, spent a few more hours researching the science on how to farm more efficiently. He'd baked through days that made the grasses crackle as he walked through them, learning how clumps of trees and restored watercourses could make a difference. Skills that had added a premium to his wage. When his fellow workers had partied hard, he'd saved his money looking for a bigger payoff. Not that he'd been a complete loner. There'd been parties, good times with friends, the occasional relationship that burnt out within a few months.

"How *are* you feeling?" He resisted the urge to pull her into his side, unsure how public touching fitted in their new relationship. The damnedest thing—she kissed his old scar when they made love. *Whoa—he hauled back on the thought—they had stupendous sex.* There'd been nothing and no one since Angus had died to challenge him on his goals or his methods. A lot of farmers envied his dispassion.

She slid her glasses down her nose as she turned to look at him, her eyes troubled. "Anxious. Hopeful."

She always did that—Ryan hid behind his reflective lenses—she always let the person she was speaking to see her eyes. Windows to the soul. She had a more generous soul than him.

"The indomitable Anderson spirit." He admired her tenacity. "Not afraid to confront adversity, but intent on overcoming it."

"I learned the hard way you have to fight to keep what's yours." She wasn't talking about the relentless reality of being a farmer—weather, crop prices, accidents, but about the real crime of being swindled out of land.

"Ever heard of retreat and regroup?" He also worried her single-minded determination, both a strength and a weakness, would get her into trouble. *Not his problem.* "An arsenal of weapons can be handier than a single line of canons."

"You think?" She skimmed a stone across the water. "We found the contaminant sooner than expected and with expert help removed any trace of it on land. That's a positive. We still have to weather the water analysis and another inspection."

"*We.* That sounds like ownership is uncertain." Ryan tested her temper to disguise the odd kick to the gut hearing her say *"we"* brought. He liked her new habit of confiding in him.

"The broker's term is 'under negotiation.'"

"What's the delay?" His palms itched at the broker's odd terminology at this late stage of the deal.

"Nothing I'm told." She skimmed a second stone across the river. "Due diligence by all parties, including the bank. Jake says we've got time and then some before the deadline."

"But you want faster?"

"I always want faster." Her sultry smile gave a kick to a different part of his anatomy. "On this, I just want to be able to reassure Mum and Dad. Do you think whoever did this planned to come back?"

He took her hand before she could pick up another stone and linked his fingers with hers. "Depends. You needed to know about it for it to be a threat."

"Whoever dumped it must know we found it." A frown

creased her forehead.

"There's no story. Bill's kept it quiet. Maybe the story should get out," he suggested. This was a false peace if the farm was still under attack. "Time to rattle the cage of whoever's responsible. Let the local tittle-tattles start sleuthing for us."

"That's devious. I like it." She tugged on their joined hands and faced him. "Take off your glasses, Ryan. I refuse to look into a mirror when I'm talking to you."

"Sun's fierce. A person needs some protection." He took off his shades with his free hand and slipped them into his pocket.

"When we have a conversation, I want to see your eyes."

"Can't guarantee that, but it works for now." He worried she'd see too much one day.

"Do you suspect someone?" She searched his face.

He had ideas, though ideas didn't convict. "Like Bill, I've got nothing that would count as evidence."

She nodded. "I've drawn up a list, deleted, revised and found myself with nothing concrete."

"More reason to let people know that while we've been quiet about it, we're very interested in who has you in their sights." The more Ryan considered letting the news out, the more he liked the idea. The broker's answer felt off. Grace needed more sleep, or maybe better-quality sleep. Given he had no intention of leaving her bed, certainty about the loan was the next best solution.

The suited-up experts stood while one of their colleagues sprayed them down with high-pressure hoses, then stripped off their protective gear and stored it in sealed units as they'd stored the drums and contaminated soil. The senior official approached, rubbing his hands over his face. "That's about it."

"Hot work?" Ryan asked.

"The pits." The man gave a rueful grin. "Same way out?"

"Back across the river and through my land," Ryan agreed. "Mary Gilhooleys pub does a decent lunch if you're looking for somewhere to stop."

Grace waited until the vehicle was lumbering back across the river. "Gilhooleys has more gossips per square inch than almost any pub in town."

"Is that so?"

She elbowed him in the ribs, and Ryan caught her, swirling her in a circle before setting her on her feet and kissing the tip of her nose. "Can you give me a few minutes?"

CHAPTER ELEVEN

Grace let him urge her towards the river bank further upstream. He sank to the bank, tugging her with him. He leaned back on his elbows.

At this angle, the brim of his hat shielded his face from Grace, but his glasses stayed in his pocket. They sat in companionable silence for a few minutes, the trickle of water over stones a dance tune for the tiny blue wrens darting in and out of bushes. The foul smell no longer clogged her nostrils or made her gag.

"Thanks for coming today." Grace's desire for his support warred with her need to keep some parts of herself walled off. Self-protection demanded precautions, even though it seemed she sucked at it every bit as much as self-promotion. "Are we here for a reason?"

"Nah!" He toppled them back on the bank. The sandy soil prickled through the thin cotton of her shirt, his face blocking the sun from her eyes. Braced above her on his forearms, he grinned. "Invite me."

"You want me to say please." Grace ran her tongue over her top lip, a lick of heat whipping through her when his gaze followed the movement. The flutter in her tummy shifted her world. Three weeks and he still did that to her.

Made her pulse kick up a bit, her muscles relax, made her feel edgy and pliant at the same time. She wasn't an inch closer to unravelling her affection for him. *Affection!* Going to bed with him hadn't lessened her craving. Each new touch from him intensified her longing.

"Oh, yeah. I like it when you beg." He gave his half smile, a wry twist of his lips, making her itch to see the rakish grin she remembered from their teens, that he shared in bed. Sometimes his bed, sometimes hers. Some nights they slept alone. A kind of test for both of them. *Did he miss her as much as she missed him?* Then he lowered himself inch by slow inch until his lower body nestled into hers and his mouth teased her lips. "That little panting noise works for me as well."

"You are pleased to see me." She wriggled against him, and he groaned. A simple yet dangerous pleasure, this longing to be part of him. "So maybe you should ask this time."

"What am I asking for?" He acted before she had time to answer, nuzzling against the sensitive place between her shoulder and neck, his slight stubble tickling her, before he found her mouth.

Pushing her hands into his hair, she dislodged his hat, revelling in the heaviness of his body on hers. A heaviness carrying memories of surrender and exquisite release. He rolled them over, deepening the kiss. He was a lavish lover; she had no self-doubts in his arms.

When he eased out of her embrace and lay on his back, her pulse stuttered to normal. She closed her eyes against the sun, now his body no longer shielded her. His breathing was as laboured as her own. Whatever was happening here, she wasn't alone.

She rolled onto her side, facing him. "Lucky we're outside."

"We're both fans of the open air."

"Barnyards and river banks. You do choose your moments." She giggled.

"It's where you are." His voice dropped, and she had to

strain to hear him.

More romance and Grace's heart stumbled and fell further. So she pushed. Because it seemed like the right time and place. He'd isolated himself after Danny's death. He said he'd talked to Angus. One person in the eight years he'd been away, and Angus had been dead a few years. Being a loner had become a badge of honour for Ryan. Knowing she'd played her part in blackballing him rubbed like a pebble caught in her boot, a constant irritant until it was dealt with.

"I couldn't come here for a long time after Danny died." She'd fumbled, blind, for months after her friend's death. "Too many images, laughing, horsing about, shooting the breeze. He loved to talk."

"Yeah," Ryan said.

"Unlike his taciturn older brother," she pointed out. But Ryan had told her things she knew in her bones he hadn't told another soul. Teasing a precious memory from him made her heart beat faster and gave her hope. Another risk for her: liking him, respecting him as well as loving him.

"I can talk." Then he didn't while she waited. "I still find it hard to talk about his death."

"Does your mother?" she asked.

His head turned towards her, and his eyes narrowed to slits. When he reached for his glasses, she lifted her free hand to still the action.

"She was devastated, but you knew that," she said, holding him with her gaze. "And unsure if she knew how to keep going. Mum visited. I went with her. Sometimes I went alone. Mum did the practical stuff, casseroles and soups and sweets. I blathered—about school, about Danny, about sport, about Danny."

"She appreciates all you did." Ryan's way of saying thank you, and the air took on a new quality, filled with separate memories and shared grief. Jerking to a sitting position, he jammed his hat back on his head and braced his arms on his knees. "I guess there was a lot of talk at school."

"Some."

"You don't have to spare me. I went to that school." He was staring at the poppies. There were hundreds now, running in lines along the edge of the paddock. Individual red and white flowers popped up randomly, a hint that in time they'd take over completely.

"Then you know it housed all types." She followed the direction of his gaze, tight bands squeezing her chest, knowing the flowers cut through his rigid barriers more effectively than words. Another bond she'd forged with him. "Rednecks who salivated over every bit of gossip they could get their hands on, and others who thought it was a shit deal." She picked up another stone, skimmed it across the river, her remembered rage making her throwing arm tense, so the stone skipped once and sank.

"More than a shit deal." He picked up a few stones himself and skimmed one across the water with more success than hers. Satan ran down to the bank and back to them, barked and then flopped beside Ryan.

"I spent some time wondering about the other boy." She faced Ryan, caught the look of surprise in his eyes, and shrugged.

He lifted his hat and ran a hand through his hair. "I didn't give him a thought. And how selfish is that!" He sounded disgusted with himself. "What did you find?"

"I checked social media a few times. He moved to Sydney with his mother. He's found his own way." It had been a good day when she'd seen the happy post.

"His mother? What about his father?"

"His father was an angry man, didn't have much patience with boys who weren't 'men.'" She hesitated, but Ryan deserved the truth, in all its odious viciousness. "Blamed Danny for seducing his son, then took his son home and beat him."

"Shit!" Ryan's horror matched her own.

"The boy came to the funeral. Alone. Stood at the back. Dad told me later." She leaned into Ryan's shoulder and nudged. "Ella went to stand with him. He was distraught. Terrified to be there, yet wanting to show his support."

"I wish I'd known." Ryan brought his arm around her shoulders and gave her a quick hug.

"An amazing act of courage. His mother must have understood. She got him away from his father and the small minds in this town." Grace wished they could have spirited Danny away.

"Poor bastard. I should have gone to see him." He flipped his glasses back into place.

Her heart ached at the infinitesimal withdrawal. "It would've been hard to see past Danny."

"Was it hard to see past Chrissy?"

"Yes," she admitted. "Even though we were able to say goodbye. Cancer killed Chrissy. It wasn't easy, and your little sister shouldn't die before you. We had—have—Tessa, and we knew we did everything we could to help."

"I didn't help." His mouth set in grim lines, marking his retreat into bitterness about his brother's death.

"You weren't here."

"That says it all." He leapt to his feet.

"That wasn't an accusation," she ripped back.

He lifted a dismissive hand as if he didn't care. She knew better now. The glasses perched on his nose were a slap in the face. Her rejection had hurt him as much, if not more, than the casual gossip of strangers. Just as his absence had left an empty space in her life. As teenagers they'd taken their friendship for granted.

Grace rose to block his escape, forcing him to look at her. "Okay, it's not an accusation today. Danny was excited after school that day. Happy. Meeting someone he fancied, he said." She rested a hand on Ryan's arm, the latent strength in the rippling muscles revealing his fight for control. "Someone told the principal, who called the parents."

"That principal was a sanctimonious prick. Shit, two kids kissing and he had to call the parents, threaten expulsion.

No fucking idea about proportion." Then, as if the words were dragged from deep within him. "Do you know what the principal said to my mother and Danny?"

"Anyone with any sense knew he was a petty despot who liked to belittle." Fear made her want to shut her ears.

"He called Danny a worthless piece of shit. Said he wasn't any kind of son. Can you imagine how that made Danny feel?" Ryan's pain was raw, the poison still doing damage.

"I can." Grace spun on one heel to face the river, hot tears stinging her eyes. She blinked them away, then swung back. It was unfair to both of them to hide her outrage. "Because Danny was gay."

"Because he was gay," Ryan repeated.

"That principal was a mean bastard." She rubbed her hands together, then opened them to stare at the palms. "Enjoyed giving the cane. The education department had him out within a fortnight. Early retirement they said."

"You expect that to give me some kind of fucking comfort!" He strode back towards the vehicles, then pulled up, bending to pick a poppy that had sprung up far from the main patch. He turned back, his voice calmer. He whipped off his glasses. "Danny was a total mess, believed he'd shamed Mum, that there was no place for him here anymore. That principal made Danny's last hours hell."

"If there's a hell, I'm sure that principal will rot there." *He'd removed his glasses. Whether he knew it or not, he wanted to share himself with her.* Grace thumped Ryan on the chest. "But it's not your fault."

"I wasn't here when he needed me." He made to jam the glasses back on his nose, then dropped his arm.

"You were away working because your mother needed money to pay the bills." Grace gripped his forearms, her tears falling unchecked. "You stayed away because you could make more money elsewhere."

"Aren't you one of the 'Ryan Wilson is a heartless bastard who abandoned his family' brigade?" Frustration and anger drove his attack, when he normally hid his torment under his veneer of silent strong man.

"Past tense, Ryan, and I was angry because you abandoned me." She tried to shake him. Being judged unfairly had wounded him. *She'd wounded him.* "You can accept my apology or not."

"I didn't plan on returning to Australia. Angus convinced me to 'return to the scene of the crime.'" His admission was pain-coated. Danny's death had been a crime, although no one was ever charged.

"You haven't really, have you?" Some of the warmth went out of Grace's day. "You have no plans to stay." She scrubbed her tears away.

"I hated this place for a long time. To escape the hate I needed to detach—from the place, from the people." His sense of not belonging was collateral damage.

"Is life better being detached? Is it even possible?" She searched his face. The grim lines had returned. His expression was implacable, locking her out. Angus had died before he'd convinced Ryan to let the anger go. Ryan would sever his connection to her as he'd severed his connection to the valley. Clean, slicing with the efficiency of a razor-edged knife. Pain spread through her body with the inevitability of ripples running from one of the stones they'd thrown into the river.

"Being detached makes buying and selling painless." He sucked in air and continued, as if making a terrible confession. "Protects me from experiencing that kind of grief ever again."

"It doesn't work like that," she said gently. "What about your mother? She lost two sons that day." *What about us? What about intimacy? Friendship?*

"She said she wanted to stay. Needed to stay to be near Danny." The dog leaned against his leg, and Ryan automatically reached down a hand to fondle its ears. "I like your memorial better than the tombstone in the cemetery."

"He loves you." She nodded towards Satan, dismissing

165

the compliment as the distraction he'd intended it to be. "Without reservation. You can stop loving land. Harder to make yourself stop loving animals or people."

His fingers stilled, and he straightened. "So?"

Grace cocked her head to one side. "Danny said your dad didn't like him."

"It wasn't personal. He wasn't interested in kids, but Danny was sensitive to rejection, even as a two-year-old." Ryan was trying to pretend his four-year-old self had been too grown up for that sort of pain.

Grace picked some more at a scab needing to be knocked off for the wound to heal. "What happened?"

"He disappeared. After a few years Mum got something from a lawyer. Said he was sorry, signed over the farm to her. Said that should make them square. Pity about the colossal mortgage!" His growl screamed disgust.

"Let's see if I've got this straight. You stopped caring about your farm because you were forced to leave, and it carried bad memories anyway." She met his scowl, but she had nothing to lose. "You have a choice this time, so moving on now is different. But, hey, your father's a handy excuse this time. He was a wanderer. It's in the blood."

"I don't know what my father's like," he snapped. "Even if he's still alive."

She attacked again. Fighting for Ryan's future if he wouldn't. "I don't buy that biology is destiny crap."

"You're the one who insists on being the fifth-generation farmer on the same farm." His eyes narrowed.

"That's nurture as much as nature, Ryan. Every time I showed interest in the farm, in farming, I was rewarded, encouraged until working the land was as natural as breathing." She took a risk. "The same is true for you, if you'll accept it."

"I farm. I've got my eye on a neat little property on the south coast."

Would he have told her if she hadn't challenged him about leaving?

She paused until he wouldn't hear the ache of loss in her

voice. "For how long?"

"I haven't decided." He crossed his arms, as good a way of saying "not your business" as any other.

"You aren't responsible for Danny's death"—she drilled a finger into his chest—"and you aren't your father. You've chosen different role models—my dad, Mr. Donovan, Angus McHugh."

"You think it's that simple." He threw a hand in the air.

"I'm a pragmatist, Ryan." Or she fought hard to be.

"Don't make me laugh. You're a spitfire."

"I'm working on that," she exploded.

"Don't work too hard. It's who you are." His anger was gone. He caught her hand and turned them to continue the walk to the vehicles. "Danny said you were the second person he told he was gay." Ryan's voice was low, deep, steady, even as the words he said shocked her. "I was the first. He said you hugged him."

"He was nervous, skittish really." Her throat dried up as past and present emotions jostled for space. "Wanting to come here after school. Racing me down the track. Then he wouldn't look at me. When he did, he was so anxious." She recalled the look on Danny's face, half determination, half fear. "I didn't know I was the second. He didn't tell me that. I hugged him because he looked impossibly terrified when he was being so brave."

He pulled her into his arms and rocked her from side to side. "We're less publicly demonstrative in our family." He was talking present tense because she'd seen him with Danny.

"That's one of those things you can change." She held her breath, waiting for his answer.

"You want me to tell Mum and Bluey it's okay for them to canoodle on the couch when I drop in to say hello?" He pretended shock.

"You could tell her you approve." When he left, his mother would be comforted knowing she had Ryan's support. It hurt to think of him leaving.

"Done that." He leaned back, dropping his hands to link around her waist. "If it's okay with you, I might use this paddock for agistment until the sale is confirmed?"

"Do you have animals needing agistment?" she asked carefully, feeling the ground fall from under her until there was only business between them. Friendship might last when he left town again. When she was alone, she could almost convince herself their buzz was too strong to last. With him, she couldn't maintain the lie.

"It's good land. You'd have extra income while we're waiting to complete the sale. I can start on some of the minor building works so when we settle the sale we're good to go."

She bristled. "I don't want your charity."

"Providing agistment is a normal part of farm business. The only way I can access this land before settlement is to pay you." He'd retreated again. "No big deal. Forget it."

"You're making me feel lower than a worm again," she muttered. He'd flipped the situation on its head. Paying her way was a matter of family honour. She wasn't using the land, and it would be his within weeks. "You're already helping me enough." She replayed his comment. "What minor building works?"

"A fence to house off a corridor for the poppy field," he said, as if permanently securing her memorial to Danny didn't reach into her chest and squeeze her heart so tightly it hurt. "A pity to see them trampled."

Her resistance dissolved in a puddle of gooey sentiment. "That would be nice."

He grinned.

"You should smile more often." She ran her fingers down his cheek. "Build your fences, bring your animals over. I won't take payment. You have to let me give something back. More than agistment. I've got some ideas for vegetation improvements at your place."

"I'll listen." He slid his glasses back into position. "I need to get back to the farm."

"Me too." She fell into step as they walked back along the track.

He stopped as they drew level with her Ute, took her chin in his hand. "One more. You make me want one more, Grace."

"I like the taste of you too." Her pulse skittered wildly.

He brushed another kiss across her part-opened mouth. "Just marking my place." He moved back.

For how long? The more of himself he shared—her temporary neighbour—the more she had to lose. Loving him was like stepping off a cliff. Why hadn't she known it would be like that? She hadn't reached the bottom, but it would be foolish not to expect a crash landing. For her.

Grace's eyes opened on an inky darkness. The wind had picked up while she slept, rattling the window in its wooden frame and bringing the earthy scent of a recent downpour into the room. She lay perfectly still, warm, but with a feather of alarm brushing up her spine. Easing onto her back, she listened for the sound that had woken her. Not the window, not in the room with her.

Her great-grandfather's upright clock sounded the hour from its place at the bottom of the wide hallway running the length of the house. Its metronome-perfect tick-tock had banished many a childhood nightmare. Maybe that's what had woken her? A grown-up nightmare about losing the farm. Family ghosts taunting her with her failure to save what they'd fought to win. Pushing away her uncharacteristic defeatism, she let the clock's familiar chimes soothe her and found another sound beneath them. A muffled thud.

She flung the doona aside. Her bare feet hit the cold wooden floor and pushed forward in a single movement. Leaving windows open despite the coming storm had been thumbing her nose at nature. Never a good move. Now her mother's favourite crystal vase was collateral damage. That and the delicate pink trigger plants it contained victims to the snap of a curtain in a high wind. If she hurried, she might be able to stop the vase rolling to the floor. She hesitated at the door, the hairs on the back of her neck rising like tiny antennae sensing danger. She could find her way through the house blindfolded, yet instinct urged her to turn on every light, to check every room. Her heart raced. She was alone in the house. She reached for the door, its solid strength beneath her fingers steadying her.

They'd never had a break-in at the farmhouse, didn't lock the doors or windows. She ran her tongue across dry lips, tasting her growing uneasiness. Before last month, they'd never had contaminants dumped on their land either.

Her shallow breaths sounded frighteningly loud to her ears. With her hand gripping the knob, she peered into the darkness. The kitchen door opened. Slowly, but the squeak her father had promised to oil was unmistakable above the wind. She stared, unable to see. Each new high-pitched whine tightened the bands of fear around her chest.

She hadn't heard Bailey's welcoming bark. A picture of the dog, injured or worse, flashed through her mind. She surged forward, blood pumping through her body. With a rebel yell she ran, hitting light switches, ducking and weaving down the hall, before dropping behind the dark sideboard standing at the kitchen end of the hall.

"Bluey. There's someone in the kitchen," she shouted, pretending she had backup. "I've called the cops!" She reached behind her, rattled another doorknob, then slammed a door back hard against the wall, before dropping to the floor on the opposite side of the hall. Trembling, she counted to five and deepened her voice. "Grace. I'm here. I've got a gun."

She crawled towards the kitchen, her hands clammy, perspiration running down her back despite the damp air hitting her. *Damp air.* She stumbled into the kitchen. The back door stood open. A figure with a flashlight ran down the driveway.

"Bailey!" Two quick strides and she'd reached the dog, dropping onto her knees to check his unmoving form. His breaths were laboured and irregular. When she tried to help him stand, his body sagged limply. A faint cloying scent clung to him. Vaguely familiar, like a sickly-sweet perfume, but she couldn't place it.

Carrying him into the house, she lay him in front of the stove. She lifted the receiver from the landline hooked to the wall and sat down on the floor, her eyes never leaving the dog. The vet was on speed dial.

"George, it's Grace Anderson. I think Bailey's been poisoned. I don't know what or when. I'm guessing quick acting and in the last thirty minutes or so. He can't stand, and his breathing's rapid." She rested a hand on the dog's head, the mute distress in his eyes bringing tears to hers. Anger swirled below the anxiety. Bailey wouldn't hurt a fly. Who'd do this to a dog?

"I can't bring him in." She swallowed hard. "I need to call the police, and I can't leave the farm. There's been an attempted break-in … You will?" She sagged against the table leg in relief. "Yes, I've got some hydrogen peroxide … Yes. Yes. Thank you."

She started for the pantry, dialling triple-zero as she moved. "Where is it?"

The call connected. "Police, please." She waited for the redirection.

"There it is." She grabbed the hydrogen peroxide from the shelf and backtracked to the kitchen table.

"Grace Anderson, Blue Sky Farm. There's been an attempted break-in … Ten minutes." She pushed her hand through her hair. "Maybe ten minutes ago. I scared the person off. He ran down the driveway." At least *he'd run like a man.* "He must have had a vehicle nearby. I didn't hear it or see any lights. I have to go. He poisoned my dog … Okay.

"I have to get you to vomit, boy. George is coming, but we need to try and empty your stomach as quickly as possible." She measured out the hydrogen peroxide and mixed it with some milk as instructed, then searched the kitchen drawer for a dropper. Sitting beside the dog, she lifted his head and pushed the dropper into the side of his mouth. "I'm sorry, Bailey; I need to do this."

Then she raided the paper box beside the fuel stove, laying newspaper around the dog. The vet said to give him thirty minutes. The police might be faster. Having done all she could for Bailey, she surveyed the scene. The back door was still open, the wind whipping fresh rain into the kitchen. She shut and locked it, backtracked to the front door and locked it as well. The attacker must be far away by now. Still, the frantic pounding of her heart, the lick of fear at how close someone who wanted to harm her and her family had come, lingered. Working her way back to the kitchen, she systematically locked windows and turned on the outside lights.

Her next decision was a no-brainer.

"Ryan. Sorry to wake you." She dragged in a deep breath to steady herself. Base instinct was driving this call. "There's been an attempted break-in." Her voice wobbled. "Bailey's been poisoned."

"I'm on my way." He asked no questions, offered no argument.

Relief flooded her, dropping her to her knees. She rocked herself backwards and forwards, admitting to a weakness she couldn't afford. She wanted him here. More than the cops. More than anyone.

CHAPTER TWELVE

Grace crawled across to Bailey. The dog vomited over the paper. "Good boy. My beautiful boy." She rolled up the papers and laid out more, pushing the sodden, foul-smelling mess into a large plastic bag. Maybe they could do tests and identify the poison. Setting a bowl of water at Bailey's head, she stroked his throat gently when he lapped at it.

The roar of a utility speeding had her back on her feet. Reason told her it was Ryan, but her stomach churned, and she searched for a weapon. Adrenalin still pumped through her. She edged towards the window, keeping her body out of sight. Ryan's number plate flashed in the circle of light cast by her external lights before he doused his headlights. He'd set a speed record for the few kilometres between them, on a wet, dark road. They reached the kitchen door at the same time. She pulled the bolts as he pushed against it, and he stumbled inside, Satan at his heels.

"I locked it." She leaned forward, resting her hands on her knees.

"Good girl." He slammed it behind him, locking out the storm and shot the bolts before scanning the room. "Has he vomited yet?"

"Once."

He crouched at the dog's head, his hand gently stroking down his flanks. "Any change in his breathing?"

Grace knelt at Bailey's tail and placed her hand beside his. "Easier maybe. The vet's coming."

Satan dropped beside Bailey's back, nudging him gently.

"He's Mum's." Fresh tears filled her eyes and started to slide down her cheeks. Impatiently, she brushed them aside. "She adores him. I can't let anything happen to him."

"How are you?"

She raised her eyes to his. *No longer afraid.* Worried about the who and the why on top of the contamination. "I need a hug."

"That's doable." He rose to his feet, reaching down a hand to pull her to hers. He simply opened his arms for her to walk into.

First, she registered his warmth, then the sheer solid strength of him, the comfort of believing no one could touch her now. Then his spicy scent. She wanted to burrow into him and curl up until the aftershocks of fear drained from her body. He demanded nothing, just held her. The realisation she could get used to this kind of steady comfort as much as she could the blaze of his passion had her pushing back. "Thank you."

"My pleasure," he murmured. Flashing blue and white lights lit up the window. "Looks like the cops."

Her hands rested on his chest. "I might get some clothes on if you can let them in."

"I like what you're wearing." He grinned, and she took a step away from the heat in his eyes. "Or maybe, not wearing."

"Right." She took another step back, flustered by his husky drawl, by the remembered feel of her breasts pressed against his chest. "Pyjamas. I'll get out of my pyjamas."

"I'll let the cops in." He crossed to the back door. "Maybe you should cover your toes too. I forgot to tell you, I find your bare toes—bare anything—distractingly sexy."

Whisking herself into her bedroom, she grabbed

yesterday's clothes from the chair she'd thrown them onto. She listened with half an ear to Ryan talking to Bill, and … Pete. She couldn't hear what they were saying, only the quiet rhythm of Ryan's voice and the staccato volley of questions Bill was firing at him. She sat on the side of her bed, reaching for her socks and boots. Ryan found her toes sexy. She wriggled them—ten standard toes. Her stomach did a little jump of elation. He'd said it to distract her. To shake her out of her meltdown. The sizzle down her spine was a bonus.

Pulling a sweater over her pyjama top, she walked back into the kitchen.

"Grace." Bill nodded. "Can you tell us what happened?"

Bailey vomited again. Satan whined in sympathy. "I'll get it," said Ryan. "You talk to Bill."

"There's not a lot to tell." She gestured to the chairs around the kitchen table, not sure of her role. "Would you like a cup of tea or something?"

"Only if you're making one," Bill answered. "Sometimes it's easier to have something to do while you talk."

Grace set the kettle on the Aga to boil, then lifted the tea canister from its shelf. The teapot sat beside the stove, but she set out mugs on the table and started at the beginning. "Something woke me. I'd just convinced myself it was nothing when I heard a thud. I assumed Mum's vase had been toppled by a gust of wind, and that I could catch it before it hit the floor."

"Was that it? Did they try to come in the window?" Bill asked while Pete took notes.

"I didn't even check." Grace shook her head. "I'd reached the bedroom door when the kitchen door opened. It squeaks, you see." The kettle screamed, and she poured the water into the pot and brought it to the table. "I didn't hear Bailey. Nobody could get past that door without Bailey barking a welcome." Sitting, she huffed out a breath. *Please let Bailey be okay.*

"What happened next," Bill prompted.

"I saw red. I realised something had happened to Bailey, and I went berserk." Outrage at the thought someone had hurt an animal had propelled her into action. "I ran down the hall, flicking on lights, yelling for Bluey to help me, saying I'd called the cops."

"Was Bluey here?" Ryan asked.

"No." Automatically she played hostess, pouring tea into the cups. "Milk?"

"I'll get it." Ryan got the jug from the fridge and handed it to her before taking the seat beside her. "Finish it."

"There was no one here except me. Bluey goes home at night. I must have scared them off. Because the next thing I knew, I was alone with a cold breeze. I checked the back door and saw someone running down the drive." Her stomach heaved at the memory.

"Any chance of identification?" Bill leaned forward. "Police are a hopeful bunch."

"It's a dark and stormy night, Officer." She smiled grimly and sipped her tea. "I caught the dance of a flashlight down the drive. Not a profile I recognised." Another car pulled up behind the house. "That'll be the vet. Bailey was my first priority. Then I called you. Then I called Ryan."

"I'll handle the vet," said Ryan.

Half an hour later Grace helped the vet load Bailey into the back of his four-wheel drive. "I'll come in tomorrow." She bent and whispered in the dog's ear. "Love you, Bailey." Then kissed the dog's head.

"I can call and give you a report. Save you a trip," George answered. "Making him vomit so quickly helped a lot. His heart rate and body temperature are better, but I'll run blood tests when I get him back to the surgery. Thanks for the sample." He raised the garbage bag she'd given him.

"I want to see him." She wanted to take a Bailey-as-normal-dog photo to send to her mother along with the report of tonight's attempted break-in. The downside of being a family who talked—she'd share tonight's attempted break-in with them. She stepped back as the vet closed the door.

"You should get back inside, out of this rain." George squeezed her arm. "Try and get some sleep."

She opened the back door and conversation ceased, like flipping a switch. Tension stretched tight, leaving her unsure of the source. "Don't hold back on my account." She pushed a hand through her damp hair, hauling it off her forehead. Then crossed to stand with her back to the stove, absorbing its warmth. Her sweater smelled like wet dog. She should have worn a coat, even for that short trip.

"Bill was asking me what I was doing before I got here tonight." Ryan sat opposite the senior cop, pouring himself a cup from the second pot of tea she'd made.

"What were you doing?" She'd assumed he'd been asleep like her.

"Some overdue paperwork, checking in online with some people." Ryan had been working, probably catching up on work missed when he stayed with her.

"Maybe we can stop in at your place on the way back to town, check your search history?" Bill suggested.

"The silhouette running down my drive wasn't Ryan." Grace crossed to Ryan's side, placing her hand on his shoulder and making her allegiance clear. "That wasn't what you were talking about. Or not only what you were talking about."

"Have you checked for damage?" Pete asked.

"I … we, haven't had time." Grace was struggling to process the attack on Bailey and the house.

"I explained that while you were outside with George." Ryan stirred sugar into his tea, the clink of the spoon on china the only sound in the lengthening silence. "You may as well tell her. She'll keep badgering until you do."

Bill sighed. "We got the analysis back on the contaminants in the drums today."

"Calcium polysulphide, also known as lime sulphur. We

did tests too, Bill. Base ingredient quick lime," Ryan said. "There are bags of quick lime missing from my shed."

"Someone stole the bags," she protested, dropping on the chair beside Ryan and resting her hand on his thigh. He had proved he was a reliable friend. "And the drums."

"And quick lime is standard supply from hardware shops. It's still being sold. Got that, Grace," Bill said. "Pete's been making discreet inquiries. We're still working through the list of agricultural suppliers and salespeople who visited Ryan's place in the last few weeks. Do you always have that many visitors?" Bill asked in disgust.

"I've made some big changes. I get stickybeaks, local media looking for stories and suppliers hoping to sell me something, even school kids doing projects." Ryan admitted to running an open house.

"Smithhouse?" Bill's face was deliberately blank.

Ryan's eyebrows rose. "Not that I know of."

Hearing the name immediately raised Grace's hackles—Smithhouse had swindled her family—but she knew what she'd seen. She sat back, releasing Ryan's thigh. "He has a very recognisable profile, Bill. It wasn't him. Smithhouse can't move that fast."

"Done any business with him?" Bill directed his question to Ryan.

"He wasn't happy I bought Donovan's place before it went on the open market." Ryan leaned back in his chair, his fingers lightly linked through the handle of his cup.

Bill pursed his lips. "What makes you so sure?"

"He told me." Ryan waved his cup in dismissal. Miraculously no tea sloshed out. "Old business."

"How come you knew it was for sale?" Pete asked.

"Grace's father." Ryan glanced at her, and his mouth twisted. "Another thing you didn't know about your dad. He got my contact details from Mum and sent me a message. Why all the interest in Smithhouse?" Ryan asked.

"Your mother noticed him going into the pub with one of your short-term hires a few months ago. She said you didn't think much of it?" Bill was asking for reasons.

"The guy was straight when he worked for me. After the job finished, he needed to look elsewhere for work. You can't condemn a man for looking for work," Ryan said levelly, placing his cup on the table.

"Rochelle?" Bill asked.

"She's called by once or twice. Not for a while?"

"What did she want?" Bill held his tea cup with the delicacy of an aging duchess, a ploy to unsettle witnesses.

"It would be ungentlemanly of me to say. But the offer of sex was a means to an end." Ryan scrubbed his face with his hands.

Grace hissed, then slapped a hand over her mouth. Rochelle didn't know she and Ryan were an item. *No one knew they were an item.* She knew the rules. Jealousy was ridiculous.

"Take her up on it?" Bill asked conversationally.

"I hate being used for my body, Bill." Ryan's jaw jutted forward. "You know how it is."

Bill whistled. "Got any *other* enemies around here?"

"Not that I know of," Ryan repeated his earlier phrase, and Bill snorted his disbelief.

"But you've put a few noses out of joint," Pete replied.

"That's part of the territory when you do something different." Ryan sounded indifferent, while Grace was seething on his behalf.

"Where are you heading with this, Bill?" Grace couldn't make the pieces fit.

Bill drained his tea, set the cup on the table. "You caused gossip when you took off, Ryan, gossip when you returned and gossip when you splashed cash around." Bill was digging for something.

"And?" Ryan shifted, a subtle movement of mind and body. He was on guard.

"There are people who resent your good fortune." Bill was matter-of-fact.

"Leaving here had nothing to do with good fortune."

Ryan stared hard at the cop. Bill had been the first on the scene after they found Danny's body. Another crime no one was held accountable for.

"I know that." Bill frowned. "But you've got a nasty tongue when you want. Let's go back to our working theory. Someone wants to cost Grace money so she can't afford to buy the farm. What's the target tonight?"

"More contamination?" The blood turned to ice in Grace's veins. She made to rise.

Ryan reached out a hand to hold her in place. "They didn't need to come into the house for that. What's your most valuable asset?"

"My cheeses." She stared at him in disbelief. *Dumb, dumb, dumb*—she'd been trying to figure out the attacker's target in the main house.

"Where are they?" Bill demanded, focusing on the new angle.

"I've converted the back of the second farmhouse, so my production and storage are there." Her mind raced, calculating the value of what she had in storage. A pulse in her temple throbbed uncontrollably. Irreplaceable. Without her stock she couldn't meet her orders, and the dominoes fell with frightening speed. Her hands trembled. Loss of business, damage to her reputation. Worst of all, she wouldn't have the regular income to make loan payments.

"Check the house," Bill ordered Pete.

"Wait!" Grace called as the cop moved towards the door. "I started locking it after the lime sulphur was dumped."

Pete turned back. "Where do you keep the keys?"

She walked stiffly towards the keyboard inside the back door. "They're missing."

"Just those?" Ryan demanded, following her.

"No." She traced a finger over the empty hooks. "The power boxes, the machinery shed, the keys to this house."

Pete slipped out the back door. "A precaution," Bill said. "I'm guessing they tried to get in, were forced to come looking for the keys, and you disturbed them before they could go back."

"I should go with him," Grace said.

Ryan turned her back to sit at the table. She murmured a silent prayer. *Please don't tell me they got into the cheese fridges.* Repeating it like a mantra. No one could help her if her stock was adulterated.

Pete returned. "An attempt to jimmy the locks on the house. They were unlucky tonight."

"Keys will need to be changed," Bill instructed—another cost she hadn't factored into her budget.

Grace sagged against Ryan. The adrenalin that had carried her so far was gone, leaving her disoriented. He wrapped an arm around her shoulders.

"I'm buying a stretch of Grace's land," Ryan's announcement blindsided Grace.

"Dandy," Bill snapped. "Who knows?"

"Me, Grace, her family and our lawyers at this stage," Ryan said.

"You're putting yourself firmly in the frame. Stand up, Ryan, and turn out your pockets."

Ryan stood to empty his pockets—car keys, wallet, phone.

The sharp order cut through Grace's fuzziness. "Don't be ridiculous, Bill. He's buying the land at full market value so I can get the deposit to buy the rest of the farm. And he's buying the strip where the lime sulphur was dumped."

"*That's* why you were there." Bill jerked his chin in Ryan's direction. "We're struggling to find evidence against anyone. We do this strictly by the book so no one can accuse us or him in the future. I definitely want to see your internet history."

"Ryan is not responsible for the attacks on this farm," she declared, outraged on his behalf.

* * *

Ryan exchanged a look with the cop, one that said Grace was dead beat and didn't need any more of this tonight.

Bill settled back in his chair, not done yet. "You're saying you got everything you want in this little transaction? You're not interested in the whole shebang?"

"I'm saying I was already in the frame. I bought Donovan's. I'm upgrading Mum's. It's known I'm interested in farming at scale." Ryan outlined a plausible case against himself.

Bill studied Ryan through narrowed eyes, Bill's brain almost visibly processing all the angles. He was no fool. He seemed to reach a conclusion. "News of the contamination got out. All those big EPA trucks and officials coming through town. Did you have anything to do with that?"

"Coming through town was the logical route," Ryan said.

"You didn't suggest stopping for a meal and a chat?" Bill was sceptical.

"They asked for a recommendation." Ryan held up his hands as if to say "nothing to see here." "What's a bloke to do?"

"The story is now doing the rounds of every kitchen table," Bill continued. "Replacing all the locks won't be a secret either."

"Maybe someone will make a mistake, let something slip," Ryan offered.

"Maybe." Bill jammed his hat back on. "I'm also wondering if you pissed off someone enough that setting you up to take the fall suits them."

Ryan was starting to think the same thing. His advantage, as he saw it, was that Bill had an open mind, and Grace's attacker wasn't smart enough to work out Ryan would cover all her losses.

"Perhaps we can see your laptop now?" Bill rose to his feet and nodded at his offsider.

Ryan also rose. "You're welcome to go in and have a look on your way back to town. Alternatively, you can call by my place tomorrow, or I'll bring it in. I'm staying tonight to make sure there isn't another attempt at a break-in." He braced himself on both feet. They'd need to arrest him to get him to leave Grace now. "That is, unless you plan to stay here and keep watch?"

"Appreciate that." Bill gave him a vote of confidence. Not for the first time. "We don't have the resources."

"Thank you for coming." Grace followed Bill to the door. Even exhausted she seemed to produce the social niceties. She closed the door, closed her eyes and leaned her forehead on it.

"What the hell did you think you were doing, running towards an intruder?" Ryan took her shoulders and turned her to face him, pent-up fear making him sharper than he intended. "He could have been armed!"

"Bailey was hurt." She had no energy left to fight but was unrepentant. "You'd have done the same for Satan." She had him there.

"Where was your bloody phone? Why didn't you just ring the cops from your bedroom and run the other way?"

"Because I left my phone over at my place." She enunciated with care. She looked like forming words was beyond her, and seeing her helpless made his belly clench. "I was feeling a bit low tonight."

"Why didn't you call?" He released her shoulders to wrap her in his arms, where she should have been from the moment he'd walked in the door.

"I did." She snuggled against him.

Ryan disengaged her morning alarm while she was in the bathroom, knowing he wouldn't sleep again tonight. He had a lot to think about. Not just the possibilities Bill had outlined, but his reaction to Grace's frantic call. Luckily there'd been no one on the road because he would have driven through them. Imagining her hurt and defenceless had kept his foot on the accelerator until he'd skidded into the drive.

Hell! He straightened the bed and found his hands

trembling. It was far too easy to picture the intruder staying to fight and Grace tackling him single-handed and without a weapon. She could have been hurt, and he'd have known nothing about it. That shook him to his bootstraps. He'd vowed when he left the valley he'd never be powerless again, never not be there when someone he …

He didn't love Grace! He raked a hand through his hair. He cared for her. *Friends!* A friend wouldn't allow anyone to cheat or hurt her. That's all it was.

"I'm going to pass out." She stumbled towards the bedroom, mumbling as if she'd failed Entertaining Guests 101. "Maybe I should sleep in my clothes, be ready for milking."

"Take off your clothes." Ryan pulled her sweater over her head. "That's not a proposition."

"I'm still wearing my pyjama top." She yawned widely as he threw the sweater on a chair.

"Now the boots and jeans." He backed her against the bed until her knees hit the side, and she toppled backwards.

"I can do it," she protested.

"I'm closer." Ryan knelt at her feet. "Practice closing your eyes. You might find you like it."

She chuckled. "I *love* it. Give me more."

"Goodnight, Grace." He pulled off her elasticised work boots, then undid the button on her jeans, tugged down the zipper. "Lift your hips."

"You've said that before." Obediently, she did as he said, and he hooked his hands around her backside to ease the denim down her thighs.

White knickers with a dash of lace. Ryan smiled, recalling how he'd helped her out of a similar pair on the night she'd first come to him. Like winning a prize when he wasn't sure he'd bought the right ticket. The knickers were another insight into the world of Grace. She hadn't worn them to arouse him when they'd made love, hadn't been conned by the fashionistas into the myth she needed props to be wholly feminine. He should have known better. She wore them for herself. So much of her wardrobe had to be practical, she could indulge her fantasies with her underwear. The fantasies she'd shared with him so far had brought him to his knees. He grimaced at the floor. Literally.

The flimsy fabric barely hid the triangle of hair at the top of her legs. Needing the contact, he rested his cheek against her. Her hands rested on his head. Having her reach for him when she was boneless with exhaustion made him feel invincible. He didn't know what to do with the emotion. Turning his head, he pressed a last kiss to her, the scent of woman making him want to linger. Tonight, she needed tending.

"Night, Ryan."

Lifting her feet onto the mattress, he covered her with the doona. She curled onto her side and snuggled down, asleep before he could turn out the light. He shucked his boots, jeans, heavy sweater and shirt before joining her, drawing her back against him. Her purr of contentment warmed him as much as her body. He held her gently while his mind raced, reviewing people in town, people in the district. Breaking into the farmhouse while Grace was alone marked an escalation in the attacks. *Why now?*

She was still sleeping when Ryan returned from the milking. He wandered into the kitchen and stretched his arms above his head to ease the ache in his shoulder muscles. He didn't miss the early morning starts. It had been bloody brisk in the milk shed this morning. The music for milking wasn't his usual taste, still there was a certain satisfaction knowing he could still milk a herd and muck out the shed single-handed. A vehicle in the drive brought him out into the grey morning light and a sky threatening more rain.

"Where's Grace?" Bluey's immediate concern reinforced Ryan's decision to insist on lending the farmhand to Grace. The older man formed her first line of defence.

Briefly, Ryan filled him in on the night's events. "Have you seen anything suspicious?"

"I've been watching since the drums were dumped." Bluey scratched his jaw. "Done a few extra checks on the boundaries. It's been clear. If they were after the keys, it sounds like machinery theft."

"Or they were after her cheese," Ryan suggested grimly.

"Stop talking about me, and talk to me," a sleep-tousled Grace snarled at them from the kitchen door.

"Scones today." Bluey held up a basket and headed sheepishly towards the door.

"I should get back to my place." Ryan started to back away.

"Not until you explain why you turned off my alarm." The light in her eyes flicked like a whip.

"I'll put the coffee on." Bluey sidled past Grace and into the house.

Ryan sauntered towards her, took her chin in one hand and searched her face. "You look a bit better rested."

She pushed his hand away. "Is that what this is about?"

"No big deal, Grace. I did one morning's milking. You had a shit of a night and deserved the chance to get a few hours' sleep before you face the day." His reference to the attack had her swinging her gunsights toward him.

"My farm, my responsibility."

"I said I'm leaving," he snapped. She made it impossible to help her. *And that suited him fine.* He didn't want to be involved. Refused to make commitments.

"You said that from day dot, Ryan. You plan to leave. Relying on you is a mug's game." She stared him down.

Knowing she was right sparked his temper. "You called me. You opened the door."

"You're right." She huffed out a breath. "Don't make me regret it."

"Hell." Ryan rested his hand on Satan's head. "You'd try the patience of a saint. I'm here now. If you want to get rid of me, we need to stop the attacks on you."

"I don't want to get rid of you." Her soft admission made up for all her prickliness. Maybe he should call her his prickly pear: thorny on the outside and soft on the inside. "I do want the attacks to stop."

"I've got an idea we could talk about." He'd planned to work on it a bit more before he raised it.

"Then stay for breakfast." She pivoted and took off down the hall.

CHAPTER THIRTEEN

Ryan followed the scent of fresh coffee, of a freshly showered woman—soap and her perfume—and each sway of her hips had him pushing his hands further into his pockets to keep them off her. Desire was muted by the need to know she was safe and well.

"A long black for you, Gracie." Bluey set the cup in front of her.

"I'll have mine with milk, thanks," Ryan said.

Bluey set fresh scones, jam and cream on the table, a bowl of sugar, and then poured coffee for Ryan and himself. Bluey set Ryan's down opposite Grace but stayed leaning against the stove.

"What's the bank's current position?" Ryan demanded. Cosseting wasn't an approach that worked with Grace.

"They want evidence the deposit money is in my account before they approve the loan." She studied him over the rim of her coffee cup.

"When were you going to tell me?" He sat back in his chair, refusing to believe she'd risk the farm rather than tell him, but the news answered the question bothering him.

"I read the email before bed last night. It kinda slipped my mind." She waved her cup, encompassing the drama of the night before.

"You didn't remember when I told Bill I was buying a piece of your land?" Ryan remembered his surprised pride at her instinctive defence of him.

"I couldn't work out why you were sharing our business with Bill when all it did was make him suspect you?" She'd been discombobulated and had turned to him.

"Let's recap, Grace." The new information itched uncomfortably in the part of Ryan's brain that had bought and sold numerous properties. "One, you're buying the farm. Two, someone dumps contaminants. Three, news of the poisoning reaches the town's gossips. It's possible some people guess I helped in the clean-up. Maybe not. Four, the same day you get told you need twenty-five percent in the bank for your loan to be approved, your cheese store is targeted."

"Are you saying someone at the bank is sabotaging me?" She slammed her cup on the table.

"It's possible someone at the bank is indiscreet. General gossip—'What sort of deposit do you reckon Grace'll need for the farm?'"

"You're scaring me." She didn't sound scared; she sounded ready for a fight.

"We can act today. I transfer the shortfall into your account. We exchange deeds of agreement, guaranteeing I get the poppy fields when you settle on Blue Sky. Make it two separate deals. You and me. You and the bank." He'd take all necessary steps to protect her. If the goal was to break her financially and force her off the farm, then they needed to get the news out that the sale had gone through. To quash any suggestion that continued sabotage would bring her to her knees, they needed to make it clear she had a steady stream of cash to call on.

"The bank will know you made the deposit." She was thinking rather than objecting, which was another step forward. "Whoever accidentally leaked the loan requirement will know too."

"That's the aim. The bank seems to have been on a go-slow. Where are we? Week ten, eleven. This way they can't argue." He pushed because the threat was real, and he couldn't be with her twenty-four-seven.

"Eleven," she said.

"We also make sure the community knows. That you definitely have the money for the purchase because you're selling a parcel of land to me. We broadcast through every conventional and social media channel available." From where Ryan sat, the connection between the bank's email and the attack was too convenient to be a coincidence.

"If I announce the bank's given the go-ahead, that should end the acts of sabotage." *Was she uncomfortable about making the sale to him public?* "Blue Sky will be out of reach."

He shook his head. "You're still vulnerable. Managing the repayments is still a big load. People need to know your position's stronger than that. That I'm backing you." He'd need to sell some shares, slow down some purchases, but he'd make it obvious he was her backer. He wasn't interested in buying into her business, just ensuring some bastard didn't steal it from her.

"While you're here." She had even more prickles than a thorny dragon and was moving into armadillo class.

"I'm here a few years yet." Why her repetition of a truth he'd told her himself irritated him, he didn't know. "Ring Bill and see what he thinks."

"It might work." She took another sip of her coffee, as if weighing up the pros and cons. "But I want it watertight. I'm selling you a piece of my land. That's all. Blue Sky is mine."

"Of course you do." The reservation in her agreement stung. That she needed to restate her independence at the end of each conversation. She shed her caution when they made love, and he wanted to get her naked each time she put her clothes back on. "In the meantime, you can ask Bluey if he's prepared to stay over, or you get me."

"I beg your pardon," she sputtered.

"Mum might even enjoy a stint back on a farm." He swallowed half a scone and licked the cream off his lips.

"This is my life and my house you're talking about." She pushed herself upright in her chair and glowered at him.

"Until we're convinced this is over, you get company every night. You decide." He wouldn't be able to sleep if she was on her own.

"I don't take orders from you. Just because we've been to bed a few times—"

"Don't go there, Grace," he said quietly. "I don't need to be in your bed. I do need to know you're safe. I can sleep in another room."

Bluey cleared his throat. "I'll ask your mother if she'd like to stay a few days."

Ryan stared her down. "That's Bluey agreeing with me that someone should stay here. I can always call Brian. You called me. You opened the door." He left unspoken the words *you asked for my help.*

* * *

Bluey had followed Grace around the farm until she'd answered all his questions at least twice. With his blistering opinion ringing in her ears, she'd rung her parents and repeated the exercise. In her search for a single ally, she'd rung Bill. And struck out. They'd all agreed with Ryan that she shouldn't stay alone at the farm until the sale was finalised. Even after she'd confirmed the locks would be changed today. Her temper remained on simmer as she worked through her list. A new batch of cheddar, another delivery to the delicatessen, which had agreed to take her meagre production of eggs. Being right didn't excuse Ryan's high-handedness. She'd make that perfectly clear. She practised how she'd set him straight:

"Thank you for your help, but …"

"I appreciate your concern, but …"

"My home, my business and my decision to make, right down to

whether or not I sleepwalk my way through milking my own cows at four in the morning."

Somehow, he'd been there when she'd stepped out of her shower at dusk. The look in his eyes made her reach for him, as if loving him was the right way to end her working day. The heat and flash of good sex left her body loose and her mind relaxed. Before she'd realised he'd manoeuvred her into letting him stay, she was telling him about her day while he served the dinner he'd brought.

"Thanks for letting me stay," he'd whispered in her ear later that night after they'd made love again. His clever hands and mouth convinced her it was her choice.

Was falling in love with him a choice? Because she was stupidly in love with him. Also bound by the promise he'd made at the beginning—he was leaving.

A week until the farm was hers, and Grace's sense of body, heart and mind becoming disconnected from one another and floating in different directions had grown. Day and night belonged to different versions of herself.

During the day, Jake and Ryan's lawyer negotiated business and the legal niceties. Playing her part, she'd lent on the counter of every business in the surrounding towns and let the shopkeepers into a secret—her purchase of Blue Sky was a done deal. When they'd marvelled at how much money she'd made from cheese, she'd shared another secret. Ryan Wilson, you know the prodigal Wilson boy, had bought a few paddocks, gifting her financial security into the future. At night, she and Ryan entered their own magical world, where the brush of his skin across hers aroused with an exquisite agony, where the scent of their lovemaking triggered the need for more, and where his taste fuelled a hunger in her growing by the day.

She hated the disconnect more each day, hated the big lie acted out in both of her worlds—pretending she didn't love him.

He—she—hadn't anticipated the fallout from spreading the word Ryan was her banker. Anonymous and deeply personal, the whispers and social media gossip slapped at her pride and white-anted her self-belief.

"It's another attack on you," Ryan had brushed off the taunts. "Hoping to make you pull out of the deal."

Barbs were being fired from all directions, with some in her community turning on her with the viciousness of hornets defending their turf.

At the supermarket she heard the first whisper. *"She's selling more than some land."*

The next day, it was the post office. *"Ms. High-And-Mighty is prepared to roll over and spread her legs if the price is right."*

One afternoon when she was unloading her trolley, two men she didn't know well hovered, sniggering behind their hands. *"The EPA went through his land because he bankrolled the clean-up. Funny if he dumped the stuff so he could play knight in shining armour."*

Some of the comments found their way onto her business social media accounts.

"Lover! Whore more like."

"Prostituting herself to keep the farm!"

The crude viciousness of some comments disturbed her, while Ryan brushed them aside. He insisted he and she were the only judges of their relationship. She hadn't accepted every offer he made. She'd drawn boundaries—she'd accepted his improvements to the poppy fields but refused to accept payment for agistment. Her vegetation redesign plans for his property were almost complete. Paying her debts was essential. Both those secrets were known only to herself and Ryan.

Secrets preserved dignity and respect. Her father had kept Mrs. Wilson's secret that she was destitute when Ryan first left town. Ryan kept the secret Bluey was on his payroll, not hers. Grace was finding it harder to pretend none of the barbs snuck past her barriers.

A whisper, a nasty laugh, a snide remark—each one

hammering at defences stretched to breaking point because she loved him. The comments targeted her *and* Ryan. His association with her was threatening his new-found leadership in the community.

Today her first stop was the delicatessen. She pushed her loaded trolley through the front door. Seeing a crowd at the counter and in the café section, she tucked herself into a corner and waited for Bob to be free.

"You know he pushed to let her into the field day." Grace recognised the wife of a grumpy committee member. "What's in it for him?"

Grace froze. The woman was talking about her and Ryan.

"I always thought he was a deep one. Fancy setting her up so early." The woman's companion had a distinctive shrill singsong. President of the country women's association before Bess, she'd sat at Mrs. Wilson's table and at Grace's and commiserated about milk prices, the drought, and so many children being forced to work off-farm.

"I heard she seduced him." Mrs. Grumpy-By-Association dropped her voice to salacious level. "She's been begging for that stall for years. Knowing she got it by crawling into his bed must shame her parents."

"They left town pretty fast after that, although my Graham did say crowd numbers were up." Mrs. Shrill added a judicious assessment.

"They did leave fast. Do you think we should let them know what's happening—as friends?" Mrs. Grumpy spewed sanctimonious sympathy in a too-loud whisper.

"She can't be so naïve as to think he's seriously interested in her?" Mrs. Shrill's voice vibrated with disbelief.

"With Rochelle Harkiss around, he can do better. Rochelle said she was delighted his new land purchase would bring him closer to her." At public functions Mrs. Grumpy hung on Rochelle's every word.

"Grace can't compete with Rochelle in the looks department." Mrs. Shrill giggled. "Or the charm department. Have you heard talk he's not staying in town much longer?" Mrs. Shrill listened to too much talk. "He'll make a killing when he sells. His place, Donovan's and Blue Sky. Grace is as gullible as her father. She won't be so high and mighty in the future."

"Grace," Bob called her name. "I can deal with those deliveries now."

Aware the voices had stopped, Grace broke cover, pushing the trolley towards the counter with her head high. She didn't dignify the women with a glance.

Her remaining deliveries passed in a blur. Climbing into her van for the trip home, she stared into the distance.

"What's in it for him?"

"She can't be so naïve as to think he's seriously interested in her?"

"Sticks and stones," she muttered. But the overheard conversation had hit like a giant wave after a series of smaller ones. She'd withstood the earlier surges. This one sucked her under and had her fighting for clear air. These were the town's matriarchs, often kind-hearted, always small-minded, and frequently spitting out a kernel of truth with the bile.

"What do we have?" she whispered, suddenly cold. "An affair until the fire dies out or he loses interest. He plans to sell up and move on. He's never lied about his plans."

What's in it for him? She hated her doubt, but the question swirled, stinging like grit thrown in a windstorm. What's in it for him apart from the sex? The gossipy women were right. He could get sex anywhere.

She didn't know how to stop loving him. Although she knew it wasn't part of the deal, had known from the moment she'd knocked on his door and confessed to wanting him. Tight bands closed around her chest, squeezing until her heart hurt. Fear of him leaving threatened to choke her. This morning he'd held her tenderly, been reluctant to release her when the alarm sounded. He'd whispered endearments as she'd eased herself out of his arms, and she'd dared to hope that in time he'd love her too. He never used the word. She forced it back each time it rose to her lips.

Anthony Callea's version of *Save the Best for Last* signalled an incoming text message. Jake's address popped up.

There's a new condition. If you're okay to go ahead we exchange tonight. Call me when you get this.

Curiosity had her opening the attachment. Ryan hadn't mentioned any new conditions before she'd left this morning. A flicker of apprehension trickled down her spine. Trying to dismiss it, she summoned an image of her tousled lover as she'd last seen him. He'd been propped up in bed, his broad torso bare, the sheets tangled around his thighs, working on his computer, as he did every morning.

"You do your work. I'll do mine." He'd winked at her as she'd left.

He could have told her about a new condition last night or this morning. Why wait until the penultimate hour?

He hadn't told her. Why?

With a week until her parents' deadline, she'd lose everything if she pulled out.

Doubt was the evil-smelling miasma swirling above a witch's cauldron—choking her. This was the first time she'd broken her own rules. Smithhouse had smiled at her father before he'd presented him with a summons. The town's matriarchs had informed a packed café she was a tramp who'd been conned. Her stomach jittered.

What's in it for him?

She clicked on the document to open it, her hand clammy where she held the phone. Her vision blurred, so it took a few seconds to find the new clause Jake had highlighted for her. Panic coalesced into a tight ball in her chest. Her world came crashing down.

The phone sat where she'd dropped it, on the seat beside her. The words danced through her skull, like a ticker-tape newsreel on a relentless loop where you were forced to read the same breaking news again and again.

She'd been naïve. Or played by a master. Blue Sky was

the jewel in the crown in this valley. With this new clause, she'd hold ownership by the thinnest of threads.

Compromise isn't defeat until it is.

She'd compromised until she had nothing left. Nausea swirled, leaving her dizzy. She'd trusted him. Enough to surrender part of her dream. She couldn't give more, not when she'd given her heart. She focused on the road ahead, on keeping to the speed limit in the short distance to Ryan's. Stupid, really, she dashed away a tear. Ryan's final condition, offered at the eleventh hour made his motivation for everything else clear. She needed to focus on his betrayal, use her devastation to get her through this conversation.

He hadn't warned her of a new clause.

Ryan pushed through the door to stand above her on the veranda when she pulled up. Magnificent—her returning hero—legs apart, balanced, his arms hanging loosely at his sides—all cool strength and hot passion, and she wanted to beat at his chest until the bruises in her heart showed on his skin. Head bare, with the wind riffling through it, his shirtsleeves rolled up to reveal his muscled forearms, and she wanted him. Her love was her flaw. Love shattered her. She'd had such dreams. Becoming a cheese maker, owning the family farm, convincing Ryan they were good together. Not just in bed.

Satan danced against the Ute door in welcome. Pushing it open, she climbed out and bent to bury her face in his fur. She dug deep for the anger she needed to salvage some pride from this wreckage.

"Hi, boy. This is goodbye," she whispered. He whimpered as if he knew something was wrong, barked and loped up the veranda steps to his master.

"Down, Satan," he ordered. The dog dropped beside him.

She reached back into the van to pick up her phone, then rejected the prop. She dropped her sunglasses on the dashboard. He'd forced her to confront the power he had over her. She couldn't change his power over her farm. She could end one part of this lie.

"You bastard!" She walked up the steps to face him.

An eyebrow shot up. "Is there a reason for this fight? Or do you want an excuse to make up?"

"Did you ever want me?" Her throat burned with despair.

He frowned. "What are you talking about?"

"Jake sent me your new condition."

"And?" He ran a hand through his hair. A shaggy lock fell forward, shielding his eyes as effectively as his sunglasses. "Spit it out, Grace, so I know what I'm accused of this time."

"You're the only one who knew Dad and Mum gave me three months. The contracts need to be signed or the farm goes on the open market." Her words tumbled over each other.

"They'll be signed." He stood taller somehow, braced.

"Because you've backed me into a corner," she accused. "It's too late for alternatives. I have to accept your new condition." A condition making her work about as relevant as shifting a pile of hay from one side of the paddock to the other then back again.

"I don't see the problem?"

"You get first option to buy if I'm forced to sell. Was that your plan all along?" She turned and paced to the end of his veranda. Looking at his stony face should have stiffened her pride, but it made her weak at the knees. She sagged against a post. She didn't want an affair with him. She wanted forever, and she wanted to hate him. Instead she pushed herself upright and turned. "You've spent weeks finding out my weaknesses, learning exactly what my cash flow is."

"And that's a problem *because*?" His patience had bled into confusion.

"You said it yourself. Scale is everything. You know how fragile my cash flow is. This contract gives you leverage to cut my legs from under me at any time."

"Let me see if I've got this straight?" His voice was dangerously quiet. "I paid for Bluey to do farm work so he could …? I know, learn your spread so I can leave him to run it when I take over. I dumped the chemicals to force you to sell me the land, and then I cheated you on the price. Probably organised the break-and-enter at the farmhouse as well. Makes sense from where I stand."

"You went straight from my bed to your lawyer with this new condition."

"Speaking before you think is a good way to lose friends, Grace." He'd withdrawn without taking a step.

"Friends!" She threw an arm into the air, frightened she was right, terrified she was wrong. "You wanted everyone to know I was your mistress. You claimed it would protect me. It shames me. And when you take off, like you did before, you'll have taken everything. My land, my reputation, my independence."

He paled. His mouth set in a straight line. "You've said enough."

She slapped a hand against her thigh. "You didn't need to seduce me to get this far."

"As I recall, you came to my bed."

If he'd raised a fist to her, the blow couldn't be greater. He couldn't have been clearer about it being sex for him.

Arms raised, she flew at him. He reacted faster and caught her before she could land a punch, holding her while she struggled to free herself. Satan moved between them, whining in distress.

"Back," Ryan ordered, and Satan backed away. "I want you to leave." He dropped her hands as if he couldn't bear to touch her, as if every word the old women in the café had uttered was true.

"You're the one who's going. That's one thing you didn't lie about. You'll have a rolled-gold option on my farm as a nice sweetener for your buyer. I'll always be looking over my shoulder, waiting for the option to be cashed in." She'd trusted him and stood to lose everything—a reduction in the milk price, a fall-off in orders or a negative organic assessment. Her buffers were wafer-thin.

"Enough." He threw up a hand, cutting her off. "I get the caution. I understand what Smithhouse did to you and your family. I get the need to prove you can do things by yourself. I've been as driven. Sometimes I enjoy you exploding like a firecracker because making up is so much fun."

She pounded her fist against her heart. "Damn you! I love you. I'll never forgive you for tricking me."

"You don't love me, Grace. You just need something to dress up the sex." He sounded impossibly weary. "Love needs trust, and you've never trusted me." His barriers were firmly back in place. "I'm tired of walking on eggshells to prove you can."

Satan had risen to his feet to circle them, trying to herd them.

"You can't fix this, boy." She rested her hand on the animal's head when he followed her to her van. As she drove out, Ryan and the dog stood in the same place, the man keeping his dog close. Tears blurred her vision.

CHAPTER FOURTEEN

Grace unlocked her door, and the cold emptiness of the farmhouse enveloped her. Ryan had done that too. Occupied her space so she was lonely without him. *Already abandoned.* Her phone rang; she hated Anthony Callea's every ringtone and message tune.

"Hi, Ella." She tried to level her voice.

"What did you say, Grace?" Her sister skipped her usual breezy hello, her voice tight with anxiety. *Had the entire world turned upside down?*

"Oh!" She couldn't find an answer. Jake had asked her to call and confirm hours ago for the sale of the poppy fields to go through tonight. She caught sight of the kitchen clock. Jake wouldn't have gone ahead without her say so. "I lost track of the time. Is Jake with you?"

"He's redrafting the contract. The clause is gone."

Grace closed her eyes. *Why didn't Ryan's response feel like a victory?* She'd told him she loved him, and he hadn't believed her.

"Answer me." Her sister's impatience cut through Grace's misery. "The clause was my idea."

"Your idea?" Grace slumped into a chair, one hand propping up her head while she held the phone to her ear with the other. She didn't understand.

"The threats are too close. Mum and Dad have been frantic since the break-in, agonising about whether they should return, cancel the sale." Her sister's answer made no sense. Her parents had no option but to sell the farm. "Jake ran it past Ryan this morning. Ryan agreed."

Grace fumbled through her sister's clarification to the key point. "The clause *wasn't* Ryan's idea?"

"More window-dressing for the local rumour mill, making it clear Ryan had first option to buy Blue Sky if it went on the market again." Ella might look all yummy mummy, but her brain was as sharp as her husband's.

"You should have told me." Grace's stomach churned. Realising what she'd done, a wave of nausea shook her.

"We needed Ryan to agree first. Another bit of protection for you. Someone we know we can trust." Ella skewered Grace.

They did trust Ryan, a test she'd failed, with her surrender to past fears and malicious gossip. "I have to go." She had to crawl under a hay bail and hide.

"Not. Before. You. Answer. Me." Her sister separated each word with intent.

Grace heard Kit's gurgle and imagined Ella placing her hand on the child's head for mutual comfort, much like Ryan touched Satan.

Ella repeated, "What did you say?"

"You should have told me." Grace shivered, cold dread creeping through her. "Should have asked me. Should have warned me."

Should have stopped me from accusing Ryan.

"Are you crying?" Ella switched from exasperation to concern.

"No." But Grace touched her cheek and found it wet.

"Jake was going to explain to you. That's why he asked you to call." Her sister made their actions sound so reasonable.

"What did Ryan say?" Grace asked. He'd been quick,

ringing Jake within minutes of her departure. Severing his connection to her at a speed to leave her breathless.

"Not much. He'd changed his mind, didn't think it was a good idea. What did you say to him?" Ella resumed her cross-examination.

"That I didn't trust him. That he'd shamed me by letting everyone know I was his lover." Grace's breath emerged as a sob. "That I loved him."

"Oh, baby," Ella crooned, instantly Grace's supportive big sister.

"He didn't believe me." Because she'd used the words as a lash to whip him. "I'm scared of how I'll feel when he leaves town."

"So you're pushing him away." Ella's insight hit Grace like a nudge from a bull.

She loved him. She knew he'd go. A locked-in first option on the farm gave a ruthless man incredible leverage over her future. Only Ryan wasn't a ruthless man. Her emotions were as messy as when she'd shouted at him as a fifteen-year-old. She'd been trying to protect herself from a second abandonment. *Instead, she'd pushed him away.* "I ruined everything," she whispered.

Ella didn't answer, and the silence crowded Grace.

"What aren't you telling me?" Grace's hand climbed to her throat.

"He wants seventy-two hours to think about the purchase," her sister admitted.

"I don't have much more than that." The churning in Grace's stomach picked up speed.

"He wants to *think* about it," Ella emphasised. "That's all he said."

"If he doesn't buy the river paddocks, I'm finished." Grace no longer cared. Her accusation had been criminally unfair. Gossip and her uncertainty about Ryan's feelings for her had been the trigger. Ryan had told her not to let it get to her. She'd listened and absorbed the poison.

"He hasn't withdrawn the offer." Ella sounded

uncertain.

Yet! Grace heard the yet and couldn't blame Ryan when she'd called him a liar and a cheat. She covered her mouth with her hand as her stomach heaved. "I have to go."

"Will you be okay?" Ella paused. "What a stupid question. I love you, Grace. I'll ring tomorrow."

"Talk soon." She dropped the phone on her run to the bathroom, reaching the toilet in time to be violently sick. When the second bout of nausea hit, she was already on her knees, hugging the bowl, her body trembling.

She cleaned herself up, fed Bailey—back home after his stint at the vet's—and was about to crawl into bed, for the warmth, for the hoped-for oblivion, when the headlights lit the drive. A vehicle was slowly approaching the house. She hit the external lights and walked back onto the veranda, torn between hope Ryan had come to see her and fear she'd disgrace herself by throwing up again. Then she recognised Bluey's van.

Swinging himself out, he loped towards her, stopping a few feet away. "Ryan called. Said he couldn't get here tonight."

Tears spilled onto her cheeks, and she knuckled them away. "You don't have to stay. I'm fine."

"We're not having that argument again." He took her arm. "Let's get you inside."

She sat at the kitchen table, sniffled and then blew her nose. Ryan had withdrawn his support. She had the independence she'd claimed to want. She hadn't known the price she'd have to pay—this awful sensation of being hollowed out, as if some part of her was missing.

Bluey glanced at her surreptitiously from time to time as he busied himself heating soup and making toast. She pretended a confidence she didn't feel, chatting about the new calves and the seaweed-based feed she wanted to experiment with. She ran out of small talk.

Seventy-two hours. Three sleeps short of disaster. If Ryan bought the land, she'd hate herself. If he cancelled the sale, she'd hate herself. She'd messed up. Crossing her arms on the table, she lowered her head. The truth in all the obscene taunts—that he didn't love her—had festered inside her, destroying what they did have. They'd been friends.

Bluey brought the soup and buttered toast to the table. "Eat some, Gracie. You need to eat and sleep. There's another day tomorrow."

Lifting her head, she forced a weak smile. "I'll do the morning milking. You start at six as normal."

"We'll do the morning milking." He brushed a hand over her head before he went to collect his own food, as her father might, and the love in the gesture had tears spilling over. "Your only flaw, girl, is not letting people close enough to help."

"You know why." She picked up a spoon. Things were bad when Bluey chastised her.

"That was a long time ago. Bull-headed independence can be a blessing or a curse. It took me a long time to learn that. Don't make my mistake."

When they finished eating, she carried their bowls to the sink before turning to face him. "You can't stay here every night. You have your own life."

"We're talking less than a week." Bluey knew how much time she had left. "Don't know how that news got out, but it's common knowledge." He also knew Ryan didn't want to see her anymore.

She hunched a shoulder. "Ryan suspects someone at the bank is either indiscreet or deliberately providing a running commentary on the status and timing of my loan."

"If that's the case, the world will know it's on hold." Bluey pulled on his ear. *Was her entire life fodder for gossip?*

"Unless Ryan buys some land, I don't have a deposit."

"I know." He rose to his feet. "I'll sleep in the other house. See you at four." Bluey had just confirmed the seriousness of the threat against her. Ryan and her family had been trying to give her what she claimed she most wanted, and she'd thrown Ryan's help back in his face.

When she crawled into bed, she replayed every act of kindness Ryan had shown her until she fell asleep. Her dreams were filled with memories of their lovemaking, when he'd smiled at her the first time, when he'd reached for her as if touching her, holding her was all that mattered. Loving him was all that mattered to her. Afraid of waiting for him to end their affair, she'd thrown a stick of dynamite on the bonfire.

* * *

Ryan settled comfortably into what was probably Bluey's chair. With Bluey staying over at Grace's, he'd invited himself to dinner with his mother. It wasn't often he found her alone. That was a good thing, since he'd been gone eight of the last ten years and would be off again soon. She'd answered his questions about his father, his childhood, about why she'd stayed when Ryan had offered more than once to bankroll her to leave. Grace had been right about his mother not wanting to leave Danny. Plus, she had good friends in the valley and town who'd supported her emotionally after Danny had died.

"And there's Bluey." She gave a private smile.

"It took me a while to wake up to that." Ryan's only excuse was the punishing days he'd worked when he returned, using work to block out other memories.

"He's a gentle, decent man." She'd never liked idle hands and continued now with her knitting, the clacking of the needles a musical accompaniment to match the ebb and flow of conversation, sometimes fast, sometimes silent, mostly steady.

"I've worked that out for myself. Why aren't you married?"

"He wasn't sure you'd approve." Ryan's mother dropped her hands and her knitting into her lap to look at him.

"Why is my opinion even relevant?" He'd never considered they were waiting for some kind of approval from him.

"You're my son. I value your opinion. Bluey knows that." She pinned Ryan with the clear gaze he'd treasured every day of his childhood and missed every day of his exile.

"I really am a bastard, aren't I?"

"Six months after the wedding, but there was a wedding, so you're legitimate." She winked.

"I approve, for what it's worth." Ryan wanted her to be happy, and she was of a generation to value the formal commitment.

"Bluey's changed his mind lately. Now it's cold feet because 'Good heavens—marriage!'" she exclaimed.

Ryan laughed for the first time since he'd had his bust-up with Grace.

"What about you and Grace?" His mother picked up her needles again.

"What about me and Grace?" Ryan and his mother hadn't talked much about feelings since Danny's death. At first, Ryan had been absent, then they'd lost the habit, or he'd lost the habit. Grace had changed that.

"Not fair. I shared." The needles continued their steady rhythm. She waited while he squirmed like an adolescent. "We women don't know unless you tell us."

"I care." And he was telling his mother when he hadn't told Grace. That didn't feel right. "A lot. Smithhouse did a serious number on her." He sought for the right words to describe what he'd finally worked out. "She has to do everything alone because, hell, you might be trying to trap her or cheat her."

"The gossip about you and Grace has been fierce, son."

"Wilsons don't listen to gossip." Rather, he had a compartment in his brain where he parked the crap some people spewed and kept it closed. Danny had been broken by gossip.

"Some trolls have left messages on Grace's business

site." His mother was *looking for* gossip. "Bluey heard things, so I checked."

"Shit! I've learned to block it out."

"I'm guessing the gossip that says, 'Why on earth would Ryan Wilson be interested in Grace if not for the land' and then calls her a slut would hurt." She rolled up her knitting. "She's a bit like Danny that way. Uncertain of her own appeal and easily hurt."

"I thought most of the dirt would be directed at me. She's lived here all her life. Is it really bad?" Ryan had told Grace to ignore it without knowing she and her business were the primary targets.

"I walked into Bob's café yesterday shortly after Grace made a delivery. Bob was upset because he'd been busy. Grace had to wait, he said, and was forced to listen to some pretty vile stuff." Ryan's mother was making a rare intervention in his life.

"She didn't tell me about her business site or that other shit …" He hadn't asked for any details. His hand had fisted on his thigh, and he forced his fingers to straighten.

"Maybe she's afraid."

"Grace isn't afraid of anything," he protested. She'd gone back to the field day committee year after year, arguing for entry. She'd been an early adopter of organic and sustainable farming methods and stood up to the bullies in the district. He'd admired her even when her lady-of-the-manor act pissed him off.

"We're all a little afraid of falling in love," she said gently.

An image of Grace, thumping her heart and shouting that she loved him at the same time as accusing him of trying to cheat her, flashed through his mind. Never in all their lovemaking had she told him she loved him. *Her touch had been loving.* He'd been in enough beds to know the difference. "I'm not a good long-term bet, Mum." He'd sign the contract, buy the poppy fields, move faster on getting the farm ready for sale and move on.

She reached out a hand and stroked his cheek. "Speaking

as someone who's known you for the longest time, I'd back you."

"The plan has always been to sell the farm." Although he'd let the south coast property slide by him at auction on Saturday, despite the asking price being better than he'd hoped.

"Plans can change." She returned to her knitting.

"I love you, Mum." The words were easier to form than he'd expected. "I should have given you the words."

She smiled at him, the sheen of tears in her eyes. "The words are beautiful, but you've shown me, every day of your life. I'm proud of you, son. I probably haven't said that often enough."

"I've always known." Hearing her say the words made him feel taller.

Unsure of his next step, Ryan climbed into his Ute for the journey home. Grace had to know by now the clause hadn't been his idea. She hadn't tried to contact him. She said she'd been shamed by being his lover, as if what they'd shared had been dirty in some way. He'd never told her he cared, but he'd let her know making love to her had been a joy. More than sex. He didn't need the words to know it was more than sex. But love, the kind that lasted, needed trust. They didn't have that.

Vicious gossip had made Danny feel ashamed. *Was the same true for Grace?* Ryan's silence and lack of support would have been another hit to her confidence. He could have called Jake on the spot and made her brother-in-law tell her the new clause wasn't Ryan's idea. Instead, he'd asked her to leave. Because her lack of faith hurt him. Big, tough guys didn't admit they hurt.

Satan lifted his head, sniffing the air, then whimpered before rising to his feet and pressing his nose against the slightly open car window. He whined, barked and tried to get out.

"What is it, boy?" Ryan rolled down his window. "What can you smell?" He caught sight of the spiral of smoke simultaneously with catching the scent. Instead of turning in at his gate, he flattened the accelerator. Then reached for the dog. "Good boy. It's at Grace's."

The powerful vehicle ate kilometres as Ryan punched in the emergency number. Fire, police and maybe ambulance. The responder reassured him a call had been made, a tanker was on its way, with ambulance and police to follow. They confirmed the site as a paddock abutting the road.

"Fodder. The bastard!" Ryan thumped the steering wheel. This time whoever her attacker was had gone for animal feed.

The brief relief of hearing a call had already been registered evaporated as nightmare scenarios ran through his head. Grace wouldn't be waiting patiently for help. At least Bluey would keep his head. *Keep her from doing something brave and stupid.*

As Ryan drew closer, flames shot through the smoke like splinters of lightning. Fire speared in all directions, exploding where it landed. It moved with lethal randomness. Like him, she had fire-fighting equipment. Serviceable and in good condition, but would it be enough? Would she have the sense to wait for help? More flames leapt into the sky. Satan strained at the window.

"We'll find her, boy." Fear pressed his foot harder on the pedal. "We'll find her."

Silhouetted against the sky, the fire was dancing maniacally behind her as she held the hose from her knapsack steady. *His heart stopped.* He slammed on the brakes and leapt from his Ute, racing across the field to her side, Satan at his heels. The thick black smoke clawed at his throat, the heat seared his skin.

"It doesn't matter if it hits the road," she gasped, battling to direct the hose along a side fence. "Need to hold it here."

"Where's Bluey?" The fire brigade siren was getting closer.

"Moving the cows." She was breathing hard, and the crackle and pop shrieked around them.

"Shit, Grace! Why didn't you bring him with you?" He scanned the area. She'd filled her knapsack from the pump perched on the water-tank platform.

"Someone had to see to the animals," she croaked.

"Give me that." He covered her hand on the hose, gestured with his thumb that she should shuck the pack and let him take over. "Get back."

"If you want to help, there's a second knapsack near the tank." She coughed. "I'll see to the other flank."

"Get the fuck back, Grace." He couldn't fight the fire and her. "You're not wearing a mask." She needed to be safe. Blood pounded in his ears. If she didn't move soon, he'd tackle her and haul her to safety. Fuck! Fodder wasn't worth one mark on her body.

The fire tanker swerved around his vehicle and came alongside the farm tank.

"I'll speak to them." She shucked the pack and handed it to him before turning her back on him.

He didn't give a damn if she lost her temper. "Look after Satan," he demanded. She glared back. "Please?"

Ryan moved steadily up the line she'd started, the heat intense through his flimsy clothing. People spilled from the tanker, geared up, and moving fast. He was aware of someone gesticulating, of a hose being run along a different line, of foam being sprayed. *Was this another contaminant?*

Had that been the entire bloody purpose?

More contamination, more questions from the organic certifying body? A last attempt to stop the sale because people were convinced he'd pulled the plug and were prepared to take the risk. Shit! Forty-eight hours! This confirmed his suspicion someone in the bank was leaking.

The senior firefighter tapped him on the shoulder. A woman—Mel Agostini. "You've been here long enough. We can take over now."

He relinquished the hose and retraced his path to his vehicle. Despite the poor visibility, he made out the ambulance beside it, with its back open. He hadn't heard it arrive above the roar of the fire. Grace hunched on the floor with a paramedic crouched in front of her. Satan lay beside her, his head in her lap, while she absently stroked the dog's head. Ryan stopped a few feet away.

"How do you feel?" the paramedic asked.

"Fine," she rasped.

"Your throat will hurt for a few days." The paramedic rose to his feet. "You know better than to fight a fire without a mask." She was taking the raking down from the paramedic better than she'd accepted Ryan's instructions.

"Speed ... smelled petrol ... needed to hurry." She stopped, racked by another bout of coughing. Her hand paused its caress of the dog, and Satan nuzzled to make her continue. "Knew fire brigade on its way."

"Do it again, and I'll report you to your divisional captain in the bush fire-fighting brigade." The paramedic turned and spotted Ryan. "More walking wounded?"

"I'm fine," Ryan added pointedly. "I tied a handkerchief over my face."

"Pay attention, Grace." The paramedic shook his finger at her.

"Go to hell, Marty," she scowled.

"Is that any way to talk to a childhood friend?" Marty was inviting Ryan to weigh in, and a vague memory of the guy surfaced. Older than Ryan and a townie. Maybe that gave Marty special rights to chastise Grace. "Although I'm not impressed by your lack of protective gear either, Ryan."

Ryan shrugged. "None in the Ute."

"Satan wanted to go after you." Grace cocked her head to one side. "You told him to stay."

"He smelled it first. His instinct is to protect."

"I'm not arguing. Not here and now. I hoped it was over," she whispered. The uncharacteristic defeat in her voice skewered him. "Can ... save ... any of it?"

He leaned against the side of the ambulance, his heart rate slowing with the worst over. She'd pissed him off, hurt him, and he'd delayed the contract a few days. The bastard who'd been after her from the first had struck. Ryan blamed himself.

The firefighters followed a practised routine, reducing the square, watching for flare-ups. Surreal against the moonlit sky in their protective gear and masks, they moved through their well-choreographed dance. Grace coughed again, and Ryan's hand formed a fist.

"How long before I got here?" Ryan asked.

"Fifteen, twenty minutes." She was gripped by another coughing fit. "Bluey … a last check before bedtime … caught the scent."

"Why not go to the hospital? See a doctor." Rage came fast on the heels of Ryan's fear.

"I need … assess … what's lost."

"That can wait." Forever as far as Ryan was concerned.

"My responsibility." She tried to rise from the seat, and he pushed her back down.

"Most of this forage field is lost." He remembered her enthusiasm when she'd told him of the experimental crop, a mix of fescue, ryegrass, red and white cover.

"Why?" Her hair smelled of smoke, and beneath that, sweat. She was filthy, her face soot-smudged. "To poison the soil? Torch our animal feed for the next few months? Have to buy in feed now."

"Take your pick." Ryan remembered the blobs of a tar-like substance he'd avoided as he worked. "I smelled raw petrol when I arrived."

"Me too."

Grace," Mel called out.

Ryan stepped back again and turned to face the woman, leaving Grace to take the lead.

"It's under control, but it's worth posting a lookout to make sure no embers start up." Mel tucked her headgear under one arm.

"Bluey and I'll work out a roster for the rest of the night," Grace croaked.

"There'll be three on the roster," Ryan said.

"It's deliberate. But you knew that." Mel shook her head, the sweat-slicked hair remaining firmly stuck to her scalp. "Any ideas?"

Ryan answered for Grace. "There've been a few incidents in the last few months. Bill's investigating. The main theory is someone's trying to cost Grace money so she can't afford to buy the farm."

"Deadline's the end of the week." Mel looked pointedly at him. If she knew that level of detail, half the state probably knew.

"The sale will go through." Tomorrow, and he'd demand an overhaul of the bank's security and confidentiality procedures.

Grace was visibly deflated, and Ryan had something else to blame himself for. She'd thought he wouldn't go ahead. That he'd let her lose the farm. He'd been hunkering down like Satan in the months after his amputation, licking his wound. Missing her like the devil, and not having a blind clue what to do about it. He cursed himself for a selfish bastard.

"I might be able to help," he added. "With identifying the perpetrator."

They turned to him as one, the fire captain curious, Grace dumbstruck.

"I moved one of my CCTV cameras to the edge of Grace's farm. Aimed at the road," he explained.

Grace gasped. *Right!* His jaw clenched. Another point scored against him, another supposedly high-handed decision—something else to add to her list of suspicions.

"Were you expecting something?" Mel studied him with new respect.

"Bill and I agreed it was a reasonable precaution after the break-in." Ryan had been planning to move it in the next few days when the sale was complete.

"Another thing I didn't need to know." Grace's chin lifted belligerently.

"You would have told us to go to hell," he replied curtly.

"It should carry a record of the vehicles passing my place tonight, what time they passed, how long they spent in the valley."

"I don't envy Bill the job of trawling through that footage." Mel grimaced. "He'll have to cross-check with the visitors to the Centre. Rochelle won't be pleased."

The sardonic tone caught Ryan's attention. "Why would Rochelle be annoyed?"

"We did our regular inspection to make sure the place meets fire safety standards, and she assigned that gardener to show us around." The fire captain shrugged. "Prevent us looking around more like."

"Protecting her clients' privacy," Grace rasped. "Rochelle takes it seriously."

"You're probably right. However, their safety is as important as their privacy." Mel glanced over her shoulder as the police cruiser pulled in behind the ambulance. "Perfect timing. We've done what we can here tonight. I'll brief Bill on my thoughts before I head off."

Grace stretched out a hand. "Thanks. For the speed. For the help."

"It would have been worse if you hadn't been on the spot so quickly." The woman crossed to intercept Bill.

"I might make a move too." Marty waved to his assistant. The paramedic had been moving among the firefighters, doing a quick check they were okay.

CHAPTER FIFTEEN

Ryan steered Grace towards his Ute. She trembled, and he knew she wouldn't thank him for asking if she'd been terrified. It was enough to know he was. To know that seeing her single-handedly fighting a runaway fire made every fight they'd ever had insignificant. He could have lost her. *Love!* His gut rolled. He'd told himself he didn't do that anymore. But he didn't know any other word for the feeling that had rocked him when he'd arrived to find her surrounded by flames.

When she climbed onto the passenger seat, he recognised the concession she was making. She sat upright, unspeaking while they waited for Bill to finish his conversation with Mel. Her laboured breaths were loud in the eerie silence crowding them, shallow in an attempt to disguise the rasp, and Ryan wanted to smash something.

The fire captain climbed into the firetruck. Bill waved as it rumbled back onto the road, then crossed to them.

"Hi, Bill."

The officer nodded. "Your CCTV footage might stitch up this deal."

"I'll bring it in tomorrow morning." Ryan inclined his head towards Grace, signalling Bill to make it short and sharp.

"Sounds good," Bill answered. "You should get inside. Get some rest, Grace. I can talk to you tomorrow as well."

"More work to do," she whispered.

"I know, a roster," Ryan snapped. His mother was right. Bloody-minded independence was one way to survive.

Grace placed a hand on his forearm, a light grip, but it annoyed him to know he needed her touch to steady him. "I was safe. I've done the volunteer training, my gear's reliable, and I knew help was on its way."

"That's rational bullshit, and you know it." Adrenalin drained from him, leaving an impotent rage. He wanted to pick her up and carry her to bed, to keep her there until Bill solved this. But Ryan had made the mistake of thinking the extra clause in the contract was innocuous. That he'd won her trust. A monumental miscalculation he couldn't undo.

"I'll leave you to it." Bill waved a hand as he backed away. "Don't fight all night."

Ryan had refused to let himself think Grace was telling the truth when she'd said she loved him, but his mother's words made sense. He wanted to touch Grace. What he wanted counted for zilch. "I'll drive you to the house."

"Thank you." She swivelled her legs and pulled the door closed.

Satan was around the vehicle and jumped into the cab ahead of him, as if determined to keep them separate. Ryan drove in silence. Bluey waited in the kitchen.

"I'm doing the talking because her throat's a mess." Ryan pre-empted Bluey's questions by giving him a rundown on what had happened.

"I don't need a voice to mount guard."

"You go to bed, Gracie," the older man said firmly. "Ryan and I can cover this."

"My farm, my responsibility," she said stubbornly, unaware tears were running down her blackened cheeks.

"So, you fight the fire, you patrol the farm, and I guess you milk the cows tomorrow morning!" Ryan snapped.

"Yes."

"And you'd fall over if I blew on you." He stepped closer, shrugging off the fear and anger. *She was safe.* "You didn't fight Marty when he told you you were wrong!"

Her mouth opened and closed several times.

"No answer? Why do you have to fight me every time?" Ryan pulled her closer, needing the feel of her to settle the last of his fear, and to hell with the consequences. "I'm not the enemy." He kissed the top of her head. She was real. Flesh and blood and safe.

He carried her smoke scent as he patrolled the house and perimeter of the farm buildings, Satan at his side. He greeted Bluey with a coffee at four as the older man came down to start the milking. "I'll call Jake this morning, give the go-ahead."

Bluey nodded.

* * *

"So you're pushing him away."

"Why do you have to fight me every time?"

Grace fixed the teat to the waiting cow. She'd waited for Ryan to leave before joining Bluey.

"I'm not the enemy," he'd said.

She continued to move down the row, attaching one cow after the other.

"Because I'm afraid," she confessed to the next dumb beast she reached for.

Afraid of loving Ryan so much she'd cease to function when he walked away. Her father, a wiser, better judge of character than her had trusted Smithhouse and been betrayed. She'd loved Danny, and he'd gone in an instant, without giving her a chance to talk him out of it.

That's what she'd feared with Ryan—that one day he'd leave, and nothing she could say would change his mind. It was a kick in the teeth to discover cowardice had been driving her attacks on him. She'd lashed out before Ryan had a chance to, because if she kept control, his absence would be easier to bear. A different kind of kick to discover the joy and laughter had gone out of her life. She wasn't living anymore. Just going through the motions. She had her farm, her work, her family at the end of a phone, and it wasn't enough.

Missing Ryan was an ache down to the bone, a dull pain with a life of its own. It took its own form—a different form—every day. One day a throbbing headache, the next nausea. Although the tightness in the muscles, the stiffness in the joints were constant. Her limbs were so heavy she struggled to place one foot in front of the other.

The snap and flash of the fire had scared her spitless. Then she'd caught sight of Ryan striding towards her, and her world had miraculously righted itself. His furious arrival through the smoke had given her the confidence to keep fighting—the fire, him, whatever she needed to win. An unlikely hero. Except he'd saved Satan from a fire. She'd slapped him down after the fire because she was afraid if she didn't step back now, she'd shatter into a million pieces when he left the valley.

She owed him an apology for accusing him of trying to steal her farm. Another for risking his life for her last night. He'd kissed the top of her head. *Did he even know?* She'd soaked up the comfort he'd offered like parched earth soaking up rain and wished she could turn back time.

Bluey finished ahead of her and waited in the kitchen when she stumbled in. He set a cup of coffee in front of her. "You catch some more sleep. I'll take over."

Sleep would be bliss, but if she closed her eyes now, her brain would be on an endless loop of questions without answers. "That's a lovely idea. I'm better working."

He pushed a newspaper across to her, open at the crossword. "Seven across, eight letters, another anagram."

"Confused, but Bron's persistent," she read out the clue. "I'm not sure my brain can cope with a crossword clue."

"*Sure* it can. It's real topical too." He took the seat

opposite her and ran his finger over each word. "*Confused*—
that tells me the letters are all mixed up. You always ace the
anagrams. And *persistent*? We need another word meaning
persistent. That leaves us with *but Bron's*. Eight letters."

"Stubborn." She set her cup down with a snap.

"Bingo!" Bluey leaned back with a crooked smile. "Give
the girl a prize."

"I'm not stubborn," she protested.

"Nah! Just mulish, obstinate, pig-headed, stiff-necked,
or my personal favourite—bloody-minded."

"I'm afraid," she whispered.

He reached a hand across the table to cover hers. "I've
never known you to be afraid of anything, girl."

"I'm afraid of stuffing up. Of losing the farm that Dad
and every generation before him fought to keep. Of doing
something that reminds him of what Smithhouse did."

"You think Ryan's another Smithhouse?" Bluey drew
back.

"Now I've offended you by insulting Ryan." She pulled
at her hair and shook her head. "That wasn't what I meant."

"Maybe there are a few things you've forgotten from
that time."

"What things?" She wasn't thinking straight. She hadn't
managed more than a few hours' sleep since Ryan had left
her bed.

"Donovan or I dropped in every few days for a long
time. Donovan supplied agistment for the animals your dad
had to move off those pastures," he said.

She stared at him. The men had been around. They'd
casually dropped in, claimed to be passing and insisted her
father go into town for meetings. "You were keeping an eye
on him."

"He's a friend, Gracie. Friends help when they can."

"Donovan didn't charge for agistment," she said slowly.

"The Wilson place wasn't in good enough shape to help
then." Bluey shrugged, let her stew a bit. "Ryan isn't a thief."

She winced at the blunt assessment.

"He's being a good neighbour and friend."

She'd finally got that. The men Ryan had chosen as role models were honest, hard-working and for the most part stubbornly inarticulate men. They didn't boast of their good deeds. Hell, it took ten years before she'd learned her father had helped Mrs. Wilson after Danny's death.

"It's not that. Not *just* that," she amended, catching her bottom lip between her teeth. Bluey would keep her secret, and she was tired of second-guessing herself. "I'm afraid of loving Ryan so much I don't know what to do with it."

Bluey released a long low whistle and slumped back in the chair. "Have you told him?"

"Not in a way he believed me." She remembered the closed look on his face, the stiffness in his body. He'd kicked her out immediately. She'd cried all the way home, screaming her despair in the airless cabin.

"Do it again," Bluey said.

She inhaled instead of swallowing her mouthful of coffee and choked. She scowled at him until she got her breath back. "Just like that!"

He winked. "Be polite this time."

She narrowed her eyes.

"If you can remember how." He lifted a shoulder.

"You're testing the friendship, Bluey."

"Tell him you love him, and see what happens. I'll handle the farm. You do what you need to do."

"Simple!" She threw a hand in the air. *Wake Me Up Before You Go-Go* announced an incoming call, and she jumped. "I'm getting a new ringtone."

Bluey smirked. "Who could that be?"

"Ryan rang." Her brother-in-law's voice killed the leap of hope her heart had given. "We can finalise the sale today. Get the word out to whoever needs to know."

Ryan had told the fire captain the sale would go ahead, and he'd kept his word. Her dream. Until she'd had a new dream. "Give me twenty-four hours." She powered the phone down and put it in the cutlery drawer.

"What was that about?" Bluey transferred their cups to the sink.

"Ryan called Jake. He's offered to finalise today."

"You asked for twenty-four hours?" Bluey scratched his jaw. "Sure you know what you're doing?"

"Not yet. But I want to take the time to think it through. Not go off like a firecracker. I'll be in the cheese shed and don't want to be disturbed. Can you stay here again tonight, Bluey?" Her cheese shed was her happy place, the best place to think.

Mrs. Wilson arrived at six. Bluey had given Grace advance warning, and they'd both gone out to greet her. Ryan's mother had parked her small, white sedan beside Bluey's van. Grace couldn't hear the conversation, but the body language was fascinating. Sweetness and light when Mrs. Wilson leaned in and kissed him, awkward reluctance when she gestured to the boot. Bluey disappeared into her grandparents' house, while the older woman headed towards her, a large casserole dish in her arms.

"I brought dinner," she said matter-of-factly, passing Grace on her way to the kitchen.

"Thank you." Grace hurried ahead to open the oven door. "I seem to be living on my freezer and your cooking lately."

"There was a time when your mother did the same for me." Mrs. Wilson slid the dish into the oven and snapped on the timer. "It's a one-pot dish because from what Bluey tells me, you fall into your plate before you finish dinner most nights."

"I'm beyond exhaustion at this stage. My mind won't stop."

"I know what that's like too." The woman eyed Bluey as he came back into the kitchen. "I told Bluey I'm staying." She turned to Grace. "If that's okay with you?"

Grace swallowed. She couldn't win on this one. "Not my business."

"It's our first official overnight away from home as a

couple. I'm hoping whoever watches your place like a hawk gets that bit of gossip out." Mrs. Wilson wore a satisfied smile.

Bluey made a strangled sound.

The woman grinned. "Then he'll have to make an honest woman of me."

"Can I offer you a drink?" Grace filled the sudden silence. "Coffee, tea, water, wine?"

"You should have brought champagne," the irascible old man muttered.

"A red wine would suit dinner," Mrs. Wilson said. "And it's about time you called me Helen."

"Congratulations, Helen." Grace swallowed the giggle bubbling inside her, wishing Ryan was here to share the moment. "If you'll excuse me a minute, I'll get the glasses and wine." There was no shouting when she was in the living room. She collected the best crystal and one of her father's celebration reds, nudging open the kitchen door with her hip.

"Let me." Bluey took the bottle from her hand and studied the label.

Grace kissed his cheek. "Congratulations, Bluey."

"She was joking," he mumbled.

"No, I wasn't." Then Helen relented and started asking Grace questions about her mum, about Ella and the children.

When the timer went off, Bluey collected dishes and Helen served. A couple familiar with each other's rhythm. They brushed against each other as Bluey handed Helen an empty plate, took it back loaded with food, passed another. Very similar to her own parents before her mother's health deteriorated. Finding joy in simple things. A married couple without the legal piece of paper.

As they chatted about how they'd spent the day, exchanged smiles and quiet giggles, envy snuck up on her. Her latest temper tantrum had cost her precious time with Ryan. Time she'd never get back.

"You go to bed, Grace. I'll clean up," Helen said.

"My mother taught me some manners. If you cook, you don't clean." She made a shooing gesture with her hands.

"Are you sure?" Helen's smile spread.

"Take the rest of the wine." Grace waved them towards the door. "One-pot dinners leave very little cleaning up."

Grace stacked the dishwasher, then followed them outside. She stood for a while, soaking up the smells of the night. Unlike Helen, Grace's mother had spent hours on her garden. Bulbs had burst through the cold earth. With her frantic workload, Grace had missed the simple pleasure of seeing the season change. Now the scent of hyacinths filled her nostrils, urging her further into the garden. Even at the height of her drive for sustainability and a return to a natural environment, she'd never dared suggest changes to her mother's garden. The European plants and shrubs were another part of her legacy.

When Grace reached the garden gate, she turned back. The empty house stood unwelcoming in front of her, taunting her with her loneliness. She spun on her heel, setting off across the land she'd prioritised above everything else in her life. A clear night, the stars lit the sky like a million tiny fireflies swarming, making the well-worn track to the river easy to follow. Clumps of laurels were silhouetted against the sky. Occasionally she heard the low of cattle. A tawny frogmouth hooted, and she stopped, her eyes searching for the outline of the shy owl.

She'd told Ryan she was ashamed to be his lover, that she didn't trust him in business. Tears stung the backs of her eyes.

"Damn my temper," she yelled at the sky. She knew herself better than that. She'd grown out of her let-her-rip days, hadn't had a real tantrum in years. "Until Ryan re-entered my life." Temper was her way to fight fear.

"Isn't that pathetic!" She'd spent hours in her cheese shed trying to craft an apology and still hadn't found the right words.

She envied Helen's confidence in teasing Bluey about their relationship. Grace's parents had it, Ella and Jake had it, and Grace had doubted she'd find it. She had, and she'd torpedoed it. She continued to stride across the valley, familiar with the path, although the soft moonlight acted as a guide, revealing well-worn trails.

"What if he doesn't accept my apology?" She stopped. "Or doesn't believe me if I tell him I love him again?"

Slowly, the soft sound of wind rustling the leaves on the trees calmed her, a susurrus. A word learned from early cryptic crosswords and never forgotten. A susurrus, the word matching the breathy sound that turned silence into a living world. Stopping, she cocked her head. A sound too soft to hear in the city. She'd thrown herself on the ground during other tantrums, hiding in the grass, absorbing its damp green scent, unable to be found and then the sound would track her down, make her lift her head and laugh.

Grace turned towards home. Maybe, just maybe, she had an idea.

Grace was mulling her plan when she walked into the kitchen after milking the next morning. Bluey passed her a coffee, waited while she took a slow mouthful, then gave her the news Bill had called an hour earlier. She made the return call.

"I've got news. I can see you and Ryan at about six tonight if that suits you." Bill's deep bass voice almost made music, offering her the chance to put last night's idea into practice.

"Have you checked with Ryan yet? His place is closer to town. It makes sense to meet there." She needed to be on Ryan's patch, ceding him control for her idea to work.

"Works for me," Bill agreed.

Grace tried to synchronize her arrival at Ryan's with the police cruiser, but she'd been antsy about the meeting and miscalculated. There was no sign of the blue and white when she hit Ryan's gates. One of his cameras might catch her if she parked, so she sailed past towards the main junction to town. To a casual onlooker, town was her destination. She could backtrack from there, and if Bill ended up behind her, she could pretend she'd come back from town herself.

The sign stood inside Ryan's property at the junction— Leinad Farms. Two solid Australian red cedar posts and a crossbar, with the words carved deep and clear, visible from fifty metres at least. A huge sign that would age well and set down roots. A statement of ownership. He'd been content for people to refer to it as the Wilson place for more than two years. Why the sudden planting of the sign now? Retracing her route to her place, she reversed again to arrive just after Bill turned into Ryan's gate.

Ryan lounged against the veranda post, his habitual welcome, with Satan at his side. He straightened as she fell into step with Bill. When Satan raced towards her, Grace dropped to her knees to greet him, burying her face in his side. His enthusiasm helped steady her nerves. Seeing Ryan's slow smile for the cop reminded her of all she'd thrown away.

"Ryan," Bill stopped at the bottom of the steps, and she caught up.

"You'd better come in." Ryan held the front door open. Not as welcoming as Satan, but the desire to lean closer and inhale as she passed burned as strongly.

Ryan led the way into his kitchen.

"I like what you've done here," Bill wandered around, shrugged apologetically. "Haven't been here for a few years."

"I don't think I ever thanked you for how you handled Danny's death," Ryan said.

"A terrible time. No need to make it worse," Bill acknowledged Ryan's thanks.

"You were one of the few locals to see that, and I appreciate it." Ryan gestured to chairs. "Coffee, tea, something stronger?"

"Not for me." Grace chose one of the straight-backed kitchen chairs. A huge sign announcing Leinad Farms, and now talking about Danny without a hint of the anger often clouding his voice when he talked of his brother. Did that help or hinder her plan?

"I could be tempted. It's been a long day, and I'm technically off-duty. Going home after this." Bill set his hat on one chair and took the other opposite Grace. "What are you having?"

"A whiskey." Ryan held up a bottle of Lagavulin.

"A single malt. That's a rare treat," the cop said. "Just a small one."

Ryan poured two drinks, set Bill's in front of him and sat in the chair beside her. Easier, not having to look at him.

Bill rolled the whiskey over the ice, inhaled and took a sip, then raised the glass in a toast. "We've charged Smithhouse with arson."

"Smithhouse?" Grace expelled a long, slow breath. None of the suspects she'd landed on had sat comfortably. The opponents to organic farming just fed their animals more hormones and muttered darkly about her greenie credentials. While random vandalism didn't make sense, Smithhouse hadn't been on her radar. "He wasn't the person running away the night of the break-in."

"The CCTV footage nailed him. I never expected him to break cover that way," Bill explained. "He and a mate started the fire."

"Why?" Ryan sat forward in his chair.

"Sheer bastardry. Grace is not the first property owner he's leaned on. He's been at the edge of a few inquiries over the last ten years."

"Since he cheated Mum and Dad?" She jerked upright. The police's refusal to intervene had been a bitter blow. Their line then had been that they couldn't charge Smithhouse because they didn't have enough evidence to prosecute.

"About then. They weren't the only victims. He did

some suspect deals in town. Nothing technically illegal, nothing he could ever be picked up for. Your mother's tip-off started us on this cycle, Ryan." Bill nodded his satisfaction. "He organized for that short-term farmhand of yours to steal some bags of quick lime months ago. Sold him a story about you not wanting it. Said it was a harmless building product but would save him a bit of cash. Payment was fixing him up with a job further north."

"I didn't know the labourer was that desperate." Ryan downed another mouthful. "Did he cook up the lime sulphur and dump the drums?"

"Still working on that. He'd moved on by then. Unlikely to have been Smithhouse, however, we're expecting a few people to find their voices now we've charged him." Bill's beam would have lit an electricity grid.

"And the break-in?" Grace locked doors now and resented the loss of innocence she'd known all her life.

"We picked up a local guy who does some B and E, breaking and entering, and he's fingered Smithhouse. Turns out Rochelle Harkiss tipped Smithhouse off to the sale of Blue Sky after the country women's meeting." Bill had followed every lead, which explained why they'd been able to act quickly with the CCTV footage.

"Is she in on it?" Grace asked. Rochelle was pushy. Being pushy didn't make you a saboteur or an arsonist.

"No malicious intent as far as we can tell." Bill shrugged. "Ran into him soon after the meeting, shared a juicy bit of gossip, given his past interest in the property. Then he called in a few favours from a mate at the bank. Had an insider's view of all the sale negotiations. He was mightily pissed off that first Donovan's and now Blue Sky had slipped through his fingers."

"Why didn't he target me?" The leashed anger in Ryan's demand shivered down her spine. He was taking responsibility for Smithhouse's actions, giving himself another reason to sever links between them.

"You're known to have security. And no one knows how

deep your pockets are. It's likely you could have withstood minor attempts at sabotage. And your place isn't on the market, is it?" Bill feigned innocence.

Ryan didn't answer.

"Anyway," Bill continued. "Grace's place is more vulnerable, the rules for organic certification tighter."

"What's going to happen next?" Grace was too stunned to feel relief.

Bill rolled his shoulders—job done. "His lawyer's got him out on bail. The first court hearing is early next week, and we're going to argue he's a danger to the community."

Ryan asked a few more questions. Bill lingered over his drink, asking about the robotics, and Ryan offered a tour when Bill had a free day.

"Might bring my grandson," Bill said. "Lorraine's boy."

"How is she?" Ryan asked.

Bill laughed. "Happily married." Another bit of the past was put to bed. Bill set his glass on the table and stood up. "I'll be off."

"Thanks for everything, Bill." Grace stretched out her hand.

"It really should be over now." He turned towards the door, and Grace busied herself carrying his glass to the sink while Ryan escorted him out.

CHAPTER SIXTEEN

Ryan leaned against the doorway watching her, wondering why she lingered. Her scent filled his head when she wasn't here. The hit was harder when she was within touching distance. When her short curls, clear green eyes and determined chin messed with his mind. Not beautiful, but that was the word he found when he thought of her. Where had she been hiding the white, Indian-cotton dress? Short sleeves, a scooped neck, the light fabric clung to every curve. She'd sauntered towards him earlier, and the damn dress had swirled around her thighs, draining the blood from his head. He needed to haul back from fantasises of peeling the dress off her. *He didn't know she wore dresses.* If her intention had been to show him what he was missing, he was already there.

Her arrival with Bill hadn't been a coincidence. Ryan's regular scan of his front gate CCTV, a precaution he'd put in place until the police had someone behind bars, had shown her stop, take off towards the highway, double back towards her place and then come in the gate just behind Bill.

"Maybe I could have that drink now?" She looked at him and then away.

"Whiskey?" He'd never seen her drink spirits, but he'd

never seen her in this mood either.

"Red wine, if you've got some, please?"

"You know I've got some." He'd never seen her meek either and wasn't sure he liked it.

She returned to her chair, her hands neatly clasped on the table while he opened a bottle. Having her stay allowed him to say what he needed to say. Find out why she was delaying the sale.

He handed her the glass and took Bill's seat.

"I can't quite believe it's over." She studied the wall over his shoulder, as if unsure how to start the conversation.

That worked as an opening. Ryan swallowed another mouthful of his whiskey, relishing the hit to his system when it slid down the back of his throat. "I'm sorry."

Her head snapped around, and her stunned gaze met his. "What on earth do you have to be sorry for? I'm the one who owes you an apology. Several apologies. You're the only person who's acted with integrity throughout this whole business." She was babbling.

She never babbled.

"Don't go overboard with the grovelling, Grace. It doesn't suit you."

"I can go bloody overboard if I want." That sounded more like her.

"A sizeable chunk of the motivation was a vendetta against me," he pointed out.

"You're seriously not going to sit there and argue that your cock is bigger than mine?" She slapped her hands on the table, then realised what she'd said and started to backpedal. "I mean, he'd have gone for me whether or not you were in the picture."

"Bizarrely, I know what you mean." And that had been part of his undoing, discovering he liked the way her mind worked, could follow her when she disappeared down a rabbit hole seeking solutions to a knotty problem.

"I'm doing it again." She sucked in a deep breath. "I didn't mean that the way it sounded."

"How do you think it sounded?" he asked. Her readiness to "fess up" and take responsibility were because she cared too much. Her kind of passion warmed him from the inside out. He was a man who made careful plans; he hadn't planned for her.

"Ungracious." She lifted a hand and let it fall. "Argumentative. I didn't even thank you properly for the other night."

Ryan let the silence stretch, waiting for her next move because she'd come here for more than apologies and thank yous. He braced for bad news.

"The organic certifier's due next week." She picked up her drink, then set it down again without taking a sip. "The fire will probably delay certification. Hopefully not too long." She shifted nervously in her seat.

"That's good news," he agreed. But again, wasn't why she'd come. She'd needed him to bankroll her for the deposit, and he'd shamelessly used the excuse to get closer. He'd stopped needing excuses eons ago when he'd worked out life was better when she was around. Her request for a delay had rocked him. He didn't want to hear she'd found another backer, but that was the place he'd landed. "You asked Jake for twenty-four hours. What's your decision?"

"Have you changed your mind about selling your farm?" she countered.

For her, it was all about the land. *Only about the land.* The crazy thing was, he wanted her to have that dream. To have every dream she'd ever wanted, which was why he'd agreed to Ella's final clause in the contract. To future-proof the farm. If someone tried to cheat her or if she got into trouble, he could make sure she kept the farm. That plan blew up in his face. If he couldn't have her, he'd be on his way.

"Why would I change my mind?" He sipped his whiskey, crunching on the ice he'd used to dilute it. He didn't want his senses dulled.

"Naming the farms after Danny and then walking away doesn't make sense." She clutched the stem of the wineglass tightly enough for it to snap.

If she'd worked that out, Ryan had no place left to hide. "After Danny?"

"I'm a crossword freak. I thought you knew. Crosswords, word puzzles, acrostics. As soon as I saw your company name, I knew it spelled Daniel backwards." She'd kept one of his secrets for him, and he hadn't known.

He toasted her loyalty with his whiskey. "Mum hasn't worked it out."

She smiled without much humour. "I need to up my training with Bluey."

If they were clearing the decks, he'd do it right. "I missed his call."

"Whose call?" Her brows drew together. "What are you talking about?"

"Danny called me. I was working. Didn't hear it." Ryan nursed the whiskey glass in both hands, looking for redemption in the amber liquid. "Didn't expect any calls. By the time I got it, I was too late."

"You've never forgiven yourself," she said slowly, her brow clearing.

"I guessed he'd met a friend. He was excited. I'd warned him to be careful before I left." Ryan set his drink down. "Not the same as being on hand."

She nodded. "Did he say, 'All good,' because that's what he said to me?"

"Probably." Ryan raked a hand through his hair, dragging in a breath. What the hell did that have to do with anything?

"Did you try to ring back?" She pushed. She always pushed for him to share more.

"Yes." He'd been on auto-recall until he'd gotten his mother's message.

"I knew he had a meet with that boy after school. Didn't know where or what might happen. I waited at the bus stop for as long as I could," she confessed, pressing a hand to her stomach. "Your mother called Dad the next morning, asking for his help."

Ryan flinched at the unexpected blow. "And you feel guilty?"

"Why not?" Her baffled cry from the heart stunned Ryan.

Knowing you'd failed someone you loved off-balanced you. Life reduced to two steps forward, one step back. And the burden of silence got heavier. A private burden, until she'd started prodding him. "I was his brother. I should have done more."

He'd let go of every attachment to survive the grief. Let go of the land, let go of happily-ever-afters, let go of love. But she'd dragged him back. Made him care for her. Care for his land. It wasn't enough if she couldn't trust him.

"I was here. We all should have done more." She'd been fiercely loyal to his brother. "Hindsight's a wonderful thing." She smiled crookedly.

"If I'd spoken to you at the funeral, I would have spewed all that guilt and anger and hate all over you, because I was burning up with it." He swallowed another mouthful of whiskey, slapped the empty glass on the table.

"If you'd talked to me, we might both have purged the guilt a lot sooner." Hell, she was brave.

He should have guessed she'd shared the guilt, but for the moment, he could only stare at her.

* * *

Grace ached to wrap her arms around him, but she'd forfeited the right. She was here because she refused to let the past ambush them again. "That's why you cut yourself off?"

"I told you I hated this place." *Did he know he was using past tense?*

"Do you still?" Grace picked up the wine she hadn't wanted, then set it down. Attachment to the land was a big part of this equation. He'd cut himself off from the land as well as people.

"What does it matter?" he asked harshly.

"It matters to me. It matters if you want the future to be different to the past." Grace jumped to her feet, pushed her hand through her hair and spun on her heel to walk towards the sink. Leaning on it, she saw him reflected in the windows, head bent. "All these years I've carried an image of my father in my mind. We'd lost the land, Mum's recovery was touch and go, Ella gave up law to nurse her." Grace swung to face him. "He was exhausted. More than exhausted, devastated by all that was happening, and no end in sight. I knew something was about to break. I wanted to stay home that day. Dad sent me to school."

"Grace." He pushed to his feet and took a step towards her.

"He looked broken. I rode my bike to the barn, but I couldn't go in. I could hear guttural noises, the pain so raw it scraped my insides. My bones hurt." Tears stung her eyes.

"I'm sorry. It's a kick in the gut when you can't help the people you love." Was he still clinging to defeat?

"Do you know what I did?"

"What did you do?" He was listening.

"I got angry. With him. I learned something about myself that day. If someone I love is hurt, my default position is anger. How ridiculous is that? Instead of being sensitive and sweet, I'm irritable and bad-tempered. I snap at the person I love."

"Freud probably has an explanation for it," he muttered.

"When I'm afraid, I get angry." She hugged herself as she laid bare the source of every attack she'd ever made on him. "When I'm facing loss, I get angry."

"You're allowed to be angry, Grace, so long as you understand not everyone's the same. Men like your father are hard-wired to protect. You feel less of a man when you fail," he said.

Men like Ryan Wilson were hard-wired to protect. She'd forgotten that when the town's title-tattle had fed her fear he didn't care for her.

"After Danny died, I made a vow that with the exception of my family, I'd lock myself away. After Smithhouse, I vowed I'd never let anyone take another piece of our land. I focused on helping Dad make the farm viable. On making sure it stayed Anderson land. Not letting anyone in," she cried passionately. "That's arrogance for you."

"You were a child." He excused her but not himself.

"We were all children. You, me, Danny." She jabbed a finger at him. "You turned your back on this land. I fixated on it."

"Smithhouse is a world-class, lowlife bastard. He took advantage of your father. From what Bill said, your father wasn't alone. You can't let one mistake shape your life." Ryan's jaw set. He gripped her upper arms, shook her gently.

"You think I don't know that!"

"At this stage, I don't know what the hell you think!"

"It was my dream, the goal that kept me moving forward." Grace brought her hands together as if in prayer, pleading for his understanding. "Is there anything you're attached to, Ryan?" She took a step closer, gripping his wrists. Each time she'd sensed the possibility of intimacy with him, true intimacy, not just making love, he'd backed away. His hesitation had fuelled hers. "Are you planning to stay?"

He didn't answer. He kept secrets, and who was she to question his decisions? Sometimes secrets and dreams were the same thing. Too afraid to speak them aloud in case they were snatched from you.

"I've apologised so many times without explaining why I lash out. I'm trying to explain now. I was wrong to fixate on the land." She blew out a long breath. She needed him to make this journey with her. "We were both wrong," she continued. "Me to fixate, you to turn your back."

He scowled. "Why are you still here?"

Grace returned to the table and sat down. "I want to change the contract." This was the riskiest part of her plan.

"Of course you bloody do!" he roared. "Why did you drive backwards and forwards outside my place earlier?"

"I was using Bill as my Trojan horse." Grace lifted her chin. So, he had seen her.

"You still see me as an enemy who needs to be beaten." Satan left his position and came to Ryan's side, sensing his master's distress.

"I wasn't sure you'd let me in if I came alone," she confessed, but the sign had given her hope. "Driving backwards and forwards meant I spotted the sign. Is it temporary or permanent?"

"Why does it matter?" He rested his hand on Satan's head.

"Because it might make a difference to my proposition," she said. If he'd decided to stay, maybe he'd forgiven her. Maybe there was a chance they could share more than Blue Sky.

"Tell me the proposition first." He collected the bottle of whiskey from the sideboard, set it on the table between them and sat down.

Grace eyed it cautiously and caught her bottom lip between her teeth. "Maybe I should come back tomorrow."

"We'll finish this tonight!" he roared. Satan crawled under the table.

"No sale on the poppy fields!" Her words came out in a rush.

He shot to his feet, the violent movement causing her to jump. "You've found another backer!"

"Of course not!" She leapt to her feet, to face off across the table. "I'm changing the deal. I'm offering you a partnership in Blue Sky. Fifty-fifty. The landholding isn't split and you get fifty percent of all profits." *I trust you Ryan, with my land, with my love.*

His head jerked backwards, as if she'd landed an uppercut to his chin. "What did you say?"

She ran her tongue over dry lips. "You heard." A heartbeat was forever when she was taking the biggest risk of her life.

He circled the table to stand in front of her, his body loose, the glint in his eyes speculative. "What if I said I only wanted the poppy fields?"

Grace had to tilt her head to look at him and work to keep her voice level. "This way you get a share in them. You can move cattle there, access the land to go to and from your farm."

"What if I don't want to share?" he growled, sliding his hand into her hair to brush a curl off her face.

"If you plan to stay, it could work out well for you." Her heart pounded, her nerves popped, and his gentle caress made her yearn. "If you leave, you'd have a half share in a profitable business." She hadn't expected she'd need to explain. Her grand plan to show him what was in her heart lay trampled between them.

"That's a larger investment than I'd planned," he mused.

She'd bared her soul, and he was calculating odds. She stepped out of reach of the spell he was casting, gathering her pride around her like the skirts of the dress she'd worn for him. "Isn't that your overall plan? Investments all over the country. A finger in many pies."

"That's the point. Many pies. That's why having the poppy fields as part of Leinad Farms makes this property more saleable." *He was talking business when she'd offered her heart.*

Grace shrugged as if she was indifferent, but her muscles were stretched beyond tight. Offering him half of Blue Sky was her public declaration of trust. *And love.* "I'll let you think about it." She turned to leave.

He caught her arm. "Is that the only offer on the table?"

The heat on simmer between them flared into a dangerous fire. *You,* the want reverberated through her body. *Just you. To hold me at night, to wake beside me in the morning. To talk to me about my dreams and share yours with me.* Pride didn't ease the gaping hole where her heart should be. What they'd shared was worth fighting for. "Can we go back to where we were?"

"To a no-strings-attached affair?" He scratched his chin. "That won't work anymore."

"Why not?" Rejection hurt, and she'd dished it out to him often enough.

"You said being with me shamed you."

She closed her eyes on the memory, understanding why there was no way back for her, for them. "That was unforgivable."

"Fuck forgiveness! Was it the truth or temper talking?"

"Fear."

A shutter came over his expression. "You're afraid of me."

"Afraid of what you make me want." She fisted a hand on her chest. "Of what you make me feel. Everything happened in quick succession. Danny's death. Your departure. Mum's tractor accident and the Smithhouse swindle. My way of surviving was to rely on myself. I use temper to hide fear, but I can't be afraid anymore. I don't want to use anger as a shield. Everything snowballed that day. I overheard some particularly vicious gossip about us in town, then I got the new clause, and I forgot for a moment we're friends."

"You also said you loved me." *Now he remembered.*

"I said a lot of things." She hadn't considered his insecurities.

"I'm not a good long-term prospect." His grip gentled. "I stopped believing in permanence."

She could say she understood, or that she'd take anything he offered. They both deserved better. "That's cowardice."

He snorted.

"You're not a coward. You only pretend to reject attachment," she said. Satan crawled across the floor and rested his head on Ryan's boot. Grace released a laugh she didn't know she had. "You didn't lock Satan out."

"He refused to be locked out."

"Doesn't that tell you anything?" She took a step closer and raised her hand to his cheek. "I've seen how you can nurture, Ryan. That's a strength, not a weakness."

"You're making me something I'm not, Grace." He took her wrist and brought her hand to his mouth, kissing her palm.

"Can I refuse to be locked out?" she whispered, tingles shooting up her arm from the pressure of his lips.

"Why would you want to get close?" His uplifted head, the narrowing of his eyes, revealed her mistake. He was too smart not to guess what she was telling him. Well damn!

She'd thrown her first declaration of love at him in the middle of a fight, making the words sound like a lie. She'd been afraid of rejection, yet each move she'd made took him further away from her. "I need to talk. You know that. I didn't talk to you about the clause. I erupted and spoiled what was precious between us. I pushed you away before you pushed me away." She crossed her arms, holding herself together, because this was her last chip in the game. "I love you, Ryan."

"I wasn't thinking of love," he said.

She squeezed her eyes shut, waiting for the earth to open up and swallow her.

"Hold on." He rested his hands on her shoulders and pulled her closer. "I wasn't thinking of love. Not when we first kissed, not when I took you to bed."

"I know that." She dropped her head on his chest, blinking to hold back fresh tears.

"But that's what was happening." He threaded his fingers through her hair. "Soft, like your skin. Like your heart. You gave me Sleeping Beauty in reverse. One kiss from you and I started to change." He used a finger to lift her chin.

She sniffed. "That's almost poetic."

"I'd like to give you poetry and flowers and romance. You deserve it." His honey-soaked drawl shivered through her.

"You're a romantic, but you try to hide it," she said. He'd given her romance the first time they'd made love and every time since.

"I wanted you close from the moment you spoke to me at the field day. The more time I spent with you, the more I cared. I hadn't got as far as staying. Just delaying my departure date." He'd fought his feelings as strenuously as she'd fought hers. "The contract clause to be your first line of defence was a godsend. Your family believed I was a good Samaritan, when I'd found a foolproof way to be there if you decided you need me."

"I thought it took you a step closer to leaving me, so I left first." She hid behind anger; he hid behind cool analysis.

"You need to work on engaging your brain before your mouth." He nuzzled against her neck below her ear, and a tremble shivered through her.

"You can be as bad when you're in a temper." She wasn't carrying the can for all the crossed wires in their relationship.

He nipped her ear.

"Okay." She blew out a breath, lifting her fringe. "You're more reflective than me. You think things through."

"Yeah. Except I didn't anticipate my delay on the final sale would result in arson."

"I'm sorry I scared you that night." She underlined her apology by sliding her hands up his chest and around his neck.

"I lost ten years off my life seeing you dancing through those flames."

"When I saw you arrive, I knew everything would be okay." She tugged on his collar-length hair. "You're my hero." She'd come here ready to risk everything on a final throw of the dice. Selling him the poppy fields and getting back into his bed wasn't enough anymore. "My offer of a partnership is making the same offer. I'm here if you want me."

"I knew … know, what you're offering." He flashed his

rare smile, his hands on her hips. "Outrageous of me to tease you. It's probably my first and last chance to see such total, willing capitulation from you. I want to stay. That's why I put up the sign. But it depends on you."

"Tell me how I can help your decision." Her hands slid around his back to urge him closer.

"Tonight was my deadline. If you hadn't come here, I was coming to see you." He wrapped her close, his cheek resting against her temple.

She leaned back to meet his gaze. "To make sure I went through with the sale?"

"To explain myself. I know you need to talk. I'm a bit rusty." He was making a commitment his way.

She brushed her lips along his jaw. "I'm good at lubricating rusty parts."

"Putting up the sign was my way of saying I want to put down roots. In the land. With you. I'll stay, if I can have you. You make me believe in tomorrows. I love you, Grace." His vow filled all the lonely, scared parts of her.

"Right back at you, Ryan Wilson." She brushed her lips across his. "I don't want to make my life alone anymore."

"Neither do I." His bedroom smile curved his mouth. "And along with the occasional fireworks, you're generous, loving, and loyal."

"I do trust you, Ryan." She gave him those words because trust and love were indivisible.

"You don't need to give me half your farm to prove that." He nibbled his way up her throat and along her jaw, scattering kisses until she lost any capacity to think straight. "Marry me?"

"Yes." Grace jumped into his arms, locking her legs around his waist.

"Don't you need to think about it?" He cupped her backside, holding her in place.

"Nah! Don't want to give you time to change your mind." The joy in her heart was reflected in his eyes.

"I don't need to own Blue Sky." He swung in a circle.

"Just to be part of your life."

"Then you keep Leinad Farms?"

"I thought we'd share." He was carrying her towards his bedroom.

"Partners in every way? We can operate the farms together, keep them on separate titles—whatever." She punctuated her sentences with kisses.

"Let's work out the details as we go along." His hand stroked down her back, a long, leisurely caress with a sting of heat.

"You *do* love me."

"Nah. Just want you naked all the time." He slid both hands under the dress. "I like this dress."

"Easy access." She smiled demurely.

"I like a woman who plans ahead."

"I asked Bluey to do the morning milking." She started to unbutton his shirt.

"Even better." He lowered her onto his bed. "We'll order a robotic unit for your place tomorrow."

"Stop talking, Ryan, and love me."

"I plan to." He smiled his special smile.

AUTHOR'S NOTE

There were a number of triggers for *Grace Under Fire* and *Taylor's Law*. One was a news item about how farming families deal with farm succession and inheritance, or more importantly, how they don't. Often a family farm will only support one child, who may work for years on low pay, but with the expectation of inheriting the farm. Far too frequently, this can lead to bitter financial disputes between siblings when the parents die and the farm is the only asset. In *Grace Under Fire*, I make those conversations explicit.

I'd like to thank the many people who have helped me write this book. In particular, I'd like to thank my editor, Yezanira Venecia, my cover designer Fantasia Frog Designs, and Melissa Keir, Inkspell Publishing for her continuing support.

Don't Miss this Award Winning book by Jennifer Raines

TAYLOR'S LAW

Tell me a secret and I'll tell you a lie.

Ella Anderson adores her niece. Despite struggling to make ends meet, accepting her dying sister's request she raise Tessa as her own is a no brainer. Until she receives a summons from a legal goliath on behalf of a wealthy stranger claiming paternity and, potentially, custody of her child.

Jake Taylor has been ripped off one too many times. Yet the letter from a woman claiming his cousin fathered her child feels real. His aunt and uncle are desperate for a grandchild. When the child's aunt shows up in his office in place of the child's mother, he smells fraud.

Secrets and lies bubble to the surface, threatening Ella and Jake's growing attraction. In a minefield of divided loyalties, can Ella trust Jake to make the right decision about custody of Tessa?

Jennifer's book is great for fans of contemporary romances where attraction blossoms into breath-stealing passion, where mutual respect leads lovers to also being friends, and where humour and tolerance enliven a deep and abiding love.

Jennifer likes to think her readers get occasional hints of the deep passion of a Nora Roberts or the unshakeable loyalty of a Grace Burrowes where love conquers loneliness, distrust and fear.

EXCERPT

"Who are you?" he demanded.

The tension in his liquid chocolate voice rippled through her. This man couldn't be Tessa's father. The ferocity of her denial rattled her. Every cell refused to accept he'd been her sister's lover. And some remnant of reasoned thought nagged at her. He'd have eaten Chrissy alive.

"Eleanor Anderson." With an effort, she gathered her professional poise. "Chrissy's sister. Ella. You must be Drew." She reached out a hand.

"You know damn well I'm not Drew."

"If you aren't Drew, who are you?" Off-balanced by his instant attack, she tried to steady her jumpy nerves. Withdrawing her hand, she turned to the older man, who was staring at Tessa. "Mr. Taylor, your letter requested Chrissy meet you here about Drew Browning's paternity and …" She stumbled to a halt over the word "custody," then shook her head as a bizarre idea formed. "You can't be Drew?"

"I'm his father, Peter." His presence confused her further but confirmed the identity of the pirate king.

She stretched out a hand for a second time. "Then you must be Mr. Taylor. Good morning."

"Where's Chrissy?" Taylor demanded.

Before she could answer, Tessa's soft voice ricocheted around the room. "Mama's in heaven."

AVAILABLE AT ALL BOOK RETAILERS IN EBOOK AND PRINT

ABOUT THE AUTHOR

Australian Jennifer Raines writes contemporary romances set mainly in Australia, but not exclusively—think Malta, Finland, New Zealand or ?. A dreamer and an optimist, her stories are a delicious cocktail of mutual respect, passion and loyalty because she still believes in happily-ever-afters. Jennifer loves those days when words flow and the joy of writing makes the hard slog worthwhile. She's always made up stories about strangers in the street, in a café or strolling through an airport terminal; finding inspiration in snippets of conversation, news items and the sheer puzzle of human interactions.

Jennifer is a member of Romance Writers of Australia and is a three times finalist in the Emerald competition,

2017, 2018 (Taylor's Law) and 2022. She's a member of Romance Writers of New Zealand, winning the Pacific Hearts competition in 2017 and 2019 (Grace Under Fire). She's also a member of Romance Writers of America and has been a finalist in chapter competitions in 2019, 2020 and 2021 (Taylor's Law).

Jennifer lives in inner-city Sydney, Australia, with the requisite number of partners (1) and animals (2). Her desk overlooks a park which nourishes her soul when she raises her head from her keyboard. She gets some of her best insights during long yin yoga poses or walking—anywhere. Jennifer adores historical romance but chose to write contemporary because she thought (wrongly) it needed less research.

Jennifer can be reached through her webpage https://jenniferrainesauthor.com, via Facebook https://www.facebook.com/jenniferrainesauthor and Instagram - romanceauthorjen

Her book(s) are available through major providers.